DEATH IN ROME

WOLFGANG KOEPPEN

————————

DEATH IN ROME

TRANSLATED WITH AN INTRODUCTION
BY
MICHAEL HOFMANN

W. W. Norton & Company
New York London

For information about permission to reproduce selections from this book, write to
Permissions, W. W. Norton & Company, Inc., 500 Fifth Avenue, New York, NY 10110

ISBN 0-393-32194-0

W. W. Norton & Company, Inc.
500 Fifth Avenue, New York, N.Y. 10110
www.wwnorton.com

W. W. Norton & Company Ltd.
Castle House, 75/76 Wells Street, London W1T 3QT

1 2 3 4 5 6 7 8 9 0

INTRODUCTION

It was the painter Kokoschka who said, 'If you last, you'll see your reputation die three times, and even three cultures.' This is just what has happened to Wolfgang Koeppen, whose career has spanned six decades, from Weimar to post-Unification Germany. Important critics have repeatedly hailed him as – with Grass – 'the greatest living German writer', but in spite of that, he has remained vastly less known and less read, a victim of call it what you will: Kokoschka's 'Law of Longevity', the censorship of fashion, the tyranny of neglect, the neglect of fashion, the fashion of neglect . . . Articles on him have been published with titles one might translate as 'Wolfgang Koeppen: the Anatomy of a Failure'. However, the failure is not Koeppen's but Germany's, and its circumstances are both specific and illuminating.

Koeppen was born in 1906 in Greifswald on the Baltic coast. He studied, in the German manner, various subjects at various universities he doesn't seem to care to have publicized, and probably never took his degree. From 1931 to 1934 he had what he described as the only regular employment of his life, when he worked as a journalist for the *Berliner Börsen-Courier*. He published a novel, *Eine unglückliche Liebe* (*An Unhappy Love Affair*), left Germany for Holland in 1935, published another, *Die Mauer schwankt* (*The Tottering Wall*), but returned to Germany before the war broke out. He then dropped out of view until the 1950s, when, in the space of four years, he published the three novels that (perhaps for the second time!) made his reputation, all of them written very quickly, in no more than three or four months apiece, he says. These books are among the best things to have come out of post-war Germany: *Tauben im Gras* (*Pigeons on the Grass*; there is an English translation by David Ward, published by Holmes & Meier in 1988), set in Munich in a single day, a modernist jigsaw in 110 pieces and showing 30 figures; *Das Treibhaus* (*The Hothouse*), about the dilemma of a Socialist member of the Bundestag during a rearmament debate, and something of a *succès de scandale*; and *Death in Rome*, the most accessible and I think the best of the three, about a German family reunion in Rome. The three books form a loose trilogy, an interrogation of the Federal Republic's phoenix act, the famous *Wirtschaftswunder*. Since then, in almost forty years, Koeppen has published only one short work of semi-fiction, *Die Jugend* (*Youth*), three travel books about Russia, America and France, and some essays and reviews. His silence – which is perceived as such – is one of the loudest things in German literature today.

So much for the fast-forward version. Taken a little more slowly, it shows the troubling shape of a career in twentieth-century German letters. Where Chancellor Kohl congratulated himself on being born late, Koeppen could lament being born early. He was formed by the 1920s, the great decade of modernism, late expressionism and *Neue Sachlichkeit*. He read Proust, Kafka, Faulkner and Woolf as they appeared. *Ulysses* – the 1926 small-press edition of the first German translation – was the stuff his dreams were made of. By the 1930s his own career had begun. He went abroad. He wasn't a Nazi. He returned. He didn't have the reputation, the contacts, the command of foreign languages to enable him to make his way in exile. Nor did he lay claim to the condition of 'internal exile'. Along with the poet Gottfried Benn and a very few other significant writers he lived through the period in Germany.

This put him at a disadvantage later. One might have supposed that the *status quo ante* 1933 would be restored as a matter of urgency, but that isn't what happened. Instead, the story was one of discontinuity. It was as though the literature had been bombed as the cities had been. It took until the 60s and even the 70s for the classic books of the 20s and 30s – a Silver Age of German letters – to get back into print, for the still-living writers from that period to be 'discovered' and the dead ones to be exhumed. Precedence was given to the returning exiles – to Thomas Mann in the West, Brecht in the East – and to the work of new writers like the *Gruppe 47*. The preferred form for literature was a clean slate, with only the distinguished markings of a very few on it – the ones with cast-iron alibis. It was a very German solution – *Schwamm drüber!* – unjust and evasive and superficial, an extension of collective amnesia.

Koeppen's position was exacerbated by the nature of the books he wrote and published in the early 50s. Far from underwriting a fresh start, they connected stylistically with the 20s and politically with the 30s. They were works of memory and continuance and criticism – and they were savaged for it by the press. The response to them was characterized by 'hostility, even revulsion and repugnance' (*Neue Zürcher Zeitung*). Their detractors squealed at their ferocity and outspokenness, their self-conscious and difficult technique, their sexual content. 'Is this really what we need at such a time in our history?' (always an obnoxious argument in literary politics) was the gist, 'let's look on the bright side!' Even those praising Koeppen were embarrassed by the political content of his books, or sold their artistry short. And so the conservatism of the modish and dirigible German public won out. Koeppen's books never had anything like the currency and acclaim they deserved.

Five years later, Grass's *Die Blechtrommel* appeared; another four, and Böll's *Ansichten eines Clowns*; and the internationally accredited commodity 'post-war German literature' had come into existence. The earliest and fullest and most drastic description of German post-war reality didn't figure in it. Anyway, whether for that reason or others, Koeppen gave up fiction. His travel books were respectfully reviewed – no one to tell him what he had and hadn't, could and couldn't see – but as a writer of fiction, in spite of the efforts of two determined publishers and a handful of *cognoscenti*, he has ceased to exist. It is a great scandal.

Death in Rome is the most devastating novel about the Germans that I have ever read, and one of the most arresting on any subject. It takes a German family – not a real German family, not even a caricature German family, but a prototypical German family that George Grosz would have had the bile but not the wit to invent, and Musil or Mann the wit but not the bile – and brings them to Rome, a city having an association with Germans that goes back hundreds of years, there to enact their conflicts. It is a history book, a family book, a book about the battle over who gets to represent the authentic face of Germany.

Significantly, this German family is all male. (Of course there are women in it too, but they are minor, though also well done.) There is the older generation, consisting of Gottlieb Judejahn, the unreconstructed and unkillable old SS man, and his brother-in-law Friedrich Wilhelm Pfaffrath, who held office under the Nazis and is once more making his way up the greasy pole, this time as democratically elected burgomaster; and there are their respective rebel sons: Adolf Judejahn, who is on his way to becoming a Catholic priest, and his cousin, Siegfried

Pfaffrath, a composer of serial music. (There is also Siegfried's conformist brother Dietrich, but let's forget about him for the moment.) These four represent the four principal areas of German achievement, or the four quarters of the riven German soul: murder, bureaucracy, theology and music. It is like having Frederick the Great, Bismarck, Luther and Beethoven in one family. Their movements, their meetings and remeetings in the alien city of Rome – which, interestingly, offers each of them what they want, so each of them sees it in a different version – are, as the novelist and critic Alfred Andersch pointed out, choreographed like a ballet: a macabre ballet of outrageous contrivance, viewed by the reader with growing horror, alarm and incredulity: how *dare* these people show their faces, how *can* they belong together . . .

This is part of Koeppen's point. Church and state. Music and the camps. You can't have one of them without the others. In the 50s when Germany wanted severance and disavowal of the past, Koeppen showed it bonds of steel and blood instead. He gave Germans a character at a time when they were supposed not to have one; he wrote the history of a period that strove for greyness, and – until invented by Fassbinder – had seemed invisible: whatever happened between 1945 and the World Cup in 1966?! There is something implacable, almost vindictive – like one of his Furies – about his pursuit of the Germans postwar, post-Holocaust, post-division, turning away from their crimes towards rehabilitation and the EC, once again exporting their goods and their culture and themselves. He shows them to us. All of them.

Death in Rome is a comprehensive and brilliant provocation of an entire nation (it's only a pity that the nation didn't respond a little better to it). It begins, like all the best German stories, with the words, '*Es war einmal . . .*',

'Once upon a time', and it ends with a dirty, tawdry version of the last sentence of *Death in Venice* (the original of which is helpfully given as an epigraph). In between there are countless glancing references to German history, from Roman times to when the novel was written in 1954. There is a whole micro-plot about the German presence in Rome, from Alaric the Goth to the Holy Roman Emperor Charlemagne (who was also Emperor of Germany, is known as Karl der Grosse, and lies buried in Aachen), Henry IV's penitential visit to Pope Gregory VII at Canossa, the cultural trippers of the Grand Tour including Goethe, and finally Hitler himself on his fraternal visits to Mussolini. In their various ways – destroyer, ruler, penitent, tourist, warrior – these are all antecedents for the various Judejahns and Pfaffraths who have descended on the city now. As I said before, Koeppen is interested in establishing continuity and pattern.

Most of the German references concern the Nazi period – although the Nazis themselves, in their hunt for legitimacy and historical validation, had a deliberate policy of reinvesting old words, old places, old habits and old wars. For instance, they set up their élite 'Napola' schools in the old Teutonic fortresses in the East – which is why Adolf and Siegfried talk about their school as the Teutonic castle or academy; they revived concepts like the *Femegericht*, the 'Vehmic Court', first used in fourteenth-century Westphalia, then applied to political killings in the 1920s; they tried wherever possible to associate themselves with the military traditions of German history. And so the great majority of these terms and references are military or power-related, and are woven in around the figure of Judejahn, whose own immaculate National Socialist c.v. takes in everything that was anything in terms of right-wing murder and thuggery in the years after 1918: the Ruhr

Uprising, the Freikorps, the Kapp Putsch, the Black Reichswehr. Of course, it's all too bad to be true – no single person can have participated in *all* of the above – but it tags, insists, calls to mind, reinforces the myth. Koeppen is calling the German language as evidence of the recurring violence and power-lust of German history.

I would like the English reader not to be too bothered by all this. If it's any comfort, I doubt whether most German readers would be able to explain half the references. It isn't necessary. You take in the principle of historical labelling and cross-referencing, feel the (foreign) texture of the word, take from the context whether it's a building or a political movement or a personality that's being referred to, and pass on. It can be read pedantically – by all means, consult an encyclopaedia – but it wasn't written in such a spirit, and the original didn't come with notes either. *Death in Rome* works as myth much better than as an agglomeration of allusions.

Koeppen seems to sit on the shoulders of his four main protagonists and parrot their thoughts and impressions: the brutal, rueful Judejahn (rueful for not having killed more); the discriminations – havering but also frank in their way – of Siegfried; pat Adolf and fearful Pfaffrath. In the modernist manner, they take up prismatically different attitudes to the same things: sex, dress, food, the gods and God, myth, Rome. Judejahn has his desert, and Siegfried the Africa for his black symphony. The spooky arms-dealer Austerlitz has his warmed milk, Siegfried and Adolf their ice-cream. Everywhere there is congruence and difference. The events and perspectives of the book are related in a wonderful, highly wrought and rhythmic prose – how many novels are there about which you can say they have rhythm? – short, spat-out sentences, and long, sweeping, comma'd-off periods, protocols of consciousness that are actually less difficult to follow than they seem. Koeppen's style commends itself both to the eye and the ear, as much as to the cells of memory and knowledge. It was the style – gorgeous, bristling, pugnacious – that got me sold on the book, and that from the very first sentence: 'Once upon a time, this city was a home to gods . . .' If that worked, then everything else had to, too.

A note on the names. Both surnames are significant fabrications: 'Judejahn' from *Jude*, a Jew, and *jahn*, not a word but like a cross between *Wahn*, madness, and *jäten*, to weed out; and Pfaffrath, from *Pfaffe*, a disrespectful term for a priest, and *rath*, council or counsel. With the first names, there is an awful irony in the way the fathers have named the sons – and been named by their own fathers before them! – as they themselves should have been named. No one likes or fits his own name. There is a narcissistic syncopation in the way the Nazis have names from the pious empire, Friedrich Wilhelm and Gottlieb (love-god); and the rebels and expatriates are called Adolf and Siegfried. Siegfried's brother Dietrich is named by Koeppen after Diederich, the creepy and servile anti-hero of Heinrich Mann's novel *Der Untertan*; while the word 'Dietrich' means a picklock. Truly, he will inherit the earth.

I have various debts to record: to the bookseller Barbara Stiess in Berlin, who first recommended Koeppen to me; to Daniel Halpern for his unforgettably impulsive agreement to publish the book; and to Joseph Brodsky, for the gift of a Mussolini T-shirt, in which I did as much of the work as was decently possible. Thank you!

Michael Hofmann
London, March 1992

DEATH IN ROME

Il mal seme d'Adamo

Dante, *Inferno*

And before nightfall a shocked and respectful world received the news of his decease.

Thomas Mann, *Death in Venice*

PART ONE

Once upon a time, this city was a home to gods, now there's only Raphael in the Pantheon, a demigod, a darling of Apollo's, but the corpses that joined him later are a sorry bunch, a cardinal of dubious merit, a couple of monarchs and their purblind generals, high-flying civil servants, scholars that made it into the reference books, artists of academic distinction. Who gives a damn about them? The tour group stand in the ancient vaults, and gawp up at the light falling on them like rain through the only window, the circular opening in the cupola that was once covered with bronze tiles. Is it golden rain? Danaë succumbs to the approaches of Thomas Cook and the Italian Tourist Board; but without much enthusiasm. She won't lift her skirts to receive the god into her. Perseus won't be born. Medusa gets to keep her head and moves into a swish apartment. And what about great Jupiter? Is he here in our midst? Could he be the old fellow in the Amex office, or the rep for the German–European Travel Agency? Or has he been banished to the edge of town somewhere, is he in the asylum enduring the questions of nosy psychiatrists, or languishing in the state's prisons? They've installed a she-wolf under the Capitol, a sick and depressed animal, not up to suckling Romulus and Remus. The faces of the tourists look pasty in the light of the Pantheon. Where is the baker that will knead them, where is the oven that will give them a bit of colour?

Wrong, the music sounded wrong, it no longer moved him, it was almost unpleasant to him, like hearing your own voice for the first time, a recording coming out of a loudspeaker, and you think, well, so that's me, that braying twit, that phoney, that smoothie, and in particular it was the violins that were wrong, their sound was too lush; it wasn't the unearthly wind in the trees, it wasn't the child's conversation with the daemon at nightfall, that wasn't what fear of being sounded like, it wasn't so measured, so well-tempered, it should be more torment-ing, more passionate, old panic fear of the green trees, of the expanse of the sky, of the drifting clouds – that was what Siegfried had meant to sing, and he had totally and utterly failed, and so now he felt weak and timid, he felt like crying, but Kürenberg had been reassuring and praised the symphony. Siegfried admired Kürenberg, the way he ruled with his baton, the plenipotentiary of the notes; but still there were times when Siegfried felt violated by him. Then Siegfried would get angry with himself for not put-ting up any fight. He couldn't; Kürenberg was so know-ledgeable, and Siegfried was green and no match for him in musical theory. Kürenberg smoothed, accented, articu-lated Siegfried's score, and Siegfried's painful groping, his search for a sound, the memory of an Edenic garden before the dawn of mankind, an approximation to the truth of things, which was by definition unhuman – all that, under Kürenberg's conducting hand, had become humanistic and enlightened, music for a cultured audience; but to Siegfried it sounded unfamiliar and disappointing, the feeling now tamed and striving for harmony, and Siegfried was worried, but then again the artist in him enjoyed the pre-cision, the clarity of the instruments, the care with which the celebrated hundred-strong orchestra were playing his composition.

6

In the concert hall there were laurel trees growing in green-painted tubs, or perhaps it was oleander; anyway the same thing that grew in crematoria, and even in high summer looked somehow wintry. 'Variations on Death and the Colour of Oleander' had been the title of Siegfried's first major composition, a septet that had remained unperformed. In the first draft he had had in mind his dead grandmother, the only member of his family to whom he had been at all close; perhaps because she had been such a strange and silent presence in the noisy and bustling house of his parents, forever echoing to the tramp of jackboots. And what a ghastly send-off they'd given her. His grandmother was the widow of a pastor, and had she been able to watch, she would have hated the technology and comfort, the hygiene and slickness, with which she had been turned to ashes, the deft and indifferent address, while the wreath, with the garish swastika ribbon that the SA Women's Section had contributed, was certainly repugnant to her, even if she would never have spoken out against it. But then, in the second version of his septet, Siegfried had tried to express something more universal and more suspect, a secret opposition, suppressed, brittle, romantic scraps of feelings, and in its posture of resistance his composition resembled a rose-garlanded marble torso, the torso of a young warrior or a hermaphrodite in the blaze of single combat: it represented Siegfried's rebellion against his surroundings, against the prisoner-of-war camp, against the barbed-wire fences, against his comrades with their boring conversations, against the war, for which he held his parents responsible, against his whole hellish and hellbent Fatherland. Siegfried wanted to pay them all back, and so, having read in an English newspaper that Kürenberg, who had been a rising conductor in Germany before the war, was now in Edinburgh, he had written to

7

him, asking for some examples of twelve-tone music, a form of composition that was considered unacceptable in Siegfried's youth, and which now attracted him for that very reason, because it was frowned upon by those in power, his hated teachers at the military academy, his feared Uncle Judejahn, the mighty man whose glowering image in the vile uniform had hung over his despised father's desk, and Kürenberg had sent works by Schönberg and Webern to Siegfried in his camp, and sent a friendly note to accompany them. The scores were in the old Universal edition, published in Vienna before Siegfried's time and then banned after the Anschluss of Austria. The music represented a new world for Siegfried, it opened a gate for him, not just in the barbed-wire prisoner-of-war compound, but in something still more constricting. And afterwards he refused to crawl back under the yoke as he called it, the war was lost, and he at least had been freed, and no longer deferred to the views of the family to have been born into which had always seemed ghastly to him.

The greenery in the concert hall looked dusty. It probably was laurel after all, the leaves had the look of dried herbs swimming in soup, moistened but still brittle and unsoftened by cooking. They depressed Siegfried, who didn't want to be sad in Rome. The leaves reminded him of a succession of soups in his life: the Eintopf at the Party school that his father had sent him to on Uncle Judejahn's recommendation, the field-kitchens of the army, to which Siegfried had fled from school; the Party's Junker school had had green bay trees too, and there were oak leaves in the barracks, proliferating on decorations and on tombstones, and there had always been a picture of that twitchy and repressed type, the Führer, with his Charlie Chaplin moustache, looking benevolently down on his herd of sacrificial lambs, the boys in uniform now ready for the slaughter. Here, among the laurel and oleander of the concert hall, in this chilly indoor grove, there was an old portrait of the master, Palestrina, looking far from benevolent, no, surveying the orchestra's efforts sternly and reproachfully. The Council of Trent had accepted Palestrina's music. The congress in Rome would reject Siegfried's. That too depressed Siegfried, depressed him while still rehearsing, depressed him even though he'd come to Rome expecting to be rejected, telling himself he didn't care.

There is a trench going round the Pantheon that was once the street that led from the Temple of All the Gods to the Baths of Agrippa; the Roman imperium collapsed, debris filled up the trench, archaeologists laid it bare again, masonry stumps rise up mossy and ruined, and sitting on top of them are the cats. There are cats all over Rome, they are the city's oldest inhabitants, a proud race like the Orsinis and the Colonnas, they are really the last true Romans, but they have fallen on hard times. Imperial names they have! Othello, Caligula, Nero, Tiberius. Children swarm round them, calling to them, taunting them. The voices of the children are loud, shrill, voluble, so appealing to a foreign ear. They lie on their fronts on the wall that runs alongside the ditch. School ribbons transform the grimy faces into little Renoirs. The girls' pinafores have ridden up, the boys wear tiny shorts, their legs look like those of statues under a patina of dust and sun. That's the beauty of Italy. Suddenly laughter rings out. They're laughing at an old woman. Compassion always has a pathetic aspect. The old woman hobbles along with a stick, bringing the cats something to eat. Something wrapped in a foul, sodden newspaper. Fishheads. On a blood-smeared newspaper photograph the American secretary of state and the Russian foreign minister are shaking hands. Myopic the pair of them. Their glasses blink. Thin lips compressed in a smile. The cats growl and hiss at each other. The old woman tosses the paper into the trench. Severed heads of sea-creatures, dull eyes, discoloured gills, opalescent scales, tumble among the yowling moggy mob. Carrion, a sharp whiff of excrement, secretions and sex, and the sweet smell of decay and purulence rise into the air, mixed with the exhaust fumes on the street, and the fresh, tempting aroma of coffee from the espresso bar on the corner of the Piazza della Rotonda. The cats fight over the leftovers. It's a matter of life and death. Foolish creatures, why did they have to multiply! There are hundreds of them starving and homeless, randy, pregnant, cannibalistic; they are diseased and abandoned, and they have sunk about as far as cats can sink. One tom with a bullish skull, sulphur-yellow and bristle-haired, lords it over the weaker ones. He puts his paw down. He doles out. He takes for himself. His face bears the scars of past power struggles. He is missing part of an ear – a lost campaign. There is mange on his fur. The adoring children call him 'Benito'.

I was sitting at a zinc table, on a zinc chair, so light the wind might have carried me off. I was happy, I was telling myself, because I was in Rome, on the pavement terrace of an espresso bar on the corner of the Piazza della Rotonda in Rome, and I was drinking a brandy. The brandy also was light and flighty, light metal, like distilled zinc. It was grappa, and I was drinking it because I'd read in Hemingway that that's what you should drink in Italy. I wanted to be cheerful, but I didn't feel cheerful. Something was gnawing me. Perhaps the awful mob of cats were gnawing me. No one likes seeing poverty, and a few pennies weren't enough to absolve you here. I never know what to do. I avert my eye. A lot of people do, but it bothers me. Hemingway doesn't seem to know the first thing about brandy. The grappa tasted mouldy and synthetic. It tasted like German black-market brandy from the Reichsmark period. Once I got ten bottles of brandy like that in exchange for a Lenbach. The Lenbach was a sketch of Bismarck; I did the deal with a Puerto Rican in GI uniform. The brandy was distilled from fuel for the V2 rockets that were supposed to destroy London: you flew off in the air when you drank it, but that's all right, the Lenbach was faked as well. Now we had the 'economic miracle' in Germany, and good brandy. The Italians probably had decent brandy too, but they didn't have an economic miracle. I surveyed the square. I saw the state being swindled. A young woman was selling American cigarettes from her dirty apron. I felt reminded of the cats. The woman was the human equivalent of those poor creatures, ragged and unkempt and covered with open sores. She was miserable and degraded; her kind too had multiplied too quickly, and they had been weakened by lust and hunger. Now she was hoping to get rich illegally. She was ready to worship the golden calf; but I wasn't sure whether it would answer her prayers. I had a feeling this woman might be murdered. I could see her strangled body, whereas she probably saw herself as a proper businesswoman, a dignified signora, enthroned in a legitimate kiosk. On the piazza, the golden calf condescended to nuzzle the woman. She seemed to be well known in the area. Like a buoy she stood in the flow of traffic, and the deft little Fiats swam boldly up to her. How the brakes squealed! The drivers, handsome men with curled, with waved, with pomaded hair, with buffed and scented scalps if they were bald, passed money out through the windows of their cars, took their packets on board, and their little Fiats would chase off to the next port of call, the next fraudulent little transaction. A young Communist woman walked up. I could tell by the bright red kerchief over her blue anorak. A proud visage! I thought, Why are you so arrogant? You deny everything, you deny the old woman feeding the cats, you deny all compassion. A youth lurked in a doorway, greasy, as though dipped in oil. He was the cigarette-seller's boyfriend, her protégé or her protector; or maybe he was her boss, a serious businessman concerned about his volumes and his margins; whatever he was, I think he was the Devil with whom Fate had paired this woman. Every so often the two of them would meet on the piazza, as though by chance. She would slip him her takings, a bunch of dirty lira notes, and he would pass her fresh, shiny cellophane-wrapped packs. A *carabiniere* was standing there in his flashy uniform like his own monument, and was looking across at the Pantheon with a bored sneer. I thought, You and that little Communist would make a fine pair, you'd nationalize the cats, the compassionate old woman would die in a state nursing home, the fishheads would be taken into public ownership, and everything would be organized out of existence. But for the moment there was still disorder and happening. Newspaper-sellers cried their wares with hoarse, pleading shouts. They've always had my admiration. They are the rhapsodes and panegyrists of crimes, of accidents, of scandals and national commotions. The European bastion in Indochina was about to fall. In those days, war and peace hung in the balance, only we didn't know. We didn't hear about the cataclysm that threatened us until much later, in newspapers that hadn't yet been printed. Whoever could, ate well. We sipped our coffee and our brandy; we worked hard to earn money, and if the circumstances were favourable, we slept with one another. Rome is a wonderful city for men. I was interested in music, and it looked as though a lot of other people in Rome were as well. They had come from many countries to attend the congress in the ancient capital. Asia? Asia was far off. Asia was ten hours' flight, and it was as big and remote as Hokusai's wave. The wave was coming. It lapped at the shores of Ostia, where a girl's body had been found washed up. The poor corpse went around Rome like a ghost, and her pallid image terrified cabinet ministers; but they managed, as usual, to save their skins. The wave was approaching the cliffs at Antibes. *'Bonsoir, Monsieur Aga Khan!'* Dare I say that it's not my concern? I have no bank accounts, no money, no jewels, I weigh as nothing in the balance; I am free, I have no strings of race horses and no starlets to protect. My name is Siegfried Pfaffrath. An absurd name, I know. But then again, no more absurd than many others. Why do I despise it so? I never chose it. I like to talk shamelessly, but then I feel ashamed: I behave rudely, and I long to be able to show respect. I'm a composer of serious music. My profession matches my name for absurdity. Siegfried Pfaffrath, it says on concert programmes. Why don't I use a pseudonym? I have no idea. Is it the hated name clinging to me, or do I cling to it? Will my family not let go of me? And yet I believe that everything that's done, thought, dreamed or ruined, everything in the universe, even invisible and impalpable things, concern me and reach out to me.

A large automobile, gleaming black, noiseless engine, a lacquered coffin, the windows mirroring and impenetrable, had driven up to the Pantheon. It looked like a diplomatic conveyance – maybe the ambassador from Pluto was nestling on the plump upholstery, or a delegate from Hell – and Siegfried, drinking his brandy on the piazza and dreaming, aware of some activity but nothing out of the ordinary, looked at the licence plate and had an impression of Arab script. Who was it just drawing up, a prince from the Arabian Nights, an exiled king? A dusky-faced chauffeur in military livery leapt from his seat, tore open the passenger door, and stayed in bustling close attendance on a man in a well-fitting grey suit. The suit was English flannel, and it was the work of an expensive tailor, but on the squat body of the man – thick neck, broad shoulders, high ribcage, round elastic belly like a medicine ball, stocky thighs – the suit took on a rustic, Alpine aspect. The man had cropped bristly iron-grey hair, and he wore large dark glasses that were everything other than rustic, that suggested secrecy, cunning, foreign travel, diplomatic corps or wanted by Interpol. Was this Odysseus, on a visit to the gods? No, it was not Odysseus, not the wily king of Ithaca; this man was a butcher. He came from the Underworld, carrion smells wafted round him, he himself was Death, a brutal, mean, crude and unquestioning Death. Siegfried hadn't seen his Uncle Jude-jahn, who had terrorized him as a child, for thirteen years. Many times Siegfried had been punished for hiding from his uncle, and the boy had come to see his Uncle Gottlieb as the embodiment of everything he most feared and hated, the personification of duress, marching, the war. Even now he sometimes imagined he could hear the scolding, forever angry voice of the man with the bull neck, but he only dimly remembered the innumerable images of the mighty and universally feared tribune – on hoardings, on classroom walls, or as a paralysing shade on cinema screens that showed the man in ostentatiously plain Party uniform and unpolished boots, with his head thrust avidly forward. Thus, Siegfried, since escaped into freedom, drinking

14

grappa *à la* Hemingway, thinking about this square in Rome and about the music which was his personal adventure, failed to recognize Gottlieb Judejahn, it never even crossed his mind that this monster had come back from the dead and surfaced in Rome. Siegfried only observed casually, and with an involuntary shudder, a corpulent, presumably wealthy foreigner, someone of consequence and unpleasant, luring the cat Benito to him, grabbing him by the scruff, and taking him off – amid the shouts and cries of the children – to his magnificent car. The chauffeur stiffened to attention like a tin soldier, and shut the door respectfully after Judejahn and Benito. The large black automobile glided silently out of the square, and in the afternoon sun Siegfried caught a glimpse of Arab script on the licence plate, until abruptly a cloud passed in front of the sun, and the car vanished in a puff of haze and dust.

Asked along to the rehearsal by Kürenberg her husband, Ilse had been sitting, unnoticed by Siegfried, in the back row of the concert hall (which was darkened except for the lights over the orchestra pit) next to one of the green potted trees, listening to the symphony. She didn't like it. What she heard were discordant, inharmonious, mutually antagonistic sounds, a vague searching, a half-hearted experiment in which many paths were taken and none followed to its end, in which no idea asserted itself, where from the outset everything was brittle, full of doubt, doomed to despair. It seemed to Ilse that the person who had written these notes didn't know what he wanted. Did he despair because he was lost or was he lost because whichever way he went, he spread the black night of his depression, and made it impassable for himself? Kürenberg had talked a lot about Siegfried, but Ilse had yet to meet him. Up until now, she had been merely indifferent. But now Siegfried's music disturbed her, and she didn't want to be disturbed. There was something in it, some tone that made her sad. But life had taught her that sorrow and pain were best avoided. She didn't want to suffer. Not any more. She had suffered long enough. She gave beggars unusually large sums, without asking what had forced them to beg. Kürenberg could have conducted elsewhere in the world for more money, in Sydney or New York; and Ilse hadn't advised him against putting on Siegfried's symphony for the congress in Rome, but now she was sorry that he was taking trouble over something inchoate and hopeless, an expression of naked and unworthy despair.

When the rehearsal was over, the Kürenbergs went out to eat. They liked to eat; they ate often, plentifully and well. Happily it didn't show. They did well on their good and abundant food; both were solid, not fat, well-nourished and sleek like healthy animals. As Ilse didn't say anything, Kürenberg knew that she'd disliked the symphony. It's difficult to argue with a silent opponent, and before long Kürenberg was hailing Siegfried as the most gifted composer of his generation. He had invited him back for that evening. Now he wasn't sure how Ilse would respond. He mentioned it in passing, and Ilse said, 'You asked him to our hotel?' 'Yes,' said Kürenberg. Then Ilse knew that Kürenberg, who was a passionate cook, even on the road, and they were always on the road, was going to cook for him, and that was proof that he genuinely did admire Siegfried and was courting him, and once more she was silent. But why shouldn't she join him in inviting Siegfried? She didn't like to be left out. Nor did she want to quarrel with Kürenberg. They hardly ever quarrelled. Their union was harmonious, they had been all over the world together, often travelling in grim and dangerous circumstances, without friction. Very well, Siegfried could visit them in their hotel, and they would give him dinner, that was fine by her. Kürenberg assured her Siegfried was a pleasant man, and perhaps he was; but his music, unless it were to change – and Ilse refused to believe that it could change, because these notes, however incoherent and disagreeable to her, were in their way a true reflection of a particular human destiny, and that made them unalterable – his music, however nice Siegfried might be, she would never get on with. Ilse looked at Kürenberg, walking along at her side, in his stout shoes and suit of coarse Scottish tweed, grizzled, balding, but with bright eyes in his good, solid face, a little heavy but with a firm stride and agile amid the bustle and confusion of the Roman streets. Kürenberg appeared taciturn, or, perhaps more accurately, firmly anchored in himself. Living on an intellectual plane, he was never impatient and never sentimental, and yet Ilse was convinced that his support for Siegfried was emotionally inspired; it had somehow moved him that in '44 a German prisoner-of-war in an English camp had turned to him, the voluntary émigré, and involuntary volunteer infantryman in the First World War at Langemarck, and asked him for samples of the new music. For Kürenberg, Siegfried's prisoner-of-war letter had been a sign, a message from a Europe that had collapsed into barbarism, the dove that signalled that the floodwaters were receding.

They sat down in the sun, they enjoyed the sun, they sat down on the terrace of the wickedly expensive restaurant on the Piazza Navona, they enjoyed sitting there. They looked out into the calm harmonious oval of the one-time arena, they were glad that violent era was at an end, and they lunched. They lunched on little prawns crisply fried in butter, on tender grilled chicken, dry salad leaves dressed with oil and lemon juice, large sensuous red strawberries, and with their lunch they drank a dry lively Frascati. They enjoyed the wine. They enjoyed the food. They were serious and calm eaters. They were serious and blithe drinkers. They hardly spoke, but they were very much in love.

After lunch, they took the bus to the station district where they were staying. The bus was overcrowded as ever. They stood pressed against one another, and against other passengers. They stood in silence, calm and satisfied. At the station, they decided to pay a short visit to the National Museum in the ruins of the Baths of Diocletian. They loved antiquity. They loved the solid marble, the exalted forms made by man in his own image, the cool sarcophagi, the delicious rondure of the mixing-bowls. They saw the Eroses, fauns, gods and heroes. They studied the mythical monsters and gazed at the lovely body of the Cirenian Venus and the head of the Sleeping Fury. Then they stepped out into the cool, sleepy lane, shaded by high buildings, behind their hotel, nothing special but comfortable enough. They went into a butcher's shop, saw the bodies hanging on cruel hooks, bled, fresh, cool, and saw the heads of sheep and oxen, dumb, quiet sacrificial victims, and from the clean and beautiful diagonally hewn marble slab of the butcher, they ordered tender matured steaks, once Kürenberg had poked and prodded them with his fingers to test their hanging; they bought fruit and vegetables at open-air stands; they purchased oil and wine in old cellars; and, after looking for some time, and testing it with his teeth, Kürenberg found a type of rice that promised not to turn soggy when cooked. They carried their parcels home and took the lift up to their large bright room, the hotel's best suite. They were tired, and they enjoyed their tiredness. They saw the wide bed and they enjoyed the prospect of the cool clean linen. It was broad afternoon. They didn't draw the curtains. They undressed in the light, and lay down between the sheets. They thought of the beautiful Venus and the leaping fauns. They enjoyed their thoughts, they enjoyed the memory, then they enjoyed one another, and fell into a deep sleep, that condition of anticipated death that takes up a third of our lives; but Ilse dreamed she was the Eumenide, the sleeping Eumenide, appeasingly called the Kindly One, the Goddess of Revenge.

It was time, he ought to go, he had said he would go, it was the agreed hour, they were waiting for him, and he felt unwilling, reluctant, afraid. He, Judejahn, was afraid, and what was his favourite saying? 'I don't know the meaning of the word fear!' That saying had a lot to answer for, a lot of men had bitten the dust, always the others of course; he had issued the orders and they had fallen, on pointless assaults or holding doomed positions to satisfy an insane sense of honour, holding them to the last man, as Judejahn then reported to his Führer with swelled breast, and anyone who was chicken swung for it, dangled from trees and lamp-posts, swayed in the stiff breeze of the dead with his confession round his broken neck: 'I was too cowardly to defend my Fatherland.' But then whose Fatherland was it? Judejahn's? Judejahn's arm-twisting empire and marching club, hell take it. And there weren't just hangings, there were beheadings, torturings, shootings, deaths behind closed doors and up against walls. The enemy took aim, yes, of course the enemy was peppering away as well, but here it was your comrade who dispatched you with a bullet, you'll not find a better; it was your compatriot ranting, your greatly admired superior, and the young, condemned man didn't start thinking until it was too late about which was the enemy and which his comrade. Judejahn addressed them in fatherly fashion as 'my lads' and Judejahn said crudely, latrine-style, 'Kill the cunt,' he always had the popular touch, always a hell of a guy, great sense of humour, old Landsberg assassin, in bloody charge of the Black Reichswehr camps on the estates of Mecklenburg, death's head on his steel helmet, but even they, the old gods, had turned their coats, Ehrhardt the captain dining with writers and other such shitheads, and Rossbach with his troupe of pale-skinned boys, putting on mystery plays for the delectation of headmasters and clerics, but he, Judejahn, had taken the right road, unwavering and straight ahead, to Führer and Reich and full military honours.

He strode through his room, the carpets were thick, the walls were silk, silk screened the streetlights, on the damask bed lay Benito the mangy cat, looking blinkingly, sardonically up at Judejahn, as if to purr, 'So you've survived,' and then looking in disgust at the fried liver on a silver dish by the foot of the bed. Why had he brought that animal in here? Was it some kind of magic charm? Judejahn didn't believe in ghosts. He was just a sentimental bastard, he couldn't stand to see it, it had infuriated him, a kingly animal like that being tormented. Benito! Those snotnoses! Judejahn was staying on the Via Veneto, staying in an ambassador-class hotel, a billet for NATO generals, lodgings for presidents of US Steel, home from home for directors of chemicals companies, showcase for award-winning wide-screen epic bosoms, blackmailers and poules had their little coops here, all odd birds went to Rome, weird beards and wasp waists, fantastically expensive outfits, waists you could strangle the life out of with one hand, but it was better to grab the firm tits and ass, feel the arousing, palpitating flesh under the nylon skin, the wispy garter-belt stretched tautly over belly and thighs to the sheer-textured stockings – there were no cardinals staying here.

He had taken off his dark glasses. Runny eyes, watery blue. Was it foolish of him to stay here? He laughed. First, he was in the right, and had always been in the right, and secondly, well, the wind blew, didn't it? Forgiven and forgotten. It was a little joke of Judejahn's, and Judejahn liked his little jokes, like putting up at this particular hotel, albeit with a passport in which the name given was not his real name, and the country of birth was not his real country of birth, but apart from that the document was genuine enough, it was stamped with diplomatic visas, he was Someone, he had always been Someone, and he was now. He could afford to stay here, and enjoy the memory of his palmy days: he had resided under this roof once before, it was from here that he had sent messages to the Palazzo Venezia, it was in the hall of this building that he had ordered the hostages to be shot.

What was he to wear? He had a full wardrobe, he had suits of fine English cloth, tailored by nimble Arab fingers, he had become a cosmopolite, he put on perfume before going to the brothel for a relieving poke, the sheikhs had taught him that; but in whatever garb, he remained unmistakably the old Judejahn, an infantile type, a grim Boys' Own hero, unable to forget that his father, a primary schoolteacher, had beaten him for being bad at school. What about the dark suit? The reunion should be kept formal. But leave the perfume out. People didn't reek of musk where he was going. They kept the wild man out of sight. The Germans had recovered themselves. Were respectable people once more. Would they be able to tell where he had been? Once knee-deep in blood, and now, in the final frame, the desert sand?

There were jackals where he came from. Nights they howled. Unfamiliar stars pricked the sky. What did he care? They were orienteering aids. Otherwise he didn't need them. He couldn't hear the jackals, either. He slept. His sleep was tranquil, peaceful, dreamless. Every night he dropped into it like a stone into a deep well. No nightmares plagued him, no remorse, no skeletons. The sleeper woke when reveille sounded. That was welcome, familiar music. There was a storm blowing in the desert. The sound of the cornet wavered and died. The fellow was a slacker; he wanted bringing up to the mark. The sand clattered against the barrack walls. Judejahn rose from his narrow camp bed. He liked hard beds. He liked the white-washed room with the metal wardrobe, the folding table, the washing unit, the rattle of rusty ewers and basins. He could have lived in a villa in the capital, highly paid, sought-after expert that he was, put in charge of reorganizing and training the king's army. But he preferred the barracks. It gave him confidence and a feeling of security. The barracks were home, comradeship, security and order. In fact it was words that held him together. Whose 'comrade' was Judejahn really? He liked the view of the desert. It wasn't its endlessness that drew him, more its barrenness. For Judejahn the desert was a great exercise ground, a front, a continual challenge that kept him in trim. In the capital, tiptoeing servants would have hovered at his elbow, he would have fornicated with warm-bellied girls, wallowed between their thighs, he could have bathed in aromatic waters like a pasha. But in camp he soaped himself, scrubbed himself down with a stiff brush till his skin was raw, he shaved with the old German pocket razor that had accompanied him all the way from the Weiden-damm Bridge to the desert. He felt good, like a scorched wild boar, he thought to himself. He heard man sounds:

water splashing, buckets clanging, whistling, oaths, jokes, orders, boots scraping, doors banging. He smelled the barracks smell compounded from detention, service, leather polish, gun grease, strong soap, sweet pomade, sour sweat, coffee, heated aluminium dishes and piss. It was the smell of fear, only Judejahn didn't know it: after all, he didn't know what fear was. He told himself so in front of the mirror; naked, thick-bellied, he stood in front of the fly-blown glass. He did up his belt. He was old school in this. The belt held in his paunch and hitched up his buttocks. An old general's trick. Judejahn went out into the passage. Men flattened themselves against the walls, dutiful shadows. He ignored them. He was going outside. A blood-red sun floated on the sandstorm. Judejahn inspected the front. The wind tore at his khaki uniform. Sand cut into flesh like shards of glass, and rattled against tanks like hailstones. The sight amused Judejahn. See the sons of the desert on parade! He looked them over and saw dark, moist, treacherous almond eyes, brown skin, burned faces, blackamoor countenances, Semitic noses. His men! His men were dead. They lay buried under grass, under snow, under rock and sand, they lay near the Arctic Circle, in France, in Italy, in Crete, in the Caucasus, and a few of them lay in boxes under the prison-yard. His men! Now that meant these here. Judejahn had little appreciation of the irony of fate. He did the old troop-inspector's strut and looked firmly and severely into the moist, treacherous and dreamy almond eyes. Judejahn saw no reproach in those eyes. He saw no accusation. Judejahn had taken the animal gentleness from these men. He had taken their pride, the natural dignity of these male harem children. He had broken them by making them obey. He had planed them down, by the book. Now they stood in front of him, upright and braced like tin soldiers, and their

23

souls were gone out of them. They were soldiers. They
were troops. They were ready for action and expendable.
Judejahn hadn't wasted his time. He hadn't disappointed
his employers. Wherever he went was Grossdeutschland,
where he was in command it was Prussia's old glory. The
desert sand was no different from the sand of Brandenburg. Judejahn had been forced out, but he hadn't been
uprooted; he carried Germany around with him in his
heart, Germany still one day the saviour of the world. The
flagstaff soared in the storm, it soared up alone towards
the sand-occluded sun, it soared alone and tall into a godless void. Orders were given. Shouts ran through the ranks
of soldiers like electric shocks. They stood up even
straighter and stiffer as the flag climbed once more! What
a majestic symbol of meaninglessness! The red morning
star glowed on a green ground. Here you could still flog
used goods, nationalism, fealty and hatred for the Israelis,
those perennially useful people through whom Judejahn
had once more come to money, position and respect.

The dark suit wasn't right, either. It made Judejahn look
like a chubby confirmand and it enraged him as he
remembered how his father, the primary schoolteacher,
had forced him to dress up like that and walk up to the
altar of the Lord. That was in 1915 and he had had enough
of school, he wanted to fight, only they wouldn't take
little Gottlieb. But then he had his revenge on them, they
gave him his leaving certificate in 1917, and he got a place
on the officer training course, not the battlefield, but later
there were bullets aplenty whistling round the ears of Judejahn, the Freikorps, Annaberg battles, Spartacist uprising,
Kapp Putsch, Ruhrmaquis, and finally the assassination
squad in the woods. That was his seed-time, his bohème
(Youth, sweet youth, said the song), and he never got
another. In Hitler's service Judejahn became respectable,

he made it, he put on weight, he got fancy-sounding titles, he married and acquired a brother-in-law: that opportunist Kapp comrade-in-arms, camp follower and carpetbagger, the Oberpresident and Oberbürgermeister, the Führer's money man, denazified and now once again top dog, the old mayor re-elected by the people, by strictly democratic procedures. That was his way of doing things, that was his brother-in-law Friedrich Wilhelm Pfaffrath, who in his opinion was an asshole, and to whom, in a weak moment, he had written a letter: they weren't to shed any tears over him, he had landed on his feet. And then he had agreed to this idiotic reunion in Rome. His brother-in-law wrote that he'd fix everything. Fix what? His return, his decriminalization, his pardon, and then a little job at the end of it? The man was a windbag. Did Judejahn even want to go home? Did he require a certificate of acquittal, the freedom of a pardon? He was free anyway, here was his shopping list to prove it. He had weapons to buy, tanks, guns, aeroplanes: leftover gear that was no longer suitable for the next global dust-up, but pretty handy for a little desert fighting, for use against palace coup or popular uprising. Judejahn was accredited with banks, he had powers of attorney. He was meeting arms dealers from two hemispheres. There were old pals to try to recruit. He was in play. He enjoyed it. What did family matter against that? Shitty lot. You had to tough it out. Eva had been faithful to him, a faithful German woman, the type of womanhood one said one lived and fought for; and sometimes one even believed it. He was afraid. He was afraid of Eva, her unmade-up face and her hair-knot, the SA woman, the believer in Final Victory: she was all right, certainly, but nothing drew him to her. Besides, she was probably spent. And his son? That rat. What was going on behind that weird dumbshow? The letters he got hinted at changes.

He couldn't fathom them. He spread out a map of Rome in front of him, like a general-staff map. He had to go up the Via Ludovisi, then down the Spanish Steps, from whose height he could control the city with a single cannon, yes, and then to the Via Condotti, to the middle-class hotel where they were all staying, waiting for him. They had supposed he would be staying there too, in the German auberge, as the guide books called it, with its cosy atmosphere of back home. And Friedrich Wilhelm Pfaffrath, the sensible advocate of sensible and realistic national policies, Pfaffrath who had made a comeback, and maybe even thought he was the cleverer of the two, because he was back at the tiller, and was in position for a new career in the new Germany, brother-in-law Pfaffrath, Oberbürgermeister and respected West German citizen, had wanted to take him under his wing, him, the supposed fugitive. That was probably how he'd sketched it out, he wanted to hold the vagabond in his arms, with all his past misdeeds and evasions forgiven him. But Judejahn would tell him where he could stick it, he'd been through too much for this idyll to charm him: dead or presumed dead, the bombed-out Berliner, the man who went missing in the cleaning-up operation, condemned at Nuremberg *in contumaciam*. But the High Court that passed judgments on fate, human destiny and the blind actions of history, was itself reeling about in a maze of its own, was not a Justice with blindfolded eyes, just a silly woman playing blind man's buff, who, since she administered justice where there was no justice, had herself sunk in the morass of events that were without moral. The High Court had no evidence as to whether Judejahn was alive or dead, and so the High Judge had carefully donned the black cap and condemned to death Judejahn, accused before all the world as a monster, *in absentia*, with the result that the accused man avoided the rope, which was as well because people in those days were far too quick to reach for it, and for the Court, ultimately, the fact that Judejahn escaped hanging was just as well because the monster Judejahn had been earmarked for re-employment, war being a dirty business. The Oberbürgermeister had probably gone to Rome in his own car, he could probably run to a Mercedes again by now, or maybe the city had provided him with the vehicle for the scenic ride, Italy, land of longing, land of Germans, and Pfaffrath the German had his leather-bound Goethe on his shelves, and tax-commentaries well-thumbed next to the man from Weimar, a dubious type, what good ever came out of Weimar, and it irritated Judejahn having to imagine his brother-in-law with his snout in the trough again – it was treason, the fellow had committed base treason and should have swung for it. But Judejahn had a car at his disposal also, it wasn't that he had to walk, no, but he wanted to, he wanted to make the pilgrimage to bourgeois life on foot, that was appropriate here, appropriate in this city and this situation, he wanted to gain time, and Rome, they said, Rome where the bishops had settled and the streets crawled with surplices, Rome, they said, was a beautiful city, and now Judejahn was going to see it for himself. He hadn't been able to hitherto, he'd been here on duty, given orders here, gone on the rampage here. Now he could stroll through Rome, could pick up what the town had to offer by way of balmy air, historical sites, sophisticated whores and rich food. Why stint himself? He'd been in the desert a long time, and Rome was still standing, not in ruins. The eternal city, they called it. That was professors' and priests' talk. Judejahn showed his murderer's face. He knew better than that. He'd seen plenty of cities go under.

She waited. She waited by herself. No one helped her to wait, no one shortened the time by talking to her, and she didn't want the time to be shortened anyway or for them to concern themselves with her, because she alone was in mourning, she alone was distressed, and not even her sister Anna understood that Eva Judejahn was not weeping for lost possessions, or rank or respect, still less was it grief over Judejahn, whom she had seen as a hero entering Valhalla, that paled her countenance; she was grieving for Grossdeutschland, she was shedding tears for the Führer, lamenting the fact that treachery and betrayal and unnatural pacts had brought down the Germanic idea of world-salvation, the millennial Third Reich. The sound of laughter came up from the lobby through staircases and corridors, in at her window from the courtyard came the smell of cooking and an American dance tune sung by an Italian kitchen boy; but she wasn't reached by the laughter or the lively new nigger song embellished by bel canto, she stood in her widow's weeds in the stone cage of her room, madness, incomprehension and fleeting time, she stood wolf-throated, pregnant with vengeance, in the delirium of a myth she'd helped to concoct, prey to her innermost fears, her greying straw-blonde hair, sheaf of wheat left to stand when the frightened farm hands fled at the approach of a thunderstorm, her hair tied in a stern womanly knot over the pale face, long-skulled face, square-chinned face, sorrow face, terror face, ravened, burned out, a death's head like the insignia Judejahn wore on his peaked cap. She was like a ghost, not a Eumenide, but a northerly ghost, a foggy ghost that a madman had brought to Rome and locked into a hotel room.

She was in a small room, the smallest one in the hotel, that had been her desire, for brother-in-law Friedrich Wilhelm, who wouldn't understand that it was she who had to remove the blot from the name of Germany, Friedrich Wilhelm had undertaken the journey for her sake, so Anna said too, and Friedrich Wilhelm Pfaffrath patted Eva Judejahn gently on the shoulder and said, 'There, there, Eva, we'll get our Gottlieb back, just you see,' and she shuddered and bit her lip because he had said Gottlieb, he'd never dared to do that before, and it was treason to call the standard-bearer, SS-general and one of the highest figures in the godless Party Gottlieb, because Judejahn hated the name, priestly slime left on him by the schoolmaster his father, and he didn't want to love God. Family and friends called him Götz, while officially and in public he was G. Judejahn, Götz was an abbreviation of Gottlieb dating from his wild Freikorps days, but Friedrich Wilhelm, the pedant and owner of the leather-bound edition of Goethe, had found Götz unworthy, though it was pithy and Germanic, but it also summoned up the famous lines in his mind,* and it was a borrowed, occupied name, one should just carry whatever name one was baptized with, and so, daring and flush with confidence, he again said Gottlieb, although he too found the name ridiculous and unmanly. Black-clad she walked. Walked clad in black from the window overlooking the courtyard to the mirror over the wash-basin, stalked like a caged beast in a cell. She had kept her mourning all through the years, except in the detention camp, because she'd been arrested in her travelling-clothes, but once she was released, she borrowed a black dress from her sister, because her own clothes had disappeared, her wardrobes looted, and the houses Judejahn had owned had been taken away from her. And when her husband got in touch, to the perplexity

* 'Er Aber, sags ihm, er kann mich im Arsch lecken' – Goethe, *Götz von Berlichingen*, Act 3.

29

of the family she did not put aside her mourning, because she hadn't been mourning her husband, the hero missing in action, and the fact that he was alive only added to the reason for mourning, he would ask after their son, she had been unable to safeguard him, and maybe Judejahn himself had gone to Canossa and was living like a prince; she didn't mind him sleeping with other women, he had always done that and told her about it, that was part of a warrior's life, and when he made babies, then they were warrior babies and good stock, recruits for the storm troopers and the Führer, but it disturbed her that he had hidden away in the Levant. She guessed that he too had perpetrated treason, blood-treason and racial betrayal in the soft enemy climate, in rose-scented harem darkness, in garlic-reeking caves with Negresses and Jewesses, who had been waiting for revenge, and were panting for German sperm. Eva would have liked to raise an army to fetch these children, Judejahn's bastards, home: to put them to the test, and have them live as Germans or die as half-castes. The kitchen boy in the yard was whistling again, it was another nigger song, brash and cheeky and scornful, and the laughter in the lobby rolled up the stairs and along the corridor to her, plump, complacent, and sometimes cackling.

Oberbürgermeister Friedrich Wilhelm Pfaffrath was sitting with Anna his wife and Dietrich his younger son in the lounge of the German hotel, and already they had made contact with visiting compatriots, with Germans of similar background and outlook, fortunate survivors but with short memories like themselves. VW-owners, drivers of Mercedes, redeemed by German efficiency and now once more valued bringers of foreign currency, they were conversing and drinking sweet vermouth, and on the table were street maps and guidebooks, because they were planning expeditions to Tivoli and to Frascati, but also to the rebuilt monastery of Monte Cassino; they meant to visit the battlefields, which held no terrors for these people, and one of their number would look and find and shout, 'This was our battery position, we were spitting down from here, here is where we were dug in, here is where we held the line.' And then he would show what a fine fellow he was, hats off, because he admired himself as an upright warrior, a sporting killer, so to say, he would talk about Tommy Atkins and GI Joe, and maybe even about Anders and his Polish army, but only maybe because Polacks were still Polacks. And in the military cemetery they would pay tribute to themselves and the dead with exalted feeling all round. The dead didn't laugh, they were dead; or they had no time and didn't care who among the living came to see them, they were changing phases, they climbed out of life dirty and guilty, perhaps not even personally guilty, into the wheel of births to a new repentance, a new guilt, a new pointless incarnation. Friedrich Wilhelm Pfaffrath thought it rude of Judejahn to be late. But perhaps he wasn't yet in Rome, perhaps he had experienced difficulties getting there, trouble with a passport maybe, his case was sensitive and required careful handling. Things shouldn't be rushed, but Pfaffrath was convinced that the time had come, seeing as his brother-in-law had succeeded in staying alive, to lose the file on Judejahn, carefully, discreetly, without fuss – one might still be compromised, some unpatriotic type might squeal – but the time of hanging was definitely over, for them at least, the Americans had come to their senses, they now had a truer measure of German circumstances and German usefulness, and vengeful judgements and hatred were no longer wise or appropriate. Roosevelt was dead and suspected of Communist

31

collaboration. And who was Morgenthau? A nebbish! Anyone who'd survived up until now would survive in future. And maybe Judejahn could be found a job in the Agricultural Union, just to begin with, and Eva would snap out of her craziness, because, no question, he, Friedrich Wilhelm Pfaffrath, was a nationalist, but mistakes had been made, you had to own up to them and make a fresh start. Hunger had made Prussia great! And wouldn't that apply to the rest of the country too? They'd come on a lot already. Not in terms of hunger – that was a figure of speech, a fortifying legend from past times of pride and shortages – because hunger was just the rumbling of empty bellies after wars that had been lost through deceit, best not to think about that, but in terms of prosperity, that was real and tangible and worth pursuing. And might the new standard of living not finally convince the sons, the lost sheep of the break-up of Germany, those driven away by a happily brief period of chaos, to come home to the ancestral way of their people? The Federal Republic had its democratic weaknesses, certainly, and for the moment it was hard to do anything about them, but overall there was order in the occupied land, and everything was ready for a tighter rein. Soon they would be able to see a little further, prospects weren't bad, and Pfaffrath had the right kind of track record; but as far as the sons were concerned, their lack of common sense, their neuroses, the way they followed their so-called consciences, that was just a sign of the times, a sickness of the times, and in time it would be cured like an overlong puberty. Friedrich Wilhelm Pfaffrath had in mind less his nephew Adolf Judejahn than Siegfried, the elder of his two sons, who had left him, while with Dietrich, the younger, he was content: he was now a Goth, had joined his father's fraternity, had learned corps regulations, acquired connections, was approaching his final exams, and was looking forward to the visit to the battlefield at Monte Cassino, as was only right for a young person. But Siegfried was somehow degenerate. All right, if he had to – let him be a kapellmeister: there were well-paid jobs in music too. Friedrich Wilhelm Pfaffrath was a well-informed man, and it had come to his ears that Siegfried was in Rome. That seemed to him like a good omen for a possible clearing of the air and reconciliation. It wouldn't be easy, because Siegfried still seemed to be wading in a swamp, figuratively speaking, and the programme of the musical congress was full of surrealism, cultural Bolshevism and negroid newfangledness. Was the boy blind? But perhaps that was the way you made your name nowadays, now that the Jews were back in business internationally, dishing out fame and prize-money once again. Pfaffrath had also read somewhere that Kürenberg would be conducting Siegfried's symphony, and it came back to him. 'Do you remember that Kürenberg,' he asked his wife, 'who was our General Musical Director in '34, and was all set to go on to Berlin?' 'He married that Aufhäuser woman,' replied Anna. 'Yes,' said Pfaffrath, 'that's why he couldn't go to Berlin, and we weren't able to keep him, either.' And Pfaffrath had the impression that at that time, before the gauleiters had acquired all power for themselves, when he was Oberpresident of the province, he had supported Kürenberg, and that pleased him now, because it suggested that in choosing to conduct and promote the work of the son, Kürenberg was gratefully acknowledging the help of the father. But

up in the cage of her room, Eva listened out for the avenger's footfall.

Spinning out of the revolving door, the porter's hand, white-gloved lackey's hand, hangman's hand, death's hand had given the carousel of ingress and egress momentum, most respectfully, your humble servant, always at your service, sir, a tip for death, sir. Spun by his hand out of the revolving door, Judejahn felt he'd been thrown out of the hotel, out of the security of money and rank, out of the safety of power that stood behind him, borrowed power to be sure, foreign power, the power of another race even, dusky Levantine power, but nevertheless state power with suzerainty and its own flag – all at once he felt powerless. It was the first time in a very long time that Judejahn had stepped out, a man among men, a civilian, without protection, without an escort, without a weapon, a stout elderly fellow in a dark suit. It threw him the way no one paid him any attention. Passersby touched him, brushed past him, knocked into him and muttered a quick desultory 'Pardon'. Pardon for Judejahn? He took a couple of strides. No one was keeping a respectful distance. Judejahn could have gone back inside the hotel, he could have rung the diplomatic mission of his employers, and he would have been sent the automobile with the Arab licence plates. Or he could have merely waved to the hotel porter, and the white-gloved and serviceable fellow would have whistled up a taxi-cab with his shrill little flute. Back then – how stiffly they had stood, his guard of honour! Two lines of black uniforms. Twenty outriders, a car in front of him, another behind him. But he wanted to walk. He probably hadn't walked through a city for thirty years. When Berlin was a glowing inferno, when the whole world was on Judejahn's heels, he had walked a little, had crawled through debris, climbed over bodies, romped through ruins and then he'd been rescued. How? Brought low by chance, or, as his Führer would have said, by fate, doused with petrol, burned to ashes, and then not finished after all, the Phoenix resurrected itself, fate had rescued Judejahn and led him to the Promised Land, not the land of Israel, but that of some other dusky tribe. And there Judejahn hadn't been on foot either, only on the exercise ground, taking a few steps in the desert.

He got a grip on himself of course, old dreadnought, and if he fell, here was a railing to hand. Wrought-iron palings rose like spears into the sky – a palisade of power, wealth and rejection. A large automobile slid across the gravel drive. Judejahn remembered. He too had driven up here, more sweep, more gravel crunch, but he had once driven up here. A sign informed him that he was standing in front of the United States Embassy. Of course, Judejahn hadn't been to see the Americans; they hadn't invited him, they hadn't even been there at the time. But he had, definitely, so there must have been something Fascist in the building, some big production, and they had failed to exercise the necessary rigour. What was the Duce? A sentimental indulgence on the part of the Führer. Judejahn had a particular loathing for Southerners. He approached the cafés on the Via Veneto, and there they all were, not just the despised Southerners, the whole international clique was sitting there, sitting together as they had once done on the Kurfürstendamm, sitting there playing peace on earth, cooing in each other's ears, the deracinated ones, international, homeless golden jetsam, flying, restless and greedy, from one city to another, snooty vultures, escapees from German order and discipline. Judejahn detected mainly English spoken, the American version predominated, they were the ones who had benefited from the war, but he also heard Italian, French and other sounds, occasionally German – not so much here, for they were off on their own patch, making themselves pleasant to one another. Scum, rabble, Jews and Jew-slaves! The words frothed in his mouth like gall, and coated his teeth. He beheld no uniforms, no insignia on chest or shoulders, he looked out into a world without distinction or honour; there were only the epaulettes on the monkey jackets worn by employees of the gastronomic trade. But hello, what was this formation, scarlet-red, advancing against the street of the exploiters, against the plutocratic boulevard? Was the scarlet column a symbol of authority, an emblem of power? Was it the golden horde, the Young Guard, the Giovinezza, coming to clean up? Alas, it was a bitter deception that had been practised on Judejahn; they were surplices, drifting about the gaunt forms of young priests, and, far from marching, the red horde was walking in a disorderly rout, and to Judejahn it even appeared as though they had a swaying and effeminate walk, because it had escaped his notice, while in power, the manly and determined way priests faced death under a dictatorship, and fortunately he did not guess that the scarlet-robed ones were alumni of the German Seminary in Rome – that would have disturbed him even more. Money governed the Via Veneto. But didn't Judejahn have money? Could he not throw his weight around and buy as others bought? Some chairs stood outside a bar, extraordinarily flimsy-looking yellow chairs, they were ridiculous, chairs not built to be sat on, they looked like a flock of crazy canaries, you could almost hear them twittering. And Judejahn felt drawn to this bar, because, for some reason, it was empty at this hour. He didn't take a seat outside, he scorned the perilous chairs, went into the gaping interior and stood by the bar. He propped his elbow on it, he felt weary, it must be the climate that was sapping his strength, and he ordered a beer. An effeminate fellow in a purple tailcoat indicated to him that if he wanted to drink his beer standing at the bar, he would have to buy a coupon for it first, from the cashier. Behind the cash-desk sat the smiling Laura. Her lovely smile was famed up and down the street, and the owner of the bar would not let her go because of this smile that shone in his bar, which gave it a friendlier atmosphere and made the cash-desk a font of joy, even though Laura was stupid and couldn't add. What did it matter? No one cheated Laura, because even the homosexuals who made up the clientele of the bar late at night and on Sunday afternoons felt graced by Laura's steady smile. Judejahn was struck by it too. But inhumanity made him blind, and so he failed to realize that here was a childlike creature who was giving her best for no return. He thought, Nice-looking cunt. He saw hair black as lacquer, a doll's face lit up by the smile, he saw her red lips and red fingernails, he wanted to buy her, and in this moneyed street you had to buy or be bought. But again he stood there helpless and foolish and didn't know how to behave, how to address her, he wasn't in uniform now, the girl showed no fear, merely beckoning wouldn't do it. He was ready to shell out a lot of money for her, and in lira any sum seemed enormous. But how should he talk to her? In German? She wouldn't understand. Judejahn spoke no Italian. He had picked up a little English. So he asked her in English, not for a beer, but for a large Scotch. Smiling automatically, Laura gave him his token and directed him automatically to the fellow in the purple tails. 'A large King George.' 'Ice?' 'No.' 'Soda?' 'No.' The conversation didn't develop. Judejahn drank his whisky down. He was angry. He could only give orders. He couldn't even say a couple of friendly words to a whore. Maybe she was a Jewess? You couldn't spot them so easily in Italy. But he was little Gottlieb again, the son of the primary schoolteacher, who couldn't keep up with his class. He stood there, as he had once stood in one of his father's hand-me-down suits among his richer classmates in their sailor suits. Should he have another whisky? Whisky was a man's drink. Great lords drank their Scotch in silence, became drunks and lost the war. Judejahn decided against another whisky, though he wanted one; he was afraid the barman and the beautiful girl behind the cash-desk would laugh at him for being tongue-tied. But how many times had the taciturn customer seen the laughter freeze on the faces of others? That was the question! Judejahn made a note of the bar. He thought, I'll get you, see if I don't. And Laura expended her sweet smile on his broad back. Nothing told her he was a killer. She thought (if she thought anything at all, because thinking was not in her nature; instead she went in for a kind of vegetative musing), Family man, here on business, straight, chance client, showing off with those dark glasses. He was bored here, he won't be back. And if he did come back, he would come back on her account, and she would realize that it was on her account, and she would like him in spite of the dark glasses, because the homosexuals who came here in the evening bored Laura, they put their trust in any man who smelled of man, even if she had nothing against homosexuals, who, after all, provided her with a living.

Now Judajahn's thoughts returned to his in-laws, who were waiting to welcome their hero back from the dead. He took a look at the street map which he had folded up and taken with him. He quickly got his bearings, as he had learned to do: in forest, swamp and desert, he was incapable of getting lost. Nor would he get lost now in the jungle of the city. He walked down the Via di Porta Pinciana, parallel to a high old wall, behind which he guessed was a large, beautiful shady garden, perhaps belonging to one of the wealthy aristocrats, the royalist clique that had betrayed the Duce. It was warm and there was a smell of rain in the air. A puff of wind whirled up the dust and made his skin tingle. There were posters stuck on the garden wall. The next year's intake was being called up for military service. That could only be of benefit to the weaklings. Uncle Sam would provide the weapons. But where were the German trainers? Without German trainers, every dollar was wasted. Had Uncle Sam forgotten how to count? A red CP poster burned like a beacon. Judejahn thought of the night of the Reichstag fire. That was the uprising! They had answered the call! The beginning of an era! An era without Goethe! What did the Russian–Roman commune want? Judejahn couldn't read the text. Why should he read it? They should be put against the wall: up against this very wall here. In Lichterfelde they'd been put against the wall. Judejahn took a hand in the shooting, just for the hell of it. Who said all men were brothers? Those weaklings with their demands! What if there'd been an agreement with Moscow? There were no weaklings in Moscow. If the two big, strong brothers had come to an understanding, a wider, more sweeping Stalin–Hitler pact? Judejahn's head hurt. Missed opportunities, or had they really been conclusively missed, and 'The World will be Ours' belted out into a bright dawn. On Sunday there was some race, Rome–Naples, Naples–Rome. Gladiatorial bouts for weak nerves. What were their names, the fighter with the net and trident, and the other one with the sword? Germans pitted against wild animals in the circus. Germans were too good-natured, they were outwitted. There was a Church decree printed on white paper with a black cross. The Church always won out in the end. Priests were cunning and stayed on the sidelines. Let everyone else exhaust one another. After wars, they built up their own strength. Grave-robbers. Jesuit jiu-jitsu. Green paper. *Olio Sasso*. To grease the wheels. War? Mobilization? Not yet. Not for a while yet. No one dared. Little rehearsals in deserts, jungles and remote territories. As once in Spain. The coyote beckoned from the ground floor of a swanky apartment house. A coyote was a prairie wolf; Judejahn remembered his Karl May. In this instance, the Coyote was an American bar. There was plenty of polished brass on the door, and it looked exclusive and expensive. Judejahn had money, but he wouldn't venture into the bar. Judejahn was thirsty, but he wouldn't venture into the Coyote. Why not? Little Gottlieb was in the way, and he wouldn't do anything out of uniform. Judejahn went on. He came upon a *fiaschetteria*. Straw-wrapped bottles lay in heaps, the floor was awash with wine. This was where the common people drank. There was no cause to fear the common people. You could control them. There was no reason to talk to the common people. The people were gunfodder. The Führer stood over the people. Judejahn called for a Chianti. He gulped it down. The wine did him good. He ordered another glass. He didn't taste the wine, but he felt reinvigorated. He strode out, to the famous square in front of the Trinità dei Monti church. The church had two pointed towers. Nuns from the Sacré Coeur cloisters stood on the church steps. Judejahn was revolted by their long skirts, their cloaks, their coifs. Witches! Now he had the Spanish Steps at his feet, and Rome, and in the background the mighty dome of St Peter's – the old enemy. He wasn't beaten. No one was beaten. The game had been drawn – thanks to treachery: the Führer had held all the trumps, gnomes stole them from him, orders hadn't been carried out – only Judejahn had carried out every order he had been given.

He had left no mess. Had he cleaned up everywhere? Unfortunately not. In fact, as it happened, nowhere. The hydra had more than nine heads. It had millions. One Judejahn was not enough. He returned from the war, no conqueror, a beggar, a nobody. He had to support himself on the parapet. His fingers gripped the crumbling masonry. Pain welled up inside him. Rome swam before his eyes, a sea of dissolving stone, and the dome of St Peter's was a bubble adrift on the wild sea. An old lady with blue-rinsed hair pointed with her umbrella at the great panorama of the Eternal City. She called out, 'Isn't it wonderful!' The left tower of Trinità dei Monti rang out its benediction.

He went down. He went down the Spanish Steps, climbed down into picturesque Italy, into the idling population that was sitting on the steps, lying, reading, studying, chatting, quarrelling or embracing one another. A boy offered Judejahn some maize, yellow roasted kernels of maize. He held out a paper cornet to the foreigner, to the barbarian from the north, said 'cento lire' in a wheedling voice, and Judejahn knocked the bag out of his hand. The maize scattered over the steps, and Judejahn trod it underfoot. He hadn't meant it. It was clumsiness. He felt like giving the boy a thrashing.

He crossed the square and reached the Via Condotti, panting. The pavement was narrow. People squeezed together in the busy shopping street, squeezed in front of the shop windows, squeezed past each other. Judejahn jostled and was jostled back. He didn't understand. He was surprised that no one made way for him, that no one got out of his road. He was surprised to find himself being jostled.

He looked for the cross street, looked for it on the map – but was he really looking? His years on the fringe of the desert seemed to him like time spent under anaesthetic, he had felt no pain, but now he felt sick, he felt fever and pain, felt the cuts that had pruned his life to a stump, felt the cuts that severed this stump from the wide flourishing of his power. What was he? A shadow of his former self. Should he rise from the dead, or remain a spook in the desert, a ghost in the Fatherland's colour magazines? Judejahn was not afraid to keep the world at bay. What did it want with him, anyway? Let it come, let it come in all its softness and venality, all its dirty, buzzard lusts, concealed under the mask of respectability. The world should be glad there were fellows like himself. Judejahn wasn't afraid of the rope. He was afraid of living. He feared the absence of commands in which he was expected to live. He had issued any number: the higher he'd been promoted, the more he'd issued, and the responsibility had never bothered him; he merely said, 'That's on my say-so,' or 'I'm in command here,' but that had been a phrase, an intoxicating phrase, because in reality he had only ever followed orders himself. Judejahn had been mighty. He had tasted power, but in order to enjoy it, he required it to be limited, he required the Führer as an embodiment and visible god of power, the commander who was his excuse before the Creator, man and the Devil: I only did what I was told, I only obeyed orders. Did he have a conscience then? No, he was just afraid. He was afraid it might be discovered that he was little Gottlieb going around in boots too big for him. Judejahn heard a voice, not the voice of God nor the voice of conscience, it was the thin, hungry, self-improving voice of his father, the primary schoolteacher, whispering to him: You're a fool, you didn't do your homework, you're a bad pupil, a zero, an inflated zero. And so it was as well that he had stayed in the shadow of a greater being, stayed a satellite, the shining satellite of the most powerful

42

celestial body, and even now he didn't realize that this sun from whom he had borrowed light and the licence to kill had himself been nothing but a cheat, another bad pupil, another little Gottlieb who happened to be the Devil's chosen tool, a magical zero, a chimera of the people, a bubble that ultimately burst.

Judejahn felt a sudden craving to fill his belly. Even in his Freikorps days he had had bouts of gluttony, and shovelled ladles of peas from the field-kitchen down his throat. Now, at the corner of the street he was looking for, he scented food. A cheap eating-place had various dishes on display in its windows, and Judejahn went inside and ordered fried liver, which he had seen in the window under a little sign, 'Fritto scelto'. And so now Judejahn ordered the liver by asking for 'fritto scelto', but that means 'fried food on request', and so, at a loss what to do, they brought him a plate of sea-creatures fried in oil and batter. He gulped them down; they tasted like fried earthworms to him, and he felt nauseated. He felt his heavy body turning into worms, he felt his guts squirming with putrescence, and in order to fight off his disintegration, and in spite of his nausea, he polished off everything on the plate. Then he drank a quarter-litre of wine, this too, standing up, and then he was able to go on

no more than a few paces, and there was the German hotel where his in-laws were staying. Cars bearing 'D' licence plates stood in tidy ranks outside the hotel. Judejahn saw the emblems of German recovery, the sleek metal of the German economic miracle. He was impressed. He was attracted. Should he go inside, click his heels together and rap out, 'At your service!'? They would receive him with open arms. Would they? But there was also something that repelled him about these shiny cars. Recovery, life going on, going on fatly and prosperously after total

43

war, total battle and total defeat, it was betrayal, betrayal of the Führer's plans and his vision for the future, it was disgraceful collaboration with the arch-enemy in the West, who needed German blood and German troops to ward off its former Eastern allies and sharers in the stolen victory. What to do? Already the lights were going on in the hotel. One window after another was lit up, and behind one of them Eva would be sitting and waiting. Her letters, with their obscure turns of phrase that spoke of the disappointment that awaited him, the degeneracy and the shame, allowed him no hope of finding Adolf his son here. Was it worth going home? The desert was still open to him. The net of the German bourgeoisie had not yet been thrown over the old warrior. Hesitant, uncertain, he strode in through the door, came into the wood-panelled lobby, and there he saw German men, his brother-in-law, Friedrich Wilhelm Pfaffrath, was among them, he had hardly changed at all, and the German men stood facing one another in the German fashion; they were holding glasses in their hands, not mugs of German barley brew, but glasses of Italian swill, but then he Judejahn drank swill like that himself and God knows what else besides, no blame attached to that away from home. And these men, they were strong and stout, he could hear that, they were singing 'A Fortress Sure', and then he felt himself being observed, not by the singers, he felt himself being observed from the doorway, it was a serious, a seeking, an imploring, a desperate look that was levelled at him.

It didn't shock him, but it did abash Siegfried to see the broad unmade bed, which drew his eye though he tried in vain to avert it, the broad bed, the marriage bed standing four-square in the spacious room, it was shameless and

44

undeniable, without sensuality and without shame, cold,
clean linen laid bare, and it bore witness coldly and cleanly
to functions that no one wanted to disavow, to embraces
of which no one was ashamed, to deep and healthy sleep

and all at once I realized that the Kürenbergs were ahead
of me, they were the people I wanted to be, they were
without sin, they were at once old-fashioned and new,
they were antique and avant-garde, pre-Christian and
post-Christian, Graeco-Roman citizens and airline passengers crossing the oceans, they were locked up in bodies,
but in bodies that were well-explored and -maintained:
they were excursionists who had made themselves at home
in a possibly inhospitable planet, and who took pleasure
in the world as they found it.

Kürenberg was attuned to nomadism. In shirt sleeves and
white linen trousers with a rubber apron tied over them, he
was bustling about at a pair of extra tables the hotel had put
at his disposal, and I was made to ask myself what special
arrangements he had come to with the management,
because they must have had new wiring put in for him,
he had adaptors with three and four plugs in the sockets,
and electric leads ran like intertwining snakes to gleaming
electrical gear, grills, ovens, infra-red cookers, steamers,
pressure-cookers; it was the most comprehensive of
mobile kitchens, which delighted him and went everywhere with him, and he was preparing the dinner to which
he had invited me, he was mixing, tasting, beating and spic-
ing, his face was firm and manly, it had a massive calm that
did me good to look at, while Frau Kürenberg, having given
me her hand and spoken a few welcoming words, 'How
do you like Rome? Is this the first time you've been here?',
twittering swallows of small talk, low swooping flights,
was laying the table, bustled about, went to the bathroom,

leaving the door ajar behind her, rinsed glasses, put flowers in a vase, and left the wine to chill under running water.

I didn't want to stand around idly. I asked Kürenberg what I could do to help, and he gave me a bowl, a cheese-grater and a piece of Parmesan, and told me to grate it. At first the cheese merely crumbled away into the bowl in hard lumps, and Kürenberg showed me how it should be done, and then he asked me whether I hadn't ever helped my mother in the kitchen at home. I said no. And I remembered the great cold kitchen in our house, the floor tiles always damp and just washed; the boots of the uni-formed messengers and the friends of the domestics were forever making new marks on the wet, gleaming tiled surface to the irritation of the servants, who always seemed to be flying off the handle, hectically noisy and hectically nervous. 'Where are you from originally?' asked Küren-berg. I told him the name of the place, and I was going to add that nothing tied me to it any longer, nothing but the accident of my birth, when I noticed Kürenberg looking at me in surprise. And then he cried, 'Ilse comes from the same town,' and she, wiping glasses, now turned to me, with a look that went right through me. And I thought, She can see the old avenue, the avenue with the cafés and the trees which have burned down now, but the cafés have probably been reopened, and people are sitting in them again, under parasols maybe because the trees burned down, or they've planted new trees, fast-growing poplars, she can see that just as I see it, objectively but with some emotion as well; or does she not know the trees burned down? I wanted to ask her, but she bustled out again into the bathroom, and Kürenberg was making a sauce using an egg-whisk, but I noticed his thoughts were elsewhere, he was upset, and then he said, having looked across to the bathroom as though to check she wasn't too close by,

46

'I was once the conductor there. They had a good orchestra, good singers, a fine hall.' 'It's in ruins,' I said. 'They play in the castle now.' He nodded. The sauce was finished. He said: 'There was an Oberpresident Pfaffrath. Are you any relation?' I said: 'He's my father, but he's the bürgermeister now.' He peered into a steaming pot and called, 'Ilse, quick, the colander.' And she brought the colander from the bathroom, a sturdy mesh, sturdy like herself, and he shook the rice out into the colander, leapt with it full of steaming rice across to the tub, poured cold water over it, shook it dry again, and hung the colander and rice in the steam rising from the saucepan, and said to me: 'It's a Javan recipe, the rice cooks and stays crunchy.' They had got around a lot, he had conducted orchestras all over the world, and they had settled into this life, they had no house, no permanent residence, they owned suitcases, fine, large suitcases, and lived in hotel rooms like the one I was standing in. And then I realized that I'd known Kürenberg for far longer than I'd thought, I remembered, of course I wasn't aware of it at the time, I was a child, I didn't understand what was going on, but now I saw it as though it was before my very eyes: I saw my father showing Kürenberg out, I was playing in the hall, and the way Father shut the door behind Kürenberg I could tell by his reddened face that he was angry and he told me off for playing in the hall, and he went in to Mother, and I followed him, because I didn't know where in the big house I was supposed to go, and I was curious as well, even though I knew he was in a bad mood, as he generally was when people came to him for help, they didn't seem to understand him in our town, because they often came to him for help, and it never even crossed his mind to intervene in lost causes. Not out of hatred, no, he wasn't twisted (he didn't like them, that was probably true

47

enough), but he was afraid of them since they had been declared lepers. And most of all, even at that time, he feared Uncle Judejahn. And as though it were yesterday, I could hear him saying to Mother: 'Our General Musical Director' – he always expressed himself in long-winded ways, and titles never failed to impress him – 'paid me a call, and asked me to try to obtain the release of old Aufhäuser, his father-in-law. I urged him to be mindful of his career and apply for a divorce –' And then Father caught sight of me, and sent me out in a rage, and today I know that old Aufhäuser had just been arrested for the first time; it was the day of the first little anti-Jewish boy-cott, and it wasn't till later, the Kristallnacht, that Aufhäu-ser's store was set on fire. I got the day off at the Junker school and I saw it burning, the first building I saw burned down. And Aufhäuser was back in protective custody, and my Father sat at the head of the table, ladling out soup, he liked to play the patriarch occasionally, and Göring and Goebbels were spitting venom on the wireless, and my mother said: 'I must say it's a shame about all the beautiful things that were lost to the flames.' And old Aufhäuser was once again in protective custody, and later on I came across his library; it lay in disorderly heaps in the attic of the *Hitlerjugendheim*, somebody must have carted it off there and then forgotten all about it. Aufhäuser was a bibliophile, and I found first editions of the Classics and Romantics, precious old German and Latin volumes, first editions of the Naturalists, of the Mann brothers, of the works of Hofmannsthal, Rilke, George, bound volumes of periodicals like *Blätter für die Kunst* and *Neue Rundschau*, the literature of the First World War, the Expressionists up to Kafka. I helped myself, and later whatever was left was burned, was blown up by bombs along with the rest of the *Hitlerjugendheim*, and Aufhäuser, the captive in protective custody was murdered – and this was his daughter. Could I bear to look at her? Where were my thoughts running off to? My thoughts rebelled. They said: She's in pretty good shape, she must be forty and hardly a wrinkle on her. And my thoughts went on: The Aufhäusers were wealthy, wonder if she got compensation? And then: He didn't marry her money, it was too late for that, he did it to oppose evil. And then: They love each other, they've stayed together, they're still in love. And we went to table, we sat down, Kürenberg served the food, she poured the wine. It must have been a delicious meal, the chef deserved my compliments, but I couldn't bring myself to do it, nothing had a taste – or rather, it tasted of ashes, dead ashes blowing on the wind. And I thought: She didn't see her father's store on fire. And I thought: She didn't see our houses burning down, either. And I thought: It's over over over, nothing can be done about it, nothing nothing, it's finished finished finished finished. There was fresh spinach, sautéed in fine oil, and over it we sprinkled the cheese I'd grated myself, and my steak was two fingers thick, as soft as butter, and blood ran out of the heart of it, and the wine was as cold and dry as a fresh spring, I was able to taste that still in spite of all the ash coating my tongue, we didn't speak during the meal, the Kürenbergs leaned over their plates and took their nourishment seriously, and once I said, 'This is wonderful,' but maybe I didn't say it loud enough, no one replied, and then there was a raspberry soufflé, flambéed, almost tropical and yet with the aroma of German forests, and Kürenberg said, 'We'll get coffee brought up; there's nothing like a real espresso.' Ilse Kürenberg ordered coffee over the hotel telephone; a bottle of cognac appeared on the table and we talked about Rome.

They love old Rome, antique Roman Rome, they love

the fora with their battered grandeur, they love looking at
the ancient hills in the evenings, the views of cypresses
and solitary pines, they love the now functionless pillars,
the marble staircases leading nowhere, the sundered arches
over the filled-in chasms commemorating victories whose
names figure in schoolbooks, they love the House of
Augustus and they quote from Horace and Virgil, they
adore the Rotunda of the Vestal Virgins, and they pray at
the Temple of Fortune. I listen to them, speaking know-
ledgeably of new finds, discussing archaeological digs and
museum treasures; and I love them too, love the old gods,
love beauty long buried in the ground now visible once
more, I love the proportions and the smooth cold stone
skin of the old statuary, but still more I love Rome as it is
now, alive and manifest to me, I love its skies, Jupiter's
fathomless sea, and I imagine we're drowned, we're
Vineta, and up on top of the element that washes around
us are ships never seen by us, sailing on dazzling seas, and
Death casts his invisible net over the city, I love the streets,
the corners, the stairways, the quiet courtyards with urns,
ivy and lares, and the raucous squares with daredevil Lam-
bretta riders, I love the people sitting on their doorsteps
of an evening, their jokes, their expressive gestures, their
gift for comedy, their conversation which is lost on me, I
love the bubbling fountains with their sea gods, nymphs
and tritons, I love the children sitting on the marble edge
of the fountains, those tumbling, garlanded, cruel little
Neros, I love the bustle, friction, barging, and shouting
and laughter and looks on the Corso, and the obscenities
that are whispered to ladies in passing, and I love the stiff,
empty larvae of the ladies' countenances, which the dirt
helps to form, and I love their replies, their humiliation
and their pleasure in these indecent tributes, which they
bury underneath their street-masks in their real faces, and

carry home with them and into their women's dreams, I love the gleaming affluent shopfronts, the displays of the jewellers and the bird hats of the milliners, I love the snooty little Communist on the Piazza della Rotonda, I love the long, shiny espresso bar with the hissing, steam-belching machine and the men sitting there, drinking hot strong bitter-sweet coffee from little cups, I love hearing Verdi's music booming out in the passage in front of the Piazza Colonna from the loudspeakers of the television studios and echoing back from the *fin de siècle* stucco façades, I love the Via Veneto, the cafés of Vanity Fair, with their funny chairs and colourful awnings, I love the leggy, slim-hipped models, their dyed hair the colour of flame, their pale faces, their great staring eyes, fire that I can't touch, I love the happy, stupid athletic gigolos in attendance, traded by the wealthy corseted ladies, I love the dignified American senators who get audiences with the Pope and can buy anything they want, I love the gentle, white-haired automobile kings, who spend their fortunes on supporting science, art and literature, I love the homo-sexual poets in their tight drainpipe jeans and pointy thin-soled shoes, living off awards and shaking their jangling silver bracelets coquettishly back from the overlong cuffs of their shirts, I love the old mouldering bathing-ship anchored in front of the Castle of the Angels on the turbid Tiber, and its naked red light-bulbs in the night, I love the small, secret, incense-steeped, art- and ornament-crammed churches, even though Kürenberg finds baroque Rome disappointing, I love the priests in their robes of black, red, violet and white, the Latin Mass, the sem-inarians with fear in their faces, the old prebendaries in stained soutanes and beautiful greasy Monsignore hats with funny red cords round their waists and fear in their faces, the old women kneeling at confessionals with fear

51

in their faces, the poor cracked hands of the beggars in front of the carved and worked portals of the chapels and their fear trembling like the vein in their throats, I love the little shopkeeper in the Street of the Workers, cutting great slices of mortadella like leaves, I love the little markets, the fruit-sellers' stalls all green red orange, the tubs of the fishmongers full of obscure sea-creatures and all the cats of Rome prowling along the walls

and the two of them, two firm silhouettes, had stepped up to the window, the tall French window, and they looked down into the illuminated pit of the street below, and they looked across at other hotels like their own in many-storied stone buildings by the station, full of travellers, electrical signs flashed their temptations, and Rome was ready as ever to be conquered, and Kürenberg was thinking about Siegfried's music, the flow of feeling he wanted to tighten and compress and cool for this city tomorrow, and Ilse stood beside him and looked at the roofs of automobiles creeping along the bottom of the street like an armoured column of cockroaches, she saw the brief, harmless flash of lightning in the wires over the electric trolleybuses, she saw through the convention of pretending death didn't exist, the unanimous agreement to deny terror, the ownership of the buildings she saw was set out in the land register, and even the Romans, well acquainted with ruin and the devastation of former splendour, believed in the everlastingness of this particular arrangement of stones on the old earth, she saw the mystery plays of trade, these also based on the delusions of eternity, inheritance and certainty, she saw the blooming and withering miracles of advertisements, whose colours had played on her own childhood too, quicksilver lights or dragon candles, and how simple-minded of her father it had been to put up a wall of books, music and art between her girlish life and the store, a false bastion, mild lamplight extinguished for ever. She shivered and thought how cold everything felt. It's late, she thought. And she thought: This young man has come from my home town and he writes symphonies, and his grandfather may have played the harpsichord or the flute, but his father killed my father, who collected books and loved listening to the Brandenburg Concertos. She took Kürenberg's hand, forced her own cold and inert hand into the fist of the conductor, which felt warm, dry, firm and dependable.

Kürenberg was still looking down into the street, thinking: One could tell their future. He had met analysts, sociologists, economic planners, atom-splitters, international lawyers, politicians and PR men. They were a devilish breed. The devilish breed made up his audience. They went to his concerts. He shut the window and asked Siegfried, 'Do you remember Augustine's saying about music, that it was what great men gave themselves over to when their day's work was done, to refashion their souls?' Siegfried didn't remember. He hadn't read Augustine. He was an ignoramus. There was so much that he didn't know. He blushed. Are they great, the men I know? Kürenberg asked himself. And if they aren't, where are the truly great men? And do they have souls that can be refashioned by music in the evening? Did Augustine know great men? And did those whom he thought to be great men think him one? So many questions! Kürenberg had a high opinion of Siegfried's work. He looked to him for surprise, for a wholly new language. It might sound horrible to the generality which lagged behind the times; but it would carry a new message. A new message for the few who were capable of hearing it. Were those the great men Augustine had in mind? Man wants to know, even if knowledge

53

makes him unhappy. Kürenberg smiled. But he spoke seriously: 'I don't know who you compose for. But I believe your music has a purpose in the world. Ignorant people may whistle when they hear it. Don't let that put you off. Never try to satisfy people's wishes. Disappoint the season-ticket holder. But disappoint him with humility, not with arrogance. I'm not advising you to climb the ivory tower. For heaven's sake, don't live for your art! Go out on the street. Listen. Remain alone. You're lucky to be lonely. When you're on the street, stay as lonely as you might be in the isolation of a lab. Experiment with everything, all the splendour and grime of our world, with humiliation and greatness – maybe you'll find a new sound!'

And Siegfried thought of voices, of the voices of the street, he thought of the voices of vulgarity, of fear, of torment, of greed, of love, goodness and prayer, he thought of the sound of evil, the whisper of unchastity and the shout of crime. And he thought: Tomorrow he will humble me, come to me with his laws of harmony and his schoolmasterly strictness, celebrated *chef d'orchestre* that he is, an exact reader of a score, a gardener with pruning shears, while I'm all weeds and wilderness. And Kürenberg said, as though he read Siegfried's mind: 'I believe in our collaboration. There are contradictions in me and in you that don't contradict each other.' And the life into which they had been pitched was contradictory, and they contradicted their kind.

Judejahn had felt himself under observation, and had withdrawn. He retreated, with his angular skull between his hunched shoulders – retreat or tactical withdrawal, the way a patrol between the lines in no man's land retreats or withdraws when they feel they've been spotted; no shots are fired, no flares light the night sky, fate hangs in the balance, but they withdraw, creep back through barbed wire and vegetation, back to their own position, and conclude for the moment that the enemy position is impregnable. And the murderer too, the hunted criminal, presses back into the shadows, the jungle, the city, when he senses the bloodhounds are near by, when he knows he's in the policeman's field of vision. Likewise the sinner flees the eye of the Lord. But what of the godless man who doesn't know himself to be a sinner, where does he turn? Straight past God, and into the desert! Judejahn didn't know who was watching him. He saw no spies. There was only a priest in the lobby – Rome was crawling with religious brethren – standing strangely transfixed and staring like Judejahn through the glazed double door at the animated company sitting at the table, drinking and talking. It was a German *Stammtisch*, a table established in the German way but transported provisionally to a southern latitude; and, objectively speaking, there was only the wood and glass of the double door to separate Judejahn and his brother-in-law, Friedrich Wilhelm Pfaffrath, but he had remained seated: whether he was holding forth here or in front of the town council at home, he had remained seated, whereas Judejahn had strode boldly on, boldly and blindly on with the watchword that God is dead. He had gone further than the burghers in the hall, but it was they who had made it possible for him to go so far. They had underwritten his wanderings with their lives. They had invoked blood, they had summoned him, exhorted him, the world will be won by the sword, they had made speeches, there was no death to compare with death in battle, they had given him his first uniform, and had cowered before the new uniform he had made for himself, they had praised his every action, they had held him up as an example to their children, they had summoned the 'Reich' into being, and endured death and injury and the smoke from burning bodies all for the sake of Germany. But they themselves had remained seated at their table in the old German beer hall, German slogans on their garrulous tongues, Nietzsche clichés in their brains, and even the Führer's words and the Rosenberg myth had only been exhilarating clichés for them, while for Judejahn they had been a call to arms: he had set out, little Gottlieb wanted to change the world, well well, so he was a revolutionary, and yet he detested revolutionaries and had them flogged and hanged. He was stupid, a dim little Gottlieb, worshipping punishment, little Gottlieb afraid of a beating and desiring to beat, powerless little Gottlieb, who had gone on a pilgrimage to power, and when he had reached it and had seen it face to face, what had he seen? Death. Power was Death. Death was the true Almighty. Judejahn had accepted it, he wasn't frightened, even little Gottlieb had guessed that there was only this one power, the power of death, and only one exercise of power, which was killing. There is no resurrection. Judejahn had served Death. He had fed plentiful Death. That set him apart from the burghers, the Italian holiday-makers, the battlefield tourists; they had nothing, they had nothing except that nothing, they sat fatly in the midst of nothing, they got ahead in nothing, until finally they perished in nothing and became part of it, as they always had been. But he, Judejahn, he had his Death and he clung to it, only the priest might try to steal it from him. But Judejahn wasn't about to be robbed. Priests might be murdered. Who was the fellow in the black frock? A pimply face, a haggard youth seething with lust under the womanish robes. The priest too was looking at the assembly in the lobby, and he too seemed to be repulsed by it. But he was no ally for Judejahn. Judejahn was equally revolted by the priest and the burghers. He recognized that the burghers' position was impregnable for today. But time was in Judejahn's favour, and so he would return to the desert, drill recruits for Death, and one day, when battlefields were more than tourist attractions, then Judejahn would be on the march again.

He fled the hotel. He fled the sight of the burghers, the priest, fled the eye of the unseen spy. It wasn't cowardice, it wasn't disgrace, it was a tactical withdrawal. If Judejahn had set foot in the lobby, if Judejahn had shown his face among them, the burghers would have leapt up, they would have clustered round him, but it would have been for an evening of hero-worship, and then they would have cast their bourgeois net over him. Eva might be lurking at one of the lit-up windows – a mother and a heroine, why hadn't she died that May of shame? But she was still alive; and Judejahn could imagine sitting with her in a German lounge, going to the job that Pfaffrath would fix up for him, coming home from the job that Pfaffrath had fixed up for him; they would eat roast goose and drink Rhine wine, presumably brother-in-law Pfaffrath's job would run to that, and on the Führer's birthday and on the ninth of November Eva would wear the brooch on her dress – so long as it hadn't been stolen, the occupying forces were after souvenirs and valuables, Judejahn knew that – the golden swastika brooch, a present from the Führer, and she would stare at him when the news came on the radio, and Heuss spoke, and Adenauer spoke, when their neighbours played nigger songs, and she would stare and think: You're alive you're alive you're alive. And he would be alive and think of the desert, the desert from which he would reconquer Germany. He dropped into a cookshop somewhere on his way, which was now aimless, he entered a miasma of oil and batter and sea smells, he went up to the buffet, he could have wolfed the lot down, he was racked by an incredible hunger. There were some large white beans, a German dish, a dish from his school-days and his childhood. He pointed to it, but the beans were not warm, they were not German, they were slick with oil, tart with vinegar, and they had a fishy taste as well, because what he had taken to be meat was blubbery fish; but he wolfed it all down, and then an order of pasta to follow, regular Italian-style noodles, the tomato sauce rimmed his mouth in a slobbery wet kiss, spaghetti dangled from his lips, they'd forgotten to bring him a knife, and he sucked them into his mouth like a cow eating long grass, and it took another half-litre of Chianti to cleanse Judejahn and make him human again. Or so he thought.

The human reached the Piazza San Silvestro through a maze of alleys. He saw the electric sign announcing the telephone exchange. That suited his purpose. He went inside, saw the booths with telephones in them, didn't know how to use them, he wrote down the name of the Pfaffraths' hotel on a piece of paper, gave it to a girl at the counter, who looked up the number for him in a directory and sold him a telephone coupon, then he stood in one of the booths, dialled the number, he heard 'Pronto', and he spoke German into the mouthpiece, said he wanted Pfaffrath, heard clicks and whirring and footsteps, and then Pfaffrath was there on the line, replying in the correct official style, aware of his rank. 'Oberbürgermeister Pfaffrath here. Who's calling, please?' And Judejahn felt like shouting back, 'Hello, you asshole!' Or should he rasp out his own titles, his military and party rank, or even the florid Arabian one he now held? Should he describe himself as Chief Eunuch or Harem Administrator or Desert Fox, or squeak out 'Gottlieb here'? And he was such a shrunken little Gottlieb that he didn't reach up to the mouthpiece and he merely said 'Judejahn', but he spoke the name with such emphasis that power, violence and death resonated down the line. Now it was Pfaffrath's turn to clear his throat, to change down from Oberbürgermeister to brother-in-law, presumably also getting over his terror on hearing the voice of the dear departed, pride and scourge of the family, whichever, whose resurrection he was awaiting; it probably took him a while to muster courage to confront Judejahn. And he said excitedly, 'Where are you? We've been waiting for you.' And Judejahn coolly replied that he had plenty to do and little time, and he summoned them to his own hotel for the following day, the splendid palace on the Via Veneto, there they would see Judejahn in all his glory, and he told him his assumed name, his cover name and passport name, ordered him, in the small booth – the Italian scribbles on whose walls were presumably smut as in any other booth, and Judejahn wondered whether the latrines at home had 'Germany awaken' written in them again – ordered him to 'repeat the name', and Oberbürgermeister Friedrich Wilhelm Pfaffrath duly repeated the false name, the official lie: he wouldn't appear before Judejahn as his benefactor any more, he would stand at attention, and Judejahn's creeping away from the German hotel had been no flight, his sneaking away had been a tactical masterstroke.

And once again the human being felt on top of things, in charge of his destiny. He left the telephone exchange in triumph. He was crossing the Piazza San Silvestro, on his way to conquer Rome, when there was a sound of breakage, a hullabaloo as of battle, a crashing and sundering, screams of terror and cries of death. It was a new building that had collapsed, its foundations had been miscalculated,

twisted girders protruded from clouds of dust, people ran
by in panic, and Judejahn commanded: 'Seal it off, keep
back, seal it off.' He wanted to bring a little discipline to
the accident, but no one listened to his German voice, no
one understood him, and then came the sirens and bells,
police, ambulance and fire brigade, and from the church
on the square came a priest, they stuck their noses in everywhere, and Judejahn saw that he was out of place here and
in the way, useless at best, and he stepped aside, barged
his way through the crowd, and then he remembered how
at school, in his detested Gymnasium, he had learned about
the Roman belief in omens, and this here was a bad por-
tent. There were the wailing cries of a woman. Had she
lost loved ones in the ruins? The sacrifices that Judejahn
had offered to Death had never cried. It was odd, he had
never heard any of them cry.

So he drifted away down the Corso, a long intestine
stuffed with pedestrians and vehicles. Like microbes, like
worms, like digestion and metabolism, they proceeded
down the intestinal canal of the city. The weight of traffic
was pushing Judejahn towards the Piazza del Popolo, but
he felt that was the wrong way for him, and he turned
back against the current, was jabbed and barged, but when
he turned round and looked, he saw it gleaming, white
and gold and illuminated by spotlights, and now he
remembered, this was where he had driven up, the escort
ahead, motor-cycle outriders to either side, and a long line
of vehicles behind him containing Germans and Italians,
top officials, dignitaries from the Party and the armed
services. He pushed ahead, backwards, he had lost all sense
of time and direction, the present became the past, but he
kept his goal firmly in sight, the marble steps, the mega-
lith, the white monument on the Piazza Venezia, the
national memorial to Victor Emmanuel II, which, through

some confusion or false information, Judejahn was convinced was the Capitol and moreover that it was a building of Mussolini's, a monument erected by the Duce, in honour of history, to crown the antique sites, and this was the white-and-gold-gleaming annunciation of the resurrection of the imperium. This was where he had driven up. Now he hurried towards it. Here on the right was the Duce's palace. No sentries? No sentries. In the shadow of night the walls were a grimy yellow. No one stood at the gate. No window was lit up. This was where he had driven up. A former visitor returning. Knock, knock on the door – the master of the house is dead. The heirs don't know you – they are among the bustling crowds on the Corso. Yes, he had crossed the square with the Duce, it had been Judejahn at his side, to lay the Führer's wreath at the Tomb of the Unknown Soldier. There were the sentries, feet apart, stiff and unflinching. Their posture was impeccable. But Judejahn felt nothing – no honour, no pride, no sorrow, no emotion. He was like a worshipper who feels nothing in church. He prays and God isn't there. He kneels down and thinks: The ground is cold and dirty. He sees the Virgin and he thinks: A piece of worm-eaten wood with paint on it. The people were not rejoicing. No singing, no huzzahs. Mopeds rattled past. No photographers appeared to bathe Judejahn in flashlights. A couple of tired carriage horses looked across at him from the cab-rank. Was he a ghost? He hurried up the marble steps. Behind him now were the columns of the magnificent temple which he wrongly attributed to Mussolini, and all that white splendour reminded him of something: it was a cake in the window of Süfke the baker, a cake that little Gottlieb had been fascinated by and never got to taste. And before him now was the black rump of the king's horse, Judejahn didn't know which iron-clad king it was, and he didn't care, he had never had any regard for the kings of Italy, from childhood up, influenced by the comic books of the First World War, he had thought of them as wielding umbrellas rather than swords. But as he stood there, he or little Gottlieb, he had a sense of grandeur, he thought of the Duce who had built all this and had himself been desecrated, and he felt the grandeur of the history that had had such monuments built to it, behind which stood Death, the ultimate inspiration. Judejahn was bathed in light. Rome glowed. But it seemed to him a dead city, ready for the chop, the Duce had been desecrated, history had turned its back on Rome, and so had ennobling Death. Now people lived here, they dared simply to live here, they lived for business or for pleasure – what could be worse. Judejahn looked at the city. It seemed to him to be absolutely dead.

Late at night the Via del Lavatore is a dead street. The market stalls have been tidied away, and the shutters in front of the little eating-places, grey or green with age, blind the façades of the buildings the way grey or green cataracts blind the aged eye. In the little dead-end side-streets are the simple wine-shops of the people of the area, who live in small, high-ceilinged rooms in many-storeyed tenements. They sit on benches and stools at plain un-covered tables stained by leftovers and spilled wine, and order their half-litre of red or their half-litre of white, *dolce* or *secco*, and those who are hungry bring food with them wrapped in paper or in terracotta dishes, and spread it out before them on the tables, quite unabashed. Visitors are a rare sight in this part of town. Still, Siegfried is sitting outside one of these bars in the pallid artificial moon of a white lantern. A man is busying himself at his table, work-ing an onion into a salad. Siegfried dislikes the taste of raw

62

onions, but the man peels and chops with such gusto at the young green bulb, he anoints it with oil and vinegar and salt and pepper, he breaks his bread so reverently, that Siegfried is impelled to wish him '*Buon appetito*'. This pleases the man, who promptly offers him his wine to try. Siegfried is appalled by the thought of the man's glass, and the oily and spirituous contact the man's oniony mouth has already made with it, but he overcomes his disgust and tastes it anyway. Then Siegfried offers the man some of his own wine. They drink and talk. Or rather, the man talks. He talks in long, intricate and ornate sentences whose meaning is lost on Siegfried, who has only mastered one or two expressions from phrase-books. But precisely because he doesn't understand the man, he is glad to spend time in his company. For a moment Siegfried is happy, and the two men sit together like old friends, one of whom has a lot to talk about, while the other listens to him or lets his attention stray, listening instead to some ghostly voice he doesn't understand either, but which, for the moment, he thinks he does. When the man has finished his onion, he sops up the last of the oil with his piece of bread. He gives the saturated bread to a cat which has been watching him imploringly for some time. The cat thanks him, and takes the bread under an arch; that's where her babies are. Siegfried bids '*Felice notte*'. He bows. He wishes a happy night to the man, the bar, the cat and her young. Perhaps he wishes himself a happy night also. This late hour of the evening finds him content. Now he goes into the bar to buy himself a bottle for the night. Perhaps he won't be able to sleep. If you can't sleep, it's a good thing to have some wine in the house. It occurs to Siegfried to buy a second bottle of wine. He would give it to the man he was talking to just now. Siegfried thinks the man is poor. Maybe the present will please him. But Siegfried is afraid of insulting the man if he really is poor. He doesn't buy another bottle. As he goes out, he bows once more to his table-companion. Another '*Felice notte*'. Did he do the right thing, though? Why did he feel awkward about his kind thought? He doesn't know. He's full of doubt again. It's difficult to do the right thing. His contentment has deserted him. He's no longer happy.

Siegfried's steps echo in the Via del Lavatore in the quiet of the night. His shadow runs ahead of him, his shadow merges with him, his shadow pursues him. Shortly, Siegfried is surprised by the noise and the gurgling of the Piazza di Trevi. Hordes of visitors are standing around the miraculous fountains and talking in a babel of different languages. Tour groups are industrious and offer night-classes in cultural history and ethnography. Photographers flash and click away: I was in Rome, you know. Haggard Roman youth leans over the edge of the fountain, and uses long poles to fish out the coins that the visitors threw in out of superstition, gullibility or just for fun. The tour guide says a person will return to Rome if he leaves money in the fountain. Does the visitor want to come again, does he want to return, is he afraid of dying in his own joyless country, does he want to be buried in Rome? Siegfried would like to return, he would like to stay. He won't stay, he throws no coins in the fountain. He doesn't want to die. He doesn't want to die at home. Would he like to be buried here? His hotel is close by the fountain. He can see its narrow, crooked façade reflected in the water. Siegfried goes inside. He walks through the porch. Alone

the old man behind the porch was cold. He shivered at his reception desk in the draughty entrance hall, in front of the board where the keys hang. He wore felt slippers on account of the stone floors, he had a coat thrown over his shoulders in the manner of an old veteran, he covered his small bald head with a black floppy hat in the manner of an old professor, he looked like an emigré, like an exiled liberal politician from liberal times, but he was only the manager of this little hotel. He was born an Austrian and would die an Italian, soon, in a few years, and it didn't matter to him whether he died as an Italian or an Austrian. Sometimes we would talk, and now, on my return, he greeted me with some agitation: 'A priest is waiting for you!' 'A priest?' I asked. And he said, 'Yes, he's waiting up in your room.' And I thought: There must be some mistake, and at this hour of the night. I climbed up the stairs, the stairs of the old hotel, little hollows had been worn in the stone steps, the walls were buckling, the floor on my storey was uneven. I made my way up an incline to the badly fitting door of my room. No light shone through the broad cracks in the weathered door, and I thought once more: A mistake. I opened the door, and there I saw him standing by the window in front of me, a tall, black silhouette, truly a priest, in the light of the spotlights that were still being beamed at the Trevi Fountain, its wild and fabulous creatures, its baroque, fleshy Olympus and its waters, roaring and lulling like the sea. He looked tall and gaunt. His face was pale, but perhaps that was just the spotlights. I turned on the light in the room, the naked bulb hanging over the broad bed, the *letto grande* of the hotel industry, the *letto matrimoniale*, the marriage bed that had been leased out to me, to me alone, for me to lie on, naked, bare, chaste or unchaste, alone, the bare naked light bulb over me, alone or with flies buzzing around it, and the rushing of the fountain and the babel of voices from all over the world, so they say, and he, the priest, now turned to me with a timid gesture of welcome, he raised and spread his arms, a movement which evoked the pulpit, and he was wearing a cassock, and then straight away he dropped his arms again, as though ashamed of the gesture, and his hands scuttled into the folds of his black garment like two shy reddish beasts. 'Siegfried!' he called out. And then he spoke hurriedly, falling over himself. 'I found out where you were staying, please excuse me. I don't mean to disturb you. I'm sure I'm disturbing you, and if I am I should leave right away.'

Standing in front of me, tall and gaunt, confused and in clerical robes was Adolf, Adolf Judejahn, the son of my once so mighty and terrifying uncle, and I remembered the last time I had seen Adolf, in the Teutonic castle. He was small, younger than me, a poor little soldier in the Junker school uniform, in the long black army trousers with red stripes, little Adolf in the brown Party jacket, little Adolf under the black cap, worn at an angle over the regulation cropped and parted hair. I had run around like that myself, and I had loathed it, having to dress like a soldier or an official, and maybe he had hated the get-up as well, but I didn't know that, I never asked him whether he hated the Castle, the service, the soldiers and officials; I thought of Uncle Judejahn and I didn't trust Adolf, I kept out of his way, and I even thought he was like my brother Dietrich, that he enjoyed going around in uniform or took advantage of it and had his eye on promotion, and for that reason I was amused to see him dressed now in the garb of a priest, and I thought about the disguises we liked to appear in, sad clowns in a mediocre farce. I saw him standing there and I told him to sit down. I pushed the rickety old hotel chair towards him, swept the books and newspapers and manuscripts aside on the marble-top dresser, I found the corkscrew in the drawer, opened the bottle of wine I'd brought with me and rinsed the tooth-mug in the wash-basin. I thought: Judejahn has disappeared, Jude-

jahn's copped it, Judejahn's dead. And I thought: Pity that
Uncle Judejahn can't see his son now; pity he can't see him
sitting on my rickety chair; such a pity, I think he would
have had a fit, and that's something I'd like to see even
today. Was I exaggerating? Was I giving him more significance than he really had? I poured the wine and said:
'You drink first. We'll have to share a glass. I've only got
one.' And he said: 'I don't drink.' And I: 'But as a priest,
surely you're allowed to drink a glass of wine. That's not
a sin.' And he: 'It's not a sin. But thanks, anyway. I don't
want any.' And after a while he went on, 'I'm not a priest
yet. I'm still only a deacon.' I drank the wine, refilled the
glass, and took it across to the broad bed. I lay there on
the broad bed, and it was like a hint that my life was
unchaste, which wasn't the case as far as this room was
concerned, and I don't know what unchastity is, or rather
I do, but I don't want to know, and I leaned back, rested
my head on the pillow, and I asked him: 'What's the difference?' And he said: 'I'm allowed to baptize.' And then,
as if having given the question further thought: 'I'm not
allowed to celebrate Mass yet. I have no power of absolution. I can't forgive sins. Only when the bishop has
ordained me am I allowed to forgive sins.' 'That'll keep
you busy,' I said, and then I was annoyed with myself for
having said it. It was stupid and unfunny and crude, and
actually I like priests. I like priests I don't know. I like
priests from a safe distance. I like priests speaking Latin,
because then I don't understand them. I don't understand
them, but I like it when they speak in Latin, I like the
sound of it. If I could understand what they were saying,
I wouldn't like listening to them so much. Maybe I do
understand them, just a little. Or maybe I only think I
understand them a little, and I like that, because in fact I
don't understand them at all. Maybe I even misunderstand

them, but misunderstanding them wouldn't matter, because if they're right and there is a God, then He will see to it that I take the right sense from their words, even if they are not the sense His servants mean to convey. If I could understand the words of priests as they were meant, I wouldn't like them. I'm sure priests can be just as stupid and obstinate and opinionated as the next man. They invoke God in order to rule. When Judejahn ruled, he invoked Hitler and Destiny. And Adolf? Whom did he invoke? I looked at him. He looked at me. We didn't speak. The tourists, no pilgrims, spoke in their babel. Time flowed with the water in the fountain. That was outside. There were flies buzzing inside. Buzz. Dirty flies.

There might be rats nesting in the cellar, but Judejahn felt drawn to it, he felt drawn down off the wide and monotonous Via Nazionale, down into this cellar, down the damp, dirty stone steps, gluttony drove him, thirst drove him, he was lured by a sign 'German Cooking', by a sign 'Pilsener Beer', German food for a German man, Pilsen was a German town, it had been cravenly surrendered, Pilsen was a Czech town, it had been lost through betrayal, the Skoda works were important for the war effort, beer was important for the war effort, gallows were important, conspiracy, subhumans, rats, foreign workers, danger spotted and averted by the Reich Security Office, Comrade Heydrich had taken action, Comrade Heydrich, who was like a twin to him, was dead – Judejahn survived. Always the same reproach. The voice reproaching him was Eva's. And he thought, Why is she alive, why did she survive? Thinking wasn't his business. Thinking was quicksand, dangerous, forbidden territory. Writers thought. Cultural Bolshevists thought. Jews thought. The pistol thought more rigorously. Judejahn had no weapon

68

on his person. He felt unarmed. What was the matter with him? Why didn't he go out to a good restaurant, in good clothes, with a valid passport and plenty of money, and fill his belly, fill it the way the Jews were doing again, with *pâté de foie*, with mayonnaise, with tender plump capons, and then go on to a nightclub, well-dressed, moneyed, drink a skinful and pick up something for the night? He could be well-dressed, well-accoutred, randy as the Jews. He could compete, he could make demands. So why didn't he? Guzzling, boozing and whoring, that was the Landsknechts' way, that was the way their song went: he had sung it in the Freikorps, they had sung it round the camp fire with Rossbach, in the Black Reichswehr camp they had bellowed it out, in the killing grounds. Judejahn was a Landsknecht, he was the last surviving Landsknecht, he whistled the tune in the desert, he wanted to guzzle and booze and whore, that was what he felt like doing, something was pinching his balls. Why didn't he take what he wanted? Why the cookshops, the poky bars, why this cellar? He was drawn to it. It was a fateful day. There was paralysis in the ancient air of the city, paralysis and catastrophe. It was as though no one in this city could manage a fuck any more. It was as though the priests had cut the balls off the city. He went down, Pilsener beer, he descended into the Underworld, Czech rats, barrels of Pilsener, he came upon a stone cellar, extensive and vaulted, a few tables, a few chairs, a bar at the back, rusty oxidizing beer-taps, beer-slops like vomit on the aluminium surface. There were two fellows sitting at a table, playing cards. They looked at Judejahn. They grinned. It was an evil grin. They greeted him: 'You're not from this part of the world!' They spoke German. He sat down. 'Hummel Hummel,'* said one of them. The waiter came.

* A Hamburg greeting.

'A Pils,' said Judejahn. The men grinned. With the waiter they spoke Italian. The waiter grinned. The men called Judejahn 'Comrade'. One referred to the other as 'My buddy'. Judejahn felt at ease. He knew their sort: gallows birds, desperadoes. Their faces were like faces in a morgue, ravaged by some horrible disease. The beer arrived. It tasted metallic. It tasted like fizzy lemonade mixed with poison, but at least it was cold. The glasses were frosted. The men raised their frosted glasses with the poisonous-tasting beer and drank to Judejahn. They were the right stuff. Under the table they kept their knees and heels clenched together, and their buttocks. Judejahn did too. He had always been the stuff. The waiter brought food. The men must have ordered it. Fried onions sizzled on large meat patties. They ate. They stuffed themselves. The men liked the onions. Judejahn liked the onions. They got acquainted. 'It tastes just like home,' one of them said. 'Crap!' said the other, 'it's like Barras's. Barras was the only place I got decent grub.' 'Where did you serve?' asked Judejahn. They grinned. 'Take off your glasses,' they said, 'you're no spring chicken yourself.' Judejahn took off his glasses. He looked at the pair of them. They were his true sons. He wanted to drill them. If he drilled them, they'd be useful. He thought: Pair of hard bastards. 'Don't I know you?' asked one of them. 'I'm sure I've seen you some-where. Well, never mind.' What difference did it make? They gave the name of a unit. Judejahn knew them well, a notorious outfit, trouble, heroes that went in where the Wehrmacht feared to tread. They'd wasted a lot of people. They were under Judejahn's general command. They had solved some of the Führer's population problems for him. They had committed genocide. Judejahn asked after their commanding officer, a sharp fellow, a real animal. They grinned at him. One of them traced a noose in the air, and pulled it tight. 'In Warsaw,' said the other. Hadn't Warsaw been taken, hadn't Paris been taken, wasn't Rome occupied? 'What are you doing now?' asked Judejahn. 'Oh, driving around,' they said. 'Since when?' 'Long time.' 'Where you from?' 'Vienna.' They were no Germans, they were Eastern mixed race, Austrian SS, they'd slipped through all the controls. Judejahn eyed them the way a cobra eyes a toad, and they thought he was just a big bullfrog. But he also looked at them with the calculation and benevolence of a snake-breeder, with the calculation and benevolence of a reptile-house keeper, supplying reptiles to labs for poison and vivisection. Judejahn sent men and boys to the bloody, stinking labs of history, he sent them to the testing ground of Death. Should he tell them who he was? Should he recruit them for the desert? He wasn't afraid of giving them his name; but having eaten and drunk with them, his rank forbade him to give himself away. The murderer-in-chief doesn't sit at the same table as his henchmen: that wasn't the officers' mess ethos. They said, 'We've got a car.' They said they'd 'organized' one. They'd learned to organize. They were still busy organizing. Judejahn paid the bill. It amused him because they presumed he'd pay for everything. Judejahn never paid for everything. He had various currencies in his wallet, and he couldn't find his way around all the different crumpled banknotes, the inflated denominations of a war-ruined currency. The war was Judejahn; and it was as though he'd helped to devalue money and inflate figures; it both satisfied and disgusted him. The men helped Judejahn to work out the exchange rate; they organized such money-changing transactions as well; and they could launder money, and pass off fake bills for real. Judejahn despised money and got through it. But he made sure he wasn't robbed. Little Gottlieb was impressed by the rich, and hated them. Judejahn liked their life-style, but not their lives. He had tried to do better. The rich were stupid. They had thought of Judejahn as a lackey who would do their work for them. But the lackey became a gaoler and locked them up. But in the end the prisoners managed to get away from Judejahn. The rich were rich once more. They were free. They were clever. Little Gottlieb once again stood in the corner eating his heart out. Once in a while there was a crumb from their tables for him. The constellations were not unfavourable to Judejahn. Wallenstein believed in the stars. Mars, Mercury and Clio living in rat holes. Exhausted, drained, quarrelsome, envious, covetous, selfish and forever greedy, they never stop their attentions. The press announced their abortions. Judejahn left the Pilsener cellar with the Eastern Germans, he left with the cadaver-faced, grinning men, left with the useful organizers, the Eastern Hummel-Hummel-callers, his soul-brothers and comrades-in-arms. Comrade rats. Rats climbed up to the street.

He was exhausted, and again I offered him some wine, and again he refused, and I wondered if he was this exhausted when he confessed to his superiors. I wasn't his confessor, and I couldn't give him absolution. I saw no sins. I saw only life, and life wasn't a sin. Nor could I give him any advice. Who can advise anyone? It meant nothing to me and it meant an awful lot when he exclaimed: 'But she's my mother, and he's my father!' And so I learned that they were in Rome, my parents, my brother Dietrich, my aunt and Uncle Judejahn, he too, he was alive, and there was Adolf sitting in front of me, though not entirely, I thought, because his priestly cassock set him apart from us, he had freed himself, I didn't want to know at what cost, just as I too had freed myself and didn't want to know the cost. Where should I flee to now, seeing they were here, following me, because Adolf had followed them, her at least, his mother, whom he described in dismaying terms? So when he said to me, 'He's my father, she's my mother,' I didn't want to know. I'd had enough. I'd freed myself. I felt free. I really thought I was free, and wanted to remain free – and I wasn't a Christian. I don't mean I wasn't a Christian in the sense of Uncle Judejahn, I didn't hate Christians, but I didn't go to church, or rather I went to a lot of churches but not to hear Mass, or rather I went to hear Mass, but not the way they celebrated it. But if he was a Christian now and a priest, then surely there was the injunction that one had to leave father and mother – and hadn't he left them?

He buried his face in his hands. He'd told me about the end of the Teutonic academy, the end of the Nazi indoctrination fortress where they let us stew, where they were going to get their future leadership cadres from. There'd been hand-grenades in our day, practice grenades that went off with a sharp crack and a sharp little flame on the playground, and then later they'd equipped the boys with real ones. But there weren't enough to go round, so they had to take some old and dodgy captured Greek-made grenades to make up numbers, and one boy had his belly ripped away by one because the pin had got caught up in his shoulder-strap and worked loose, that's how the teachers accounted for the mishap. And then the teachers had given them guns, captured guns with rusty barrels from victorious days, and they were to go with the old men from the Volkssturm reserve, and defend the eyrie – the fastness of the defeated but still bloodthirsty gods – but luckily the gods started eating one another and losing their heads before they could all be killed, and the old Volkssturm men sloped off into the woods and hills, or they hid in hay barns and potato cellars, and the dashing instructors ran around like mice, because now they would be called to account for the bacon they'd filched, and now they were caught in the trap, they were sitting pretty in the nets they'd helped to knot themselves. And then it was announced that there was going to be one more train, and the instructors sent the children home on it, without guns, without hand-grenades, just in their brown uniforms, and how could they get home, home was just a memory. The train didn't get far. It was attacked by fighter planes. Like furious hornets the fighters sent stinging volleys of shot through the splintering glass, metal and wood of the train compartments. Adolf was unhurt. But the train was finished, a crippled worm. The children continued on foot, along the tracks, on the gravel, stumbling over the ties. And then they ran into another train. It was a concentration camp that had been put on wheels and had also come to a halt. The children found themselves eyed by skeletons, by corpses. The children trembled in their Party school uniforms. But they didn't know why they should be afraid. They were German children, after all! They were the elect! Still, they found themselves whispering. 'They're from the camps!' they whispered, 'they're Jews!' And the children looked round and they whispered, 'Where are our men, where is our armed escort?' But there were no guards left, and the train was standing between a wood and a meadow, it was a spring day, the first flowers were out, the first butterflies were flitting about, the children in brown jackets were confronted by the prisoners in blue-and-white convict clothes, and out of their sunken eye sockets the skeletons and the corpses looked right through the Party Junkers, who began to feel they had no bones, no skeletons, as if they were nothing but brown Party jackets, which some evil charm had suspended in the

74

spring air. The children ran down from the tracks into the woods. They didn't stay together. They scattered. They went in all directions, without a word, without a salute or 'Heil Hitler!' And Adolf sat down in the grass next to a bush, because he didn't know where to go. Now a wraith had concealed itself in the bush, and the wraith watched Adolf. The wraith was exactly Adolf's age, but it had only half Adolf's weight. Adolf was crying. He had always been told not to cry. 'German boys don't cry,' said his parents and instructors. But Adolf was crying. He didn't know why he was crying. Perhaps he was crying because for the first time he was alone, and there was no one there to tell him, 'German boys don't cry.' But when the wraith saw Adolf crying, it picked up the stick that was lying beside it, and emerged from the bushes, a tottering figure, an emaciated body, with beaten skin, shaved child's skull, a death mask, and the wraith in its blue-and-white-striped felon's jacket raised the stick, and its nose stuck out large and bony in its starved face, and Adolf Judejahn remembered the *Stürmer* picture and recognized his first live Jew, even though the Jew was barely alive, and the wraith, with the stick upraised in its trembling hands, screamed for bread. Adolf opened his pack, he had bread and wurst and margerine, they had been given rations for the journey, and strangely a pound of almonds as well, because almonds happened to be in supply, and Adolf handed over his rations to the wraith, which grabbed the rucksack and sat down a little way away from Adolf and tore off large pieces of bread and wurst and crammed them into itself. Adolf watched. He had no thoughts. No thoughts at all. There was an absolute void in his head, it was as though everything he had hitherto thought and learned had been cleared out, perhaps in order to make room for new ideas, new teaching, but that wasn't definite yet. For the time being his head was empty, an empty balloon dangling over the grass. And the wraith, seeing Adolf watching it, threw him some bread and wurst and called, 'You eat, too. There's enough for both!' And Adolf ate, without appetite and without enjoyment, but also without disgust. When the other saw Adolf eating, he came nearer. He sat beside him. They ate the almonds together. The bag of almonds lay between them, and they both shyly helped themselves from it. 'The Americans are coming,' said the Jewish boy. 'Where will you go?' he asked. 'I don't know,' said Adolf. 'Are you a Nazi?' asked the Jewish boy. 'My father,' said Adolf. 'My family are all dead,' said the Jewish boy. And then Adolf thought that his own father might be dead, probably was, although nothing told him for certain. If he was crying, he was crying for himself, or maybe not even for himself, he didn't know why he was crying, perhaps he was crying for the whole world. But he wasn't crying for his father. And had he not loved his father? He wasn't sure. Had he hated him? He didn't think so. He could only see him as the official Party portrait on the wall – which left him cold. The Jewish boy was sick. He vomited back the sausage and the bread and the margerine. He vomited back the almonds as well. His teeth chattered, it was as though all the bones protruding through his paper-thin skin were rattling together. Adolf took off his brown Party jacket, and laid it over the boy's shoulders. He didn't know why he did it. Not out of pity. Not out of love. Not even out of guilt did he cover the boy. He just did it because he thought he was cold. Later they exchanged jackets. Adolf pulled on the blue-and-white-striped convict jacket with the Star of David. That touched him. His heart beat so hard, he could feel the pulse in his veins. The jacket burned. He felt it. Later they heard rumbling on the road.

'Tanks,' said Adolf. 'The Americans,' whispered the boy. His life was saved, but he lacked the strength to crawl towards the tanks. What about Adolf? Had he lost his life, did the armoured column break it as it crashed and rumbled through the German countryside? The boys lay down in the leaves, and covered themselves with branches. They lay together and kept each other warm in the night. In the morning they went into the village. The young Jew went to look for the Americans. He said, 'Come on.' But Adolf didn't go with him. Adolf walked through the village. People stared at him, a boy in the black uniform trousers and red stripe, a military haircut and wearing a convict's jacket. He sat down in the village church. He sat in the village church, because its doors were open as no other doors were, and because he was tired, and because he had no place to go. And so the priest came upon him. He came upon him sleeping. Was it a vocation? Had God called him? On Sunday, the priest's text was: 'Verily, verily, I say unto you, He that heareth my word, and believeth on him that sent me, hath everlasting life, and shall not come into condemnation; but is passed from death unto life. Verily, verily, I say unto you, The hour is coming, and now is, when the dead shall hear the voice of the Son of God: and they that hear shall live.' Did Adolf want to live? Did he want to avoid condemnation? There were women and fugitives in the church, and men who had quickly slipped on civilian jackets to avoid imprisonment. There were American soldiers in the church as well, holding their helmets in their folded hands, and their short light rifles rested against the pews. They had survived. They said they were liberators. They had come from across the ocean. They were Crusaders. Adolf Judejahn had heard about the Crusades in the National Socialist academy, but his instructors had disapproved of them.

77

The conquest of earth was their teaching, not heaven. And for them it wasn't worth it to conquer the Holy Sepulchre; and yet they had no fear of sepulchres. Adolf no longer believed his instructors. He no longer trusted human beings. He wanted to serve the Lord. God, Father, Son and Holy Ghost.

Death was at hand. He didn't want to die. He was scared. Judejahn had got into the car of his extraordinary subordinates, of the serviceable servicemen. It was a battered vehicle, almost a military vehicle, a jeep. They were in open terrain, on a reconnaissance mission, probing forward. Which way were they going? The direction didn't matter. The movement was all that mattered. Judejahn had ordered, 'To the station.' Why the station? He didn't know. But the station was an objective. It was a terrain. One could hide in it. One could find cover. One could go under, leave, disappear, fake one's death; Judejahn could become a legend like the Flying Dutchman, and Eva would be proud of him. The station, the objective, was near by. But Judejahn, sitting next to the driver – the other was sitting behind him, sitting on his tail – Judejahn sensed that they weren't going to the station at all, that their progress was rambling, they were driving around in circles, searching no doubt for dead ends and quiet alleyways, or alternatively for the roar and confusion of traffic where a gunshot might go unnoticed; they really thought he was going to pay, stupid bastards, they thought they had him in their sights, but Judejahn knew his way around, and that was the way you drove in the killing grounds: a blow from behind, a shot in the back, then the wallet plundered from the corpse and, in the lee of a wall, the car door opened and the body kicked out on to the rubble. He knew the ropes, and ultimately it was the Führer's orders

78

to kill the commander who failed, the coward who surrendered, an order to anyone, but specifically an order issued to these Austrian SS, the Führer's praetorians. But Judejahn hadn't failed, he hadn't surrendered, and it was only in Rome that he was afraid, only in that damned priests' town, but he wasn't a coward and they couldn't do that to him. They planned on going to the brothel at his expense, but Judejahn wasn't about to get himself shot while attempting flight; he'd devised the method himself, and he wasn't going to be forced to flee. He was following tactical detours, on circuitous paths, on desert tracks, jackal strategy, but his goal remained Germany, Grossdeutschland was his fata morgana, nothing would deflect him, and he gave them an earful. The car stopped right away. The rotten metal quivered. It made Judejahn feel good, giving them an earful. They were his fellows, his bloodhounds, his lads. He chewed them out. They recognized their master's voice. They didn't talk back. They denied nothing. They would have licked his boots. He got out of the car. He commanded them, 'About turn!' They turned. They roared off towards Valhalla. Judejahn would have liked to tell them to report to him. But where would he have had them come? Report in Hell? Judejahn didn't believe in Hell. He was a grown man. He was disabused. Hell didn't exist. It was something to frighten children with. The Devil was the priests' bogeyman. The only possibility was reporting to Death, to friend Death, it was Comrade Death they should report to, to Death, whom little Gottlieb feared, and Judejahn – following the school song of Andreas Hofer which little Gottlieb had learned – had sent Death into the valley many times, and not just into the valley.

Behind him was the tunnel. It lured Judejahn. He ran into it, it swallowed him up. Again, he went through a gate into the Underworld. It was the gate of Hades. The tunnel was long and lined with cool tiles, it was a sewer for traffic where buses roared and neon lights painted the Underworld in spectral colours. This was where they had meant to kill him. His instinct hadn't let him down; he'd leapt out of the jeep at the very last moment. He walked down the narrow pavement by the tunnel wall. It felt like walking through his grave. It was an elongated grave, a hygienic grave, it was a mixture of kitchen, refrigerator and *pissoir*. You got no earth to chew in the morgue. The victim of the killing grounds chewed earth. The victim had been young. Judejahn had been young at the time as well. The victim was a comrade. The field shovel quickly buried the victim. And others had swallowed earth, too. In Poland, in Russia, in the Ukraine, they had swallowed earth. They were made to dig a ditch. Then they undressed. They stood naked before the ditch. Photographs came into the possession of leadership circles, were handed round, scrutinized over breakfast; jokes were cracked, tit jokes, cock and cunt jokes. Procreation and death, union with death, the ancient myth. A professor of race and an anthropologist were dispatched to study their dying erections. The photographs appeared in the *Stürmer*. The *Stürmer* was opened out and pinned on school noticeboards, eight-year-olds read it. Eight-year-olds shot. Riddled corpses filled the ditch. Man was destroyed, man desecrated, man dishonoured, and overhead was blue sky. The next up covered the first lot with earth. Over Judejahn was earth; the tunnel ran under the Quirinal Gardens. Popes wandered in the garden. Their prayers had not been heard; or what in heaven's name was it they had asked for from God? Two thousand years of Christian enlightenment and at the finish, Judejahn! Why did they ever drive the old gods out? 'Thou shalt not kill!' Was it that resounding off the tunnel walls? The Pontifex Maximus of old Rome had been unfamiliar with that commandment. He had sat and happily watched the gladiatorial contests. The Pontifex Maximus of the new Rome served the Decalogue, he had the Commandments taught, and ordered them to be obeyed. And had the killing stopped? Or had the Christian shepherd at least set his face against it, and said before all the world, 'See, I am powerless, they kill in spite of me and my pastoral word'? 'Justice for Judejahn' echoed off the tunnel walls. At school little Gottlieb had learned that even popes allied themselves with death, and there was a time, not so very long ago, when popes engaged the services of executioners, of people like Judejahn. And how many generals had paid homage to the popes, and how often had they received blessings for their victorious standards! Justice for Judejahn! And kings had walked in the Quirinal Gardens, enjoying the sunsets. But kings were less impressive than popes. Judejahn still saw them as the caricatures of the First World War comics that little Gottlieb had just learned to read, the kings were short, sell-out was written all over their faces, and in their timid hands they held umbrellas. And hadn't Chamberlain carried an umbrella, Chamberlain, the bringer of peace, who had meant to deprive the Führer of his war, a laughable figure? Kings and their diplomats, what were they but pathetic umbrella-wielders under the massing clouds of disasters? Judejahn had no use for umbrellas. Little Gottlieb wanted to be a man; he wanted to defy God the Father and his own schoolteacher father. Men braved all weathers, they mocked at the raging heavens: men walked into the hail of bullets with heads held up, men walked through the fire-storm – that was how little Gottlieb saw it, and justice for Judejahn! The automobile headlights were like the eyes of great rodents in the tunnel. The rodents left Judejahn alone. They were off in pursuit of other booty. The hounds of hell didn't bite Judejahn. They hunted other prey. Judejahn came to the end of the tunnel. The Underworld unhanded him. He reached the end. The grave released him. Hades spat him out

he stood at the end of the Via del Lavatore, which was silent and deserted. It was a mild night. From the far end of the dead street came the sound of singing.

I wanted to shut the window, I wanted to close the sun-warped, wind-beaten wooden shutters in front of the windows, I wanted locks and bolts, because now babel was finished, they were no longer speaking Babel-fashion in the Piazza of the Trevi Fountain, one language had asserted itself over the others, and a choir of German women were standing in front of the pillared grotto, standing in front of the gods and demigods and mythic creatures in baroque costume, standing in front of the ancient myth cast in stone, standing in front of water flowing from Roman pipes, standing in the floodlight of tourism and the candelabra lights of the city, singing, 'There stands a linden tree by the fountain at the gate,' singing it in the middle of Rome, singing the song in the middle of the night, where was no rustling of lindens and no tree grew for miles. But down there by the fountain they kept the faith, kept faith with their faith, they had their linden tree, their fountain there at the gate, a sublime hour and they marked it in their song, they had saved their money and travelled far, and what could I do but shut the windows and the wooden shutters, but he came across to me by the open window, he brushed me with his cassock, and we leaned out, and he told me once more that he had seen my

82

parents, my parents and my brother Dietrich, seen them through a glass door at the hotel, and he said to me: 'Your parents are even more terrible than mine, their lives are completely lost.' And I could see them sitting behind the glass door in their hotel, I hadn't been there but I could see them, I was too proud to go there to see them, and what could I do, I said 'Keep your theology,' but what could I do? Down there they were singing the linden-tree song verse by verse, and an Italian who wanted to sleep shouted at them from his window, and a man who was with the women's choir, and was an admirer of the women's choir, yelled back, 'Shut up, you wop!' yelled 'Shut up, you wop!' to whichever window it was. What could I do? And a police car came and stopped by the fountain, and the policemen watched the singing women in silent astonishment, and then the police slowly drove off, disappeared down a side street. What could they do? And a man emerged from the Via del Lavatore and joined the women and the man who had yelled, 'Shut up, you wop!' and

he was glad to find them, glad to have bumped into them. He was glad. Judejahn had followed the song, the German song, and the once-mighty man listened in reverence to the song of the German women. Their singing was Germany, was the motherland, it was 'By the Fountain at the Gate,' it was the German linden tree, it was everything one lived and fought and died for. Not murdered for. Judejahn had never murdered. He was just an old warrior, and this was balm to his old warrior's soul, this was music to renew the soul at night. When they finished, Judejahn called out 'Bravo', and he went up to them, and introduced himself, albeit under his assumed name, and since they were standing in line like a company for inspection, he followed his instinct and addressed them briefly. He spoke of lofty singing in historic hour, of German women and a stirring encounter on Italian soil, greetings from home in the regrettably faithless land of German longings. And they understood him, they took his meaning, and the man who had called out 'Shut up, you wop!' shook Judejahn by the hand and thanked him for his pithy words, and both felt the tears well up in their eyes, and both manfully held them back, for German men don't cry being full of German hardness but they are soft-souled when they think home thoughts abroad, thoughts of the fountain at the gate, of the linden tree evoked by the voice of German women

I thought:

I don't believe you, it's not your vocation, and you know that God didn't call you; you were free, for one single night you were free, one night in the woods, and that was all you could stand, you were like a dog who's lost his master, you had to find yourself a new master; then the priest found you, and you told yourself it was God calling you.

But I didn't tell him what I was thinking. He bothered me. He bothered me with his news of the family. What could I do? I didn't want to hear his news. I didn't want to hear anything about them. I wanted my life, just my own little life, no life everlasting, I wasn't greedy, no life of sin. What was sin, anyway? I just wanted to live my selfish life, I wanted to be there just for myself alone and to get on with my own life, and he wanted to talk me into going with him, I was to go with him, he was scared on his own, and call on our family, and how I hate that word, and how I use it purposely to express my loathing – the family, the prison they wanted to lock me up in for life, but I'd escaped, I'd been sprung, I'd set myself free, I was truly free, I never wanted to go back there! Why was Adolf looking for them? And why didn't he go to them, once he'd found them, why did he come to me? Did he want to convert them? Did he want to convert me? He said: 'He's my father.' And I said: 'He's my father, but I don't want to see him.' And he said: 'She's my mother.' And I said: 'She's my mother, but I don't want to see her.' And I wanted nothing to do with my brother Dietrich. And Judejahn was dead, so I'd hoped, and if the Devil had let him go, then that was the Devil's own business. I wanted to stay out of the way of Uncle Judejahn, the mighty Party general, lord over life and death, terror of my childhood, black bogeyman to the brown adolescent.

But he said: 'We have to do something. We have to help them.' He didn't say, 'I must save them.' He lacked faith for that, and he didn't dare say it to my face, either. And I said no. And I looked at him. Gaunt, uncertain, wretched he looked in his clerical robes, the lanky deacon, not even ordained yet. And I teased him: 'How do you want to help your father Judejahn? What about baptizing him, since you're not able to forgive sins? That's what you told me, that you can't forgive sins yet.'

He trembled. I went on looking at him. He was power-less. I felt sorry for him. He thought he had God on his side, and he was powerless.

There were manuscripts on the marble top of the wash-stand, there were sheets of music, and Kürenberg was expecting me to come up with music that important men would listen to to renew their souls. Flies were dancing round the bare light-bulb. Under the light-bulb, the broad hotel bed lay exposed, chaste and unchaste, the *letto matrimoniale*, the bed of marriage and concubinage. I imagined a man and a woman copulating, and I was disgusted, because their union might produce life. I was powerless as

85

well; and I didn't even want power. A fly had drowned in the remains of the wine in the tooth-mug. It had drowned in an almighty binge, in a sea of intoxication; and what did air matter to us, earth and sea and sky! Had God guided the fly? No sparrow falls from a roof. I asked: 'Where will you sleep?' And I thought: Shall I offer to share my bed with him? And I thought: I mustn't offer him my bed. He had lodgings in the dormitory for priests. He made to leave and I saw him going towards the door, and I felt sorry for him again, and I thought: He is trying to get free of them. And I asked him what his plans were for tomorrow, and he seemed not to know, he was loath to reply, maybe he didn't want to give me a reply, and then he said he was going to St Peter's and I offered to meet him at the Angels' Bridge, by the Angels' Castle, I didn't want to see him again, but I said a time, and he said he'd be there. Now it was becoming quiet in Rome. The women's choir had gone, the tourists had left, and a man somewhere had turned a stopcock and the water in the Trevi Fountain no longer bubbled up over the baroque Olympus of gods and demigods and fabulous beings. The bubbling of the fountain stopped; it was history. The silence was audible. In it I now heard his footfall, going down the stone steps, he, the priest, the deacon, climbed down through time as through a tunnel. I looked out of the window, I saw him leave the building, I followed his progress. Like a lean black dog, he loped across the silent, dead square and turned into the passage that leads to the Piazza Colonna. I took the glass with the rest of the wine and the dead fly in it, and I tipped wine and fly down the drain. He was powerless

they were both walking down the passage, one already at the exit to the Corso, the other still near the churches in

the Via Santa Maria in Via, and workmen were cleaning
the mosaic floor of the passage, they sprinkled sawdust
over the dirt people had brought in with their shoes, and
with large brooms they swept up the mixture of dirt and
sawdust. Other workmen spread ready-mixed plaster on
the swept stones, then with a sander smoothed it into the
cracks and gaps in the mosaic. It made a sound like the
whetting of long knives. The sleeping city was a provocation to Judejahn. The city mocked him. It wasn't the
sleepers that annoyed Judejahn, let them lie in their stinking beds, in the arms of their lustful wives, let them be
sapped and lose the battle of their lives, no, he was indignant at the totality of the sleeping city, each closed
window, each bolted door, each lowered blind incensed
him; he was furious that the city was sleeping without
his say-so; there should be steel-helmeted patrols going
through the streets, with MP insignia on their chests and
submachine guns in their hands, and the patrols would see
to it that Judejahn's command to sleep was kept; but Rome
was sleeping without his dispensation, it dreamed, it lulled
itself to security. Rome sleeping was sabotage, it sabotaged
a war that was far from over, or that hadn't properly begun
yet, Judejahn's war. If he could, Judejahn would have
roused the city; he would have used the trumpets of Jericho
to rouse the city, those trumpets that made walls collapse,
the last trump, which had first impressed little Gottlieb,
and which he learned to laugh at in heathen scorn. Judejahn
was out of power. He was dismayed. He couldn't stand
it. In the desert he had lived in a dream. The barracks in
the desert were under his command; the barracks had left
him the illusion of power. A wall was stuck with fresh
posters; they were still wet, and smelled of printer's ink
and of paste. Again there was a commandment from the
Church next to a Communistic summons; the summons

87

red and aggressive, the Church's edict white and dignified. One was the work of an old power, the other of a new, but both lacked a straightforward brutality, a final disavowal of thought and persuasion, there was no clenched fist, no absolute belief in force and command, and Judejahn wondered whether he shouldn't throw in his lot with the Reds, he would teach them discipline, but little Gottlieb was against that, he hated the unpatriotic lot, he believed in Germany, and he believed in private ownership too, albeit with a reallocation of property to Judejahn's advantage and into exclusively German hands, and because of little Gottlieb's unwillingness, Judejahn couldn't join the Communists; he had once intended their elimination, only a feeble and corrupt world had got in the way. In the Piazza Colonna he took a taxi back to the Via Veneto, back to the big hotel, back to the fortress that had been his headquarters, the headquarters of the great and powerful Judejahn.

And Adolf, who didn't hear the knife grinding, and didn't see the posters on the wall, Adolf found the sleeping city quiet and giving peace to the restless soul. His way home was like a walk through a great graveyard, with imposing tombs, ivy-grown crosses and old chapels, and Adolf was glad to find the city as quiet as the grave, perhaps he too was dead, that made him glad, perhaps he was a dead man walking through the dead city, a dead man looking for the lane with the hostel for visiting clergymen, they also dead, lying dead in their dead beds in the dead hostel – it couldn't be far. And there was its light, the light everlasting. And Judejahn had the taxi stop early, and got out

the homosexuals were gone. No need for Judejahn to hear their twittering. The pretty waiters in their cute purple tails were putting the chairs on the tables, they patted the red chair cushions with their hands, and perfumed dust swirled up, lavender, cologne and spicy aftershaves, and the beautiful, smiling Laura was counting up the money in the till and the coupons of the waiters, and once more the totals didn't match, but Laura smiled her beatific smile, the serene and mindless miracle of her smile, and the heterosexual owner of the homosexual bar accepted Laura's smile and the discrepant totals with pleasure and a good grace, business was good and he was a kind person, and Judejahn, unseen by Laura, the owner, the waiters, was stalking the terrain, he hadn't forgotten how to hunt, he peered through a crack in the shuttered door, the way a thief peers or a killer, and he saw Laura, saw her smile, it touched even him, did its magic on him, but the smile tortured him as well. Laura's eyelids were night-blue, her face powdered white and her lips were hardly painted, she seemed very pale, seemed delicate and timid, spun from the night and shrinking back into it, and Judejahn turned the door handle, it moved, his great heavy hand lay on the handle, a frail handle of silver bronze; but then Judejahn withdrew his hand again, a man can't be sure, she's a Jewess, a Jewish bint, in Poland anyone consorting with Jewesses swung for it, and again he pressed the handle, and again he left it, Jewish cunt. Was he frightened? The night porter of the hotel saluted him, touched his gloved hand to the peak of his cap, saluted Commander Judejahn, the man giving orders here, albeit under an assumed name. The silky stuff shone on the walls, it was like a room in a brothel, little Gottlieb could have imagined nothing finer. Why hadn't he picked up the girl? Why didn't he take her? He would have screwed her and slung her out. Screwing her would have done him good, and it would have done him good to sling her out afterwards. On the damask bedspread lay the mangy tom, Benito. He stretched, arched his back and blinked his eyes. Judejahn ran his fingers through his thin fur. The beast stank. He stank to high heaven. The tom looked at him sardonically: You've outlived yourself, you're out of power. Could Judejahn tell the porter he wanted a girl? Once he could have done. He could have got a hundred. He could have embraced them and sentenced them. Should he call Eva? They would be petrified in her middle-class hotel. They got scared there at night. They were scared of death. Why shouldn't Judejahn scare the middle-class hotel? Perhaps he could have spoken with Eva in the night. He could have cleared the air. It was good to speak on the phone. Orders to suicide squads were phoned or wired. You never gave them in person. Eva was a German woman, a National Socialist, she would understand him, she would appreciate that Judejahn hadn't yet died, that he was walking along the edge of life. Eva was a German woman like the German women by the fountain singing the beautiful German song, but she was more than those women, she came from the élite, she was his wife – she would understand him. It had been stupid of Judejahn to be apprehensive of meeting Eva. What was there to tempt him about that Italian – maybe even Jewish – woman in the purple bar? That girl wasn't his type. She wasn't German. But there was something about her that made him want her. She was a whore. Or she was a Jewess. A hot skinny Jewish harlot. That was miscegenation. He had no need to fear the girl. He could hate her. That was it, he needed a woman to hate, his hands, his body, needed another body, another life to have and to destroy, only when you killed were you alive – and who other than a bar girl was still attainable for Judejahn's hatred? He was deposed. He was powerless

and Eva slept, slept stretched out, slept in her narrow cot in the small hotel room, slept tensely. Only the knot of her hair was loosened, yellowed corn left to stand, straw not harvested and put in a barn, whitened and grizzled. But she slept deeply, dreamlessly, with mouth foolishly agape, gurgling slightly, smelling faintly of the skin on boiled milk, the irate, sleeping Norn of nocturnal oblivion

given over to nocturnal oblivion, moved only by the commotion of his snoring, Dietrich Pfaffrath slept on one of the hotel's softer beds. The wine he had drunk in the hall with his parents and the other German guests of similar views had not made him sleepy, and his suitcase was open at the foot of his bed, for Dietrich was hard-working and ambitious, and even on a family visit to beautiful Italy he was preparing for his law exams, and he was confident of passing them, and so he had been reading in the law books he had packed in his suitcase. And Dietrich's fraternity cap had also accompanied him on his journey, because one might meet members of other fraternities in sufficient numbers to take over a bar. The cap with the coloured ribbons lay beside the law books, and Dietrich was sure that both his fraternity and the law would stand him in good stead. Then there were the road maps in the open suitcase, because Dietrich enjoyed taking the wheel for his old man, the Oberbürgermeister, and he had carefully marked the places to visit on the map, and written their names down on a separate sheet of paper, with the sites of battles in red ink, and the dates on which they had been fought. But beside the suitcase, tossed out of bed after the lights had been turned out, poorly aimed and missing the suitcase, there lay a magazine, an illustrated journal he had bought at a kiosk when he thought no one was watching, in Rome where he didn't know a soul and no one knew him, and on the cover of the magazine was a girl standing there with legs spread, standing there in full fleshy colour, with her blouse open to the waist, and in wide-meshed net-stockings over the full-colour fleshy thighs – on that evening she had taken the place of his beer for Dietrich, and he had exhausted himself between those thighs. He was powerless against the habit, but he was powerfully driven to the powerful whom he wanted to serve, he wanted to sit in the house of power, and share in power and become powerful himself

Friedrich Wilhelm Pfaffrath slept contentedly with his wife Anna, united in one bed for the holiday, though not united in any embrace, at home they had separate beds. Why should he be dissatisfied? His life appeared without blemish, and life on the whole rewarded those who were without blemish. Nationalist thoughts and feelings were once again resurgent in Germany, albeit in a Germany of two separate halves, and personal popularity, reputation, continuity and the democratic process had made Friedrich Wilhelm Pfaffrath the head of his city once more, absolutely legitimately, not by deception, electoral fraud or bribery, still less by the favour of the occupying forces; the people had freely elected him to be their Oberbürgermeister, and even though he had once been Oberpresident and the administrator of great Party sums, he was content, he was without blemish. And yet unfairly a nightmare came to haunt his blameless sleep: brother-in-law Judejahn rode up to his bedside on a snorting steed and in his black uniform, and a choir sang 'Lützow's Wild and Daring Chase', and brother-in-law Judejahn pulled Pfaffrath up on to his snorting steed, and into Lützow's wild and daring chase. And they galloped up to heaven, where Judejahn unfurled a large, luminous swastika flag, and then he dropped Pfaffrath, pushed him away, and Pfaffrath fell fell fell. And against that dream the mighty Oberbürgermeister Friedrich Wilhelm Pfaffrath was powerless

I'm powerless. I wash. I wash in cold tap water from the sink, and I think of the water flowing through the old Roman pipes, flowing to me from the sad blue hills, across the ruined masonry of old aqueducts as Piranesi drew them, into this basin – I enjoy washing in this water. I walk barefooted across the old stone floor. I feel the firm cool stones underfoot. It's pleasant to feel the stones. I lie down naked on the broad bed. It's good to lie down naked on the broad bed. I don't cover myself. It's good to lie alone. My nakedness lies bare. Naked and bare, I stare up at the naked and bare light-bulb. The flies buzz. Naked. Bare. Music paper lies white on the marble. Or maybe it's not white any more; the flies have smirched the paper. I hear no music. There is no note in me. There is no refreshment. Nothing to refresh the thirsting soul. There is no source. Augustine went into the desert. But in those days the source was in the desert. Rome sleeps. I hear the noise of great battles. It's distant, but it's a terrible tumult. The battle is still far off. It's far off, but it's terrible. It's far off, but coming ever nearer. Soon the dawn will break. I will hear the steps of workers in the streets. The battle will be nearer, and the workers will move towards it. They won't know they're moving into battle. If asked, they will say: 'We don't want to go to battle.' But they will go to battle. The workers are always there, marching into battle. The little Communist girl will be there, too. All proud people will go to battle. I'm not proud, or rather I am proud, but not in that way. I am naked. I am bare. I am powerless. Naked bare powerless.

PART TWO

The Pope was praying. He was praying in his chapel, the small private chapel in his apartment in the Vatican, he was kneeling on the purple-carpeted altar steps, the crucified Christ gazing down on him from one painting, the Mother of God looking at him from another, St Peter peering down at him from the clouds. The Pope was praying for Christians and for the enemies of Christendom, he was praying *orbi et urbi*, he was praying for all the world's priests and all the world's atheists, he prayed to God to enlighten the governments of the world according to His Holy Will, and he prayed to God to vouchsafe His Presence also to the rulers of rebelliously inclined empires, he sought the intercession of the Mother of God for bankers, prisoners, executioners, policemen and soldiers, for atomic physicists and for the sick and maimed of Hiroshima, for workers and for businessmen, for cyclists and for footballers. By virtue of his Holy Office he blessed the nations and the peoples, and the crucified Christ looked down on him in pain, and the Mother of God smiled at him sadly, and St Peter had probably lifted himself off the earth into the clouds, but there was still some doubt as to whether he had reached heaven, because the clouds are only at the very beginning of the way to heaven, floating in the clouds doesn't mean anything, the journey has hardly even begun. And the Holy Father prayed for the dead, he prayed for the martyrs, for those buried in the catacombs, for all those fallen in battle, all those who had died in prisons, and he prayed also for his advisers, for his subtle jurists, for his astute financiers and his worldly-wise diplomats, and he remembered also the dead gladiators of his city, the dead Caesars, the dead tyrants, the dead popes, the dead *condottieri*, the dead artists, the dead courtesans, he thought of the gods of Ostia Antica, of the spirits of the old gods wandering about the ruins, the pagan sites, the crumbling walls, the Christianized temples, the places of worship stolen from the old heathens. And in his soul he saw the airports, in his soul he saw the magnificent railway station of Rome, he saw hordes of new heathens arriving there every hour, and the newly arrived new heathens mingled with the new heathens who were already resident in the city, and they were more godless and more remote from God than the old heathens, whose gods had turned to shadows. Was the Pope himself a shadow? Was he on the way to becoming one? On the purple floor of his chapel the Pope cast a slim, infinitely fleeting, infinitely moving shadow. The shadow of the Pope darkened the purple carpet to blood-red. The sun had risen. It shone over Rome. Who, should the Holy Father die, would inherit the *sacrum imperium*? Who will be the inheritors of the Holy Empire? In what catacombs are they praying, in which prisons are they languishing, on what execution blocks are they dying? No one knows. The sun shone. Its rays were warming, but its light was cold. The sun was a god which had seen many gods come and go; warming, beaming and cold, it had seen them come and go. The sun didn't care on whom it shone. And the heathens in the city and the heathens in the world said sunshine was an astrophysical phenomenon, and they calculated the sun's energy, analysed the solar spectrum and measured the temperature on the sun's surface to the nearest degree centigrade. That too the sun didn't mind. It didn't mind what the heathens thought about it, any more than it minded the prayers and thoughts of priests. The sun shone over Rome. It shone brightly.

I love mornings in Rome. I get up early; I sleep little. I love the freshness of morning in the narrow lanes in the shadow of the tall buildings. I love the wind as it jumps off the crooked roofs into ancient crannies; it carries greetings from the Seven Hills, it bears the scorn of the gods into the city. The sun teases the towers and domes, it teases the mighty dome of St Peter's, it strokes the old walls, it comforts the moss in the guttering, the mice in the Palatine, the she-wolf imprisoned in the Capitol, the birds nesting in the Colosseum, the cats in the Pantheon. Mass is being celebrated in the churches. I don't need to go far to hear Mass. There's a church beside the Trevi Fountain, and another on the corner of the Via del Lavatore, and half a dozen other houses of God near by, whose names I don't know. I like going into churches. I smell the devout smell of incense, wax, dust, varnish, old robes, old women and old fear, so magnanimous and so petty. I hear the litanies, *ab omni peccato libera*, the murmuring monotone, *a subitanea et improvisa morte*, the rigid and set dialogue between the priest and the old women, who cover their heads, who prostrate themselves to be raised up, who kneel on the floor of the church, *te rogamus, audi nos*, I hear the tinkling bell of the server. I stand by the door, a stranger, a beggar almost; I stand outside the communion, and deliberately so. I see the candles burning in front of the paintings of the saints, once I bought a candle myself, lit it and put it in an empty niche where no saint yet resided; I offered up my candle to the unknown saint, the way the Romans built a temple to the unknown god, because the probability that we have failed to recognize a saint is far greater than that a god has remained unknown. Maybe the unrecognized saint is even living in our midst, maybe he's someone we pass in the street, maybe he's the newspaper vendor in the passage shouting out the headlines about the latest bank robbery or the chances of war breaking out, perhaps the policeman who stops the traffic in the Via del Tritone is a saint or perhaps the man sentenced to life-imprisonment, who will never walk through Rome again, and it could even be that the director of the Banca Commerciale Italiana, which has its grand offices on the Corso, is a saint, and an unknown one at that – the faithful say nothing is impossible for God – so perhaps the banker has also heard the call; but the Holy Father won't come to any of them and wash their feet, because the Holy Father would never guess there were saints living near him, and the Church will never hear of them, never know that they were alive, and were saints. But it's also possible that there are no more saints, the way there are no more gods. I don't know. Maybe the Pope knows. He wouldn't tell me if he knew, and so I won't ask him. There are nice things to do in the mornings. I got my shoes polished; they gleamed up at me like the sun. I had myself shaved; my face was pampered. I walked through the passage; my footsteps on the flagstones made a funny echo. I bought the paper; it smelled of printer's ink, and had the latest data on the condition of the world, material and spiritual. I went into the espresso bar in the passage, went up to the counter and stood among the men, polished, shaven, combed, brushed, clean-shirted, crisply ironed, after-shaved men, and like them I drank hot, strong steam-machine-made coffee, I drank it *à la cappuccino* with sugar and a froth of milk. I liked standing there, I was happy there and on page 6 of the newspaper I found my picture and my name, and I was happy to see in the Italian paper the picture of the composer of the symphony which was to be played that evening, though I knew no one would take any notice of it, only one or two composers would take a closer look at it to check my gormless expression, the lineaments of scant success, lack of talent or madness in my face, and then the picture would become waste paper, food-wrapping, or fulfil some other function, and that was fine by me, it had my full consent, because I don't want to remain for ever as I am today, I want to live in continual change, and I'm afraid of not existing. And so, for the last rehearsal, I go to St Cecilia, the patron saint of music. Will she be kind to me? I haven't bought a candle for her, and she may not care for my particular music. I'm on my way to Kürenberg, the sage magician, to the hundred players who perform my score and who intimidate me, I'll probably run into Ilse Kürenberg, who seems not to be affected by anything, who accepts life and death, the way the sun smiles or the rain falls. She is no patron saint, I feel that, but maybe that makes her the goddess of music, or at least Polyhymnia's number two, the muse of the day wearing the mask of flight, callousness or indifference. In the Via delle Muratte, I stop reverently in front of the Società delle Pompe Funebri. Death attracts me; but how laughable are its trappings which man buys to lay himself in the grave with dignity. The funeral director, a fine fat gentleman with curled, dyed-black hair as though his career involved the denial of everything transient, unlocks the door of his shop, and his cat, who had been dreaming on the coffins, on the bronze wreaths, on the cast-iron immortelles that spite decay, corruption, the dirty process of turning-to-earth, his little cat steps alertly up to him, and he greets her pleasantly: 'Good morning, my dear cat' – is it that the man is afraid of mice, is he afraid that mice might gnaw at his funeral pomp in the night, hold a funeral banquet on the paper funeral dress, unpetal the artificial flowers?

99

He sat at the bottom end of the dining-room table in the hostel for travelling priests, bathed in a dirty brown penumbra, because the window opened on to a small courtyard, and the curtains were drawn too, so that there was gloom, gloom barely lightened by a few weak electric bulbs, which gave the daylight its tinge of brown. All of them, they looked tired, as though they'd been travelling all night or making a rough crossing, but they'd all spent the night in the hostel, sleeping or waking, lying in their beds, sleeping or waking, and, sleeping or waking, they were proud to be in Rome, the capital of Christendom. Some had already been to early-morning Mass, and now returned to breakfast, which was included in the price, and lacked savour, like breakfast in all seminaries, hospitals and educational establishments everywhere, coffee like dishwater, jam that was without colour and without fruit, an old dry loaf, and they choked it down and pored over their travel guides and wrote out lists of addresses of places they wanted to visit or to which they had introductions, and the head of the hostel asked Adolf whether he would like to take part in a tour of the city, all places of worship would be included, the graves of the martyrs, the places of illumination, the paths of visitations, and the Holy Father was to meet the participants, but Adolf declined, thank you, he preferred to be alone. They were priests, they had been ordained, the bishop had called out their names, they had replied, '*Adsum*,' and the bishop had then asked the archdeacon, 'Do you know whether they are worthy?' and the archdeacon had replied, 'Inasmuch as human frailty may be sure, I know and affirm that they are worthy of the burden of office.' Whereupon the bishop had called out, '*Deo gratias*,' and they had become priests; they were anointed, they swore obedience to the bishop and his successors, they acquired the power of absolution:

'*Accipe Spiritum Sanctum, quorum remiseris peccata, remittun-tur eis, et quorum retinueris, retenta sunt.*' He himself was not yet a priest, he was just a deacon, he was one step below them, they were his superiors, he watched them as they ate their bread, as they made their plans for the day, how they might spend it usefully in Rome, and he asked himself whether God had chosen them, whether God had sent them, ambitious ravens and shy scarecrows, and he doubted it, because then why hadn't God done more, why didn't his servants do more to oppose the world's unhappy course? Adolf had come to them out of great unhappiness, and since it seemed to him that even as a priest he would hardly be able to prevent fresh misery, and he doubted that a pharisee's smug indifference was for him, he asked himself whether he really felt a vocation, if that was what the others felt. He could find no reply, just as he could find no reply to the question whether he should see his mother and confront his father; maybe he did love his parents, or he felt duty-bound to love them, perhaps as a priest it was his particular duty to love them, or again perhaps not, perhaps a priest had to love all men equally. His parents had given him life, but his soul he owed to God, and it wasn't for God's sake that his parents had given him life, not to serve God, not to obey God's com-mandment; they had given him life out of lust, because they were concupiscent, or out of carelessness or simply because they had wanted a child, or because it was the fashion in the Third Reich to have children, because the Führer loved children, or perhaps it was all of these, lust, carelessness, the wish for offspring and the Führer's favour. And yet God had been in attendance, invisible and unacknowledged, because there is no begetting without a miracle, and even the drunk who rapes the maid by the side of the road breeds by God's inscrutable plan, but

Adolf the deacon asked, 'Why why why?' And in the hostel's twilight of dull joylessness and sour devotion Christ did not appear to him, and he was unable to ask him as Peter did, 'Lord, whither goest Thou?'

They had packed all the picnic things into the car, bread, cold roast, some pheasant, fruit and wine. They were off to Monte Cassino, not to the monastery, but the battle-field. They had got together with other Germans, veterans of the battles, who would guide them, but they were getting behindhand, because they still had to go and see Jude-jahn first, they wanted to invite him along, too. He surely wouldn't be indifferent to the battlefield, it would be a way of bringing them closer, their enthusiasm for certain shared ideals, their victors' pride even after a lost battle, but Eva, the crucial person in all this, was making trouble, she refused to participate, refused to attend the reunion, refused to go along on the expedition; she wanted to stay in her room, the room at the back with all the kitchen noise and kitchen smells, or she wanted to return to Germany, to go and live in a tiny room there, and they were furious and pleaded with her, 'Why won't you see him, what's he going to think?' and she couldn't tell them, they who had made their peace and lived for the day, made their peace with collapse, betrayal and robbery, she couldn't explain to them that the marriage contract between herself and Judejahn was so inextricably bound up with the Third Reich, had only lived in this one faith, only been fed from this one source, that the bond was broken, it had ended automatically with Hitler's death, with the passing of the Reich, with foreign troops on German soil mocking the Führer's vision and promises. Whoever didn't understand that, whoever didn't find it inconceivable that one might think and feel in any other way, couldn't be told it, it was better to keep silent and not to insult one's own grief. She wasn't at fault, and nor was Judejahn either, neither of them was at fault in what had happened and what couldn't now be mended, but they both inevitably shared the guilt of every survivor. Eva had borne this guilt, not guilt for building the road that had led to ruin, but guilt at having outlived her salvation, that never left her, and she feared that Judejahn would now have to pick up the burden of mere existence and share it with her, and she didn't want that, she still saw him as blameless, a hero in Valhalla, but a portion of the guilt was given to each living person, and the letter from Judejahn, the news of his survival, had shocked rather than delighted her. But who was there she could tell that to, to whom could she show her dismay? Her son was her enemy. He was her bitterest enemy, if the word bitter means anything, and if she had been religious, she would have cursed him. But he was the religious one, and as a heathen she had no curse at her disposal, as a heathen she was deprived, she didn't believe in curses, or the withdrawal of blessings, she believed in the life of the race, and for anyone who trespassed against that there was only death. But she couldn't kill him. She no longer had the power. She could only forget him. Forgetting took time, and she was trying to forget him, but now Judejahn's appearance reminded her of everything, all collapse, all defeat, all severance, and she didn't want to see Judejahn. She stayed in the hotel, and she felt she was being scourged.

In the car to Judejahn's hotel, with Dietrich at the wheel, the Pfaffraths were thinking: We can't tell him, we'll have to break it to him gently, she's crazy, and no wonder after everything she's been through, we did what we could, we have nothing to reproach ourselves for, no one can blame

us, we stood by her, Judejahn will see that, we brought
her here, and now Judejahn will have to decide what will
happen. Dietrich was thinking: He's staying at a far better
hotel than we are, he must be rolling. At the Teutonic
castle I was envious of Adolf because his father had so
much more clout than mine, I wonder if he still does,
more than my father. How did he slip through the enemy
net, how did he get away, and is he still the same, will he
make a bid for power, will he fight, and is it the right
moment to throw in my lot with him, or is it still too
risky? And Friedrich Wilhelm Pfaffrath said: 'Perhaps it
was a little premature to think of his return. Perhaps he
should wait another year or two for things to sort themselves out. We'll get our sovereignty, we'll get a new
army. You have to hand it to the people in Bonn, they
haven't let us down. We're not out of the woods yet, but
once the army's in place perhaps then the time will have
come for truly nationalist forces to take over, and deal
with the traitors.' 'We'll deal with them, all right,' said
Dietrich. He grimaced and clutched the steering-wheel.
He almost ran over a gentleman with a diplomat's rolled
umbrella crossing the street at the Porta Pinciana, evi-
dently, and to his evident peril, a believer in reason.

He received them in his dressing-gown, having rubbed
himself down with alcohol and splashed a fragrant hair
tonic over his grey bristles, and he looked like an old and
unsuccessful boxer getting into the ring one last time for
a hefty purse. They were bewildered by the luxury surrounding him. They stood there like beggars, like poor
relations, the way they had always stood in front of him,
and he felt it too, it was all nicely calculated, and they saw
the silk-covered walls, felt the thick carpets underfoot, his
suitcases impressed them, and on his bed they spotted the

apogee of wealth and the stamp of arrogant independence in the form of a large mangy tomcat. 'That's Benito,' Judejahn introduced him, and he was pleased at their puzzlement and their concealed alarm. Friedrich Wilhelm Pfaffrath felt nauseated by the animal, but he didn't let it show; it was as though the black stallions in his dream of Lützow's bold hunt had been transformed into this mangy tom. Judejahn didn't ask after Eva. He saw through the Pfaffraths. He narrowed his eyelids to wicked piggy little eyes, he dropped his head like a ram's – his opponent would be advised to beware of the old pro. Up until now Eva had been the poor relation, and the Pfaffraths her benefactors; that couldn't be tolerated any longer. Judejahn decided to put Eva under his protection. He would get hold of some money, Eva was to buy herself a house, she should be independent. When the Pfaffraths started speaking about Eva, Judejahn told them to forget it. He would see to everything himself; he gestured sweepingly, dictatorially. He expressed no wish to see Eva. He understood her. He could see why she hadn't come, and he approved. They couldn't see each other, couldn't look into each other's eyes, not with the Pfaffraths looking on, those rats who had understood nothing at all, but perhaps Judejahn could see Eva secretly, like a sad secret mistress he was afraid of seeing. But then he laid himself open, failed to cover himself, he asked after Adolf, and Dietrich blurted out that Adolf had entered the priesthood, and that was like a punch in the throat. Judejahn reeled, his face twisted, he grew pale and then red, his brow and his cheeks purpled, his veins stood out, he was apoplectic, he clutched at his throat, and then there broke from him a deluge of oaths, a torrent of obscenities, he flooded them with ordure, yelled at them, the craven, conformist, greedy Pfaffraths, who stood there trembling, too terrified to move, like tame pigs faced by a wild boar. He blamed them, blamed them for betrayal, for defeat, for breach of promise, desertion and capitulation, for fraternization with the enemy, they shat their pants, they were lickspittles, collaborators, arse-lickers, they had dragged their carcasses to Canossa, lame dogs whimpering at the thought of Hell and in front of the priests, they had probably come to Rome to kiss the Pope's feet, to receive absolution, but history would condemn them, Germany would damn them, cast them out, the family deserved its fate, the Führer had seen that himself, the Führer had come to lead a cowardly people, a rotten tribe, that was his tragedy. And they listened, the Oberbürgermeister listened, his wife, Anna, Dietrich, they hung on his every word, in silence, quaking, but they hung on his lips, it was like olden days, the great Judejahn spoke, the big chief ranted, and they submitted, yes, they felt good, they felt pleasured to the quick, a lustful shearing in their bellies and their genitals, they worshipped him. He stopped. He was exhausted; previously, he wouldn't have been exhausted; previously such outbursts gave him strength. There was sweat in his bristles, sweat dampened the silk pyjamas he had on under his dressing-gown; his face was still as red as a cock's comb. But he knew how to take a punch, he didn't go down, soon he'd pulled himself round again. He slapped his thighs, laughed, what a joke, what a fantastic joke, he should have sent a few more priests to heaven, since he'd gone and supplied the Church with a new one. And then he went and poured himself a cognac, knocked it back, he offered them one too, but only Friedrich Wilhelm Pfaffrath would join him, Dietrich excused himself saying he had to drive, restraint that only produced a contemptuous laugh from Judejahn. 'What's the matter with our kids?' he cried. Then something seemed to occur to him, something amusing, and he went over to the bed and from Benito's claws he took away the Italian newspaper which the hotel had delivered with his breakfast that morning. Judejahn had leafed through it, uncomprehendingly looking at the pictures and at the captions under the pictures, and so doing had come upon his nephew Siegfried, whom he could barely remember, but he thought it was probably his nephew, Siegfried Pfaffrath. And so he held the picture up to Friedrich Wilhelm Pfaffrath, mocking and incensed, and because he had misunderstood the text accompanying it, he said his brother-in-law's son had turned out to be a violinist, which admittedly wasn't as bad as being a priest, but it was bad enough, it was a violation of the family traditions, it went against background and the training of the Teutonic school. And so Judejahn had his little revenge. Pfaffrath took the newspaper, he was shaken by this unexpected attack, and he said Siegfried wasn't a violinist at all, he was a composer, and then he regretted saying so, because it really didn't matter to Judejahn whether a fellow scraped at a fiddle in a café or wrote concerti, it was an unmanly occupation in either case, a dodgy way of life. Pfaffrath could understand Judejahn's way of thinking, but he himself had a different reaction when he saw his son's picture in the Roman newspaper, perhaps he felt reminded of his bookshelf, the edition of Goethe and the life of Wagner, he felt proud of Siegfried, proud of his progeny, and he passed the newspaper on to Anna, who clucked like a mother duck when her little duckling scuttles into its world, jumps into the pond, takes to the water and swims, and Dietrich peered over her shoulder, saw his brother and muttered, 'Incredible,' which could be taken to be an expression of astonishment, or admiration, or then again of disgust. And thus Judejahn remained compromised by his own devout offspring, whereas the

Pfaffraths actually seemed to feel pride in their fiddler- or composer-boy, although of course it wasn't apparent what opinions Siegfried had, what his vices were, what squalor he might inhabit, in unpatriotic or Jewish company, or how he had managed to secure the publicity in the paper. Judejahn stalked across the room in his dressing-gown, like a boxer pacing the ring in protest against an unjust decision. He flatly refused to accompany them to Monte Cassino. What did he care about battlefields, he mocked, all quiet and at peace, where the blood had drained away into the soil, where the bodies were buried, and plants grew and donkeys grazed, and wretched tourists swarmed round the donkey paddock. What was the battle of Monte Cassino anyway, compared to the battle for Berlin! The battle for Berlin was not over yet, nor would it be, it was still being fought; it was being fought in the soul and in the air, he wanted to say, but Judejahn had forgotten the legend of the battle of Châlons, which little Gottlieb had learned at school. He remembered something about heavenly forces, but he didn't think of ghosts, they didn't exist, nor of the dead, who did exist, but they didn't fight, they were dead, and so they must be pilots, and of course pilots fought in the air, and in the end they would fight with new weapons, with the force of the atom, because Berlin had not fallen. 'Do you believe in war?' Pfaffrath asked Judejahn. And Judejahn said he always believed in war, what else was there to believe in. Pfaffrath too believed in a new war, it had to come, justice demanded it, but Pfaffrath didn't think the time was yet ripe for it, he didn't think a war at this stage was in Germany's interest, he thought the odds were too unfavourable, but he didn't dare say so to Judejahn, lest his brother-in-law might think him a coward. 'Will you come back, then?' he asked, and Judejahn said he was always at war, always fighting for Germany. And then he put on an absurd piece of play-acting for their benefit: he rang the diplomatic representation of the country in whose service he stood, and, in a mixture of French, English and Arabic, he ordered the official car, every bit as though he were giving tyrannical commands, and was deciding war or peace in the Middle East. Friedrich Wilhelm Pfaffrath and Anna his wife did not notice that little Gottlieb was up to his tricks again, they were awed by the greatness of their brother-in-law, but Dietrich Pfaffrath winced: he couldn't decipher the words, but he suddenly had a feeling that his uncle's great days were over once and for all, and that Judejahn was now nothing better than an adventurer with uncertain prospects and shady backing. 'Careful,' said a voice inside him, Judejahn might damage his career, but Dietrich would have loved to march behind Judejahn, in a conspicuous place of trust, of course, if ever Judejahn unfurled his standard and issued his call to the nation. But for the moment there were jobs going in the Federal Republic, jobs that Dietrich would get if he passed his exams. Not until Dietrich is unemployed, without a car to play with, lying on the scrapheap of the academic proletariat, only when there is an economic crisis, will Dietrich march blindly behind any false flag, will he advance righteously to any false war.

Siegfried was late for the rehearsal. He was late on purpose, he was afraid, he was afraid of his music, he was afraid of Kürenberg, he had walked, he had taken the wrong bus in the wrong direction, he had followed a child for a while, he had been daydreaming and his feet were unwilling, his shoes had lead soles, as he approached the concert hall, and now he stood hesitantly in the foyer in front of the cloakroom, a couple of raincoats hung there on sorry hooks like corpses, a couple of umbrellas lurched against the wall like drunks, a cleaning-lady was eating a roll, and the fatty rind of the ham, melting in the heat, leaked out of the roll, and the woman's unsupported breasts rolled obscenely in her sweaty, unbuttoned blouse, and Siegfried thought of the woman's belly, and of the fact that she had borne children, and he was disgusted by the warm, moist belly, her warm, moist children, by life which was warm and moist, and the love of life to which we are condemned seemed peculiar and loathsome to him, the desire to reproduce that affects even the poorest people, the sheen of eternity which is a false eternity, the Pandora's box of hunger, fear and war, and he heard trumpets, his trumpets, and they were threatening him, and he heard harps, his harps, and they seemed to be trembling, and he heard violins, his violins, and it was as though they were screaming, and his own music seemed to him remote, remote, remote. And it terrified him, too. He walked up and down the corridor. His form was reflected in the mirrors on the walls, and he found himself ugly. I look like a ghost, he thought, but not the ghost of music. He made no effort to walk quietly. His footfall was loud on the hard linoleum flooring in the passage, it was almost as though he meant to disrupt the rehearsal, as though he wanted to rush into the hall, and shout, 'Stop! Stop!'

Then Ilse Kürenberg came towards him. She was wearing a summer dress in cornflower blue, and she looked youthful, firm-fleshed but not fat, and he warmed to her because she was childless. He thought: She has not given birth, any more than the statues in the gardens of Rome have given birth, and perhaps she is the goddess of music after all, the muse Polyhymnia, who is both experienced and virginal. But he was mistaken. Today Ilse Kürenberg seemed to be the nameless goddess of advancement, because she was in the company of a gentleman who looked like a large, captive and rather melancholy bird, whom she introduced to Siegfried as the head of the music department of an important radio station, or she introduced Siegfried to the bird, because the bird had such an important job. And Ilse Kürenberg and the bird were speaking French, they were both speaking quickly, fluently and musically, perhaps the bird was French, and Ilse Kürenberg had learned French, perhaps old Aufhäuser had chosen a French governess for his daughter, or perhaps Ilse Kürenberg had learned French in exile during the war, or perhaps both; but Siegfried now felt ashamed to be so uncultured himself, the Teutonic castle had been no help, his father had done nothing for his French, Friedrich Wilhelm Pfaffrath had no great opinion of France, no great opinion of the euphony of the French language, perhaps he had a higher opinion of French women, but then only as war-booty, and by now Siegfried was stammering, he was racking his brain for vocabulary, he didn't understand what the bird was asking him, but he was asking him something, because Ilse Kürenberg was nodding and looking to Siegfried for agreement, and so he agreed, not knowing what he was agreeing to, and he felt like rushing off, leaving the goddess of music and the radio bird standing – let them gobble each other up or whatever. But then Siegfried heard the final chord of his symphony, it sounded like the collapse of all hope, like a wave swamping a ship, leaving only a few planks and a sound of splashing. Kürenberg emerged into the corridor. He was sweating and mopping his brow. Oddly, he was using a large red handkerchief, which made him look not like a conductor, but more like a farmer labouring in his fields. People were following him, journalists, critics carrying notebooks, a photographer, who straightaway set off a flashlight on the group. Kürenberg saw that Siegfried was depressed, and he pressed his hand and said: 'Courage! Courage!' But Siegfried thought:

Courage? I don't lack courage. Courage isn't what I need, anyway. Maybe I need belief. I do believe, but what I believe in is the futility of everything. Or maybe not everything, but that my being here is futile, my speaking to these people is futile, our picture being taken is futile, the flashlight is futile, my music is futile, but it wouldn't have to be, if I only had a little faith. But what am I to believe in? In myself? It would probably be sensible to believe in myself, but I can't believe in myself even if I try to sometimes, then I feel ashamed, and yet you have to believe in yourself, only you have to do it without feeling ashamed. Does Kürenberg believe in himself? I don't know. I expect he believes in his work, and he's every right to believe in his work, but if his work is in aid of my music, in which I don't believe, is he then still entitled to believe in his work? It was nice just now, the way he looked like a farmer coming off his fields. But what field is he working on? What land? And who will harvest the crop?

Kürenberg introduced Siegfried. The critics spoke to him. They addressed him in many languages. He didn't understand them. He didn't understand them in any language. He was with them, yet not with them. He was already far away.

Approaching St Peter's, the church already fully in his sight, the squat-looking dome oddly disappointing in its grandiose setting, the rows of mighty pillars, the flanking colonnades, still in a line with the lamp-posts of the Via della Conciliazione, which leads up to the cathedral, the buildings on either side imposing headquarters of insurance firms, offices of international concerns, bureaux of flourishing trusts, with cool, well-made façades, looking as monotonous in the sunshine as sets of published accounts, prompting thoughts of expensive rents and the Saviour who drove the money-changers from the temple, in view of this world-famous, holy and – how could it be otherwise – extremely worldly scene, in front of the ancient, hallowed and busily trodden stage, which no pilgrim reaches without a shudder of reverence, and no touring party fails to tick off its itinerary, Adolf was seized by a great panic. Would he pass muster at the shrine, would he not be found wanting, would his faith be strengthened? An omnibus had dropped him here, he and the other passengers tossed out like a crateload of fowls allowed to pick. And already they were scratching away, hunting for bits of culture and lasting impressions, anxious not to miss a single grain of wonder, already they clicked open their camera lenses, greaseproof paper rustled, provisions were broken out to still hunger brought on by the star-count in Baedeker, while some swiftly plunged into souvenir shops, the *cartolerie* resembling little backhanded sinecures, the excursionists, having flown clear of their home cages, off the perch of habit, sent greetings from St Peter's before they had even set foot there, and Adolf felt sad, he was tossed around in the crowd like a piece of driftwood at sea, he was barged aside, an insignificant priest, or he was asked things because they thought he would know the answers, pointless questions for pointless bits of information. And foolishly he became aware of the lamp-posts by the roadside, and was reminded of another approach, where the posts were not crowned with cheap factory-lights like these, but where ornamental pillars were crowned with smoke and fire, with glowing fireballs, a street of blazing pillars through which he, the privileged child, the son of his father, had proudly driven. The Via della Conciliazione reminded him of Nuremberg, of the site of the Party rallies, only that parade ground had in the eyes of the boy outdone the approach to the cathedral, from which he didn't expect splendour, didn't want splendour, but which itself wanted to be splendid and challenged the universally rejected and despised splendour of Nuremberg, and lost out to it, as flambeaux had been followed by blazing houses, blazing cities and blazing countries. Certainly, in the real world, one couldn't expect hovels to be standing here by the wayside; a show of poverty, in the real world, was not to be tolerated here; mendicant monks, holding out their tin begging-bowls for bread and the love of God, have probably become extinct in the real world; but these new constructions, these buildings, evidence of clever choice of location and successful investment, were they not all too clearly a triumph of this real world, and thus a belated monument to Simon Magus, who had wrestled with St Peter in this city?

The square is no square but an oval curve, an ellipse, and Adolf wondered whether Nero might not have had his circus there, whether the obelisks pitched in the middle of it might not have seen the four-horse chariot races that still provide excitement for cinemagoers in our day, whether the cross had stood here where Peter had hung head down, and had won his tragic victory over Nero and Nero's lyre, and over all singers and all emperors to come. From the roof over the colonnades, Bernini's saints gesticulated like excited onlookers down into the oval, but they didn't seem to be crucifying anyone today, there was no animal-baiting, no retiarius finishing off the murmillo, no charioteers taking the curve, only the coaches of the travel companies vying with one another, Rome and the

Vatican and the Holy Father and the tomb of the Apostle were offered for little money and in quick time, and still to look forward to there was the Blue Grotto of Capri, Tiberius's castle, Botticelli's *Primavera* in Florence, a gondola trip in Venice, and the Leaning Tower of Pisa. Others arrived on foot, and crossed the square in groups: girls' schools, little bosoms jouncing in blue uniform blouses; scouts with little flags, bare knees and dashing cowboy hats, neckties and boyish eagerness; ancient congregations in grey and black, among the perch and the tench the occasional pike, mindful of his career; communities under the care of their vicar who wanted to get away from the village for once in his life; British women's institutes, American ladies' clubs, bored by endless afternoons of bridge, parties of German visitors, spurred on by their guides, hurry hurry, so much still to be seen, lunch was waiting for them in Monte Cassino, now please hurry. But the children are dawdling, holding their quick, avid pulses under the cool flowing water of both fountains, and here come the mothers with their newest offspring in their arms, running up the stairs with babies in white lace to be baptized.

'Feed my lambs, feed my sheep.' Christ saw them as uncomprehending, vulnerable and helpless, and He wanted to protect the unprotected, and Peter, crucified upside-down in the Circus, and buried on the slope of the Vatican Hill, was to be Caiaphas the rock, the unshakeable foundation against which 'the gates of hell shall not prevail'. He lay buried on the Vatican Hill, but the wolf likes to disguise himself as a shepherd, and the robber appears in shepherd's guise; kings, tyrants, dictators and presidents, all graze their lambs, shear their sheep and slaughter their flocks for their own ends, and the preachers of enlightenment who came forward and cried, 'You are no lambs, you are free, you are no sheep, you are men, break out of the herd, abandon your shepherd,' in what panic, in what deserts they drove the herd, which yearns for the homey smell of the stall, and even for the reek of the slaughterhouse. Adolf strode through the cathedral doors. His boyhood training strode at his side. His training was incomplete, he had broken it off, and had set his face against it. But now it was with him again, accompanying him. When he was alone, speaking to someone, to his fellow-deacons, the cultivated teachers at the seminary, to his confessor, then Adolf was freed of the past in the Teutonic castle, free of its slogans, but when he was in a crowd, surrounded by crowds, confused and embittered by them, then they stirred up in him the methods of his Nazi instructors, the principle of exploiting the masses, despising the masses, directing the masses, and the Party bosses had pastured their sheep, and very successfully, so that the lambs had flocked to them. Adolf felt a profound need to disregard the world's bustle, the frenzied processes of history, what was left was a tub of blood, the repulsive, warm blood of the victims, but each time the world and history came near and got into his thinking, he would wonder whether by putting on his priestly raiment he had really succeeded in cutting himself off from all this killing, or whether for all his rituals and devotions he wasn't part of an organization that – unwillingly, tragically, with a grotesque inevitability – found itself in league with the killers. Did salvation lie in renunciation, in flight, in solitude, was the hermit the only prototype of survival? But the solitary man always seemed a figure of weakness to Adolf, because Adolf needed support, because he was afraid of himself; he required community, even though he doubted its worth. Glorious pillars pillars pillars, Bramante, Raphael, Michelangelo, one couldn't fail to think of them here, but the pillars of their edifice were glorious but cold, the stucco majestic but cold, the ornate floor ravishing but cold. Charlemagne rode up on a horse, a cold man on a cold horse, and Adolf strode on down the nave, and there was the slab of porphyry where the emperor had been crowned, igneous rock, quartz, feldspar and mica crystals, cold cold cold. And the emperors were anointed and then took it as carte blanche to go out and extend their power, to win horrible battles, their thrones were cold and the splendour of them stolen, and the grass was trodden down in the battle, and the warriors lay there battered and cold. Why did the Church get involved with emperors and generals? Why not just ignore them all, in their purple and their frockcoats, their braided uniforms and dictator leather? Why weren't they seen for what they were, men who formed alliances with God and misused the Cross for quarrels, for gluttony and fucks, for gold and land and naked ambition? There were chapels all around, and priests were busy at the altars. They were reading Masses, saying prayers, deep in meditation, devout, clean-living men, but they were at the same time employees performing their duty, doing their day's work, and once this wicked thought had occurred to him, it put an end to all reverence, and the altars were like counters in a huge department store. To either side were confessionals, stout wooden fortresses, and confessors sat in these hallowed shrines like bank-clerks – the believer could confess his sins in any language, and forgiveness would be granted him in any language. Even the confessionals seemed cold and draughty to Adolf; as cold as the marble tops of the money-changers.

Adolf felt alone in the huge, lofty splendour that didn't seem lofty to him except in the literal sense, he felt deserted by God and by his faith in Him, he felt assailed by doubt, perhaps tempted by the Devil, who perhaps wasn't a devil, because how could a devil have made his way into the House of God, into St Peter's castle, into this hallowed and blessed shrine? And it was only the oil-lamps burning over the tomb of the Apostle that gave the chill place any warmth, but the colossal shadow of a worshipper darkened the mild, contemplative light of the oil-lamps, and made it seem like the grave of a commercial councillor. Then the sight of the admired *Pietà* gave Adolf back his breath and his faith, it freed the man struggling in snarls of ideas, suffering, shock, she seemed like compassion to him, all-embracing love, Adolf wanted to love, even if he had to force himself, he wanted to be friendly and loving to every human being he met, even his parents, even his father, the hardest case of all. Here, in front of the rightly praised *Pietà*, Adolf prayed, he prayed for the power to love; that was the only prayer he said in the principal church of Christianity, and then, gaunt, skinny and miserable, a little deacon defeated by too much splendour, he left St Peter's, whose air and aspect he couldn't take.

I forgot what time I had agreed to meet Adolf. Was it noon or was it later? I wasn't sure. I'd forgotten. Perhaps I didn't want to remember. I didn't want to see Adolf, but all the same here I was going to the rendezvous, already caught; I was angry because I felt trapped. Adolf took away my freedom, he took away my immediate sense of life, he took away my continual astonishment at things. He took me back to the oppressiveness of youth, the past, family, morning exercises and lessons in patriotism in the Nazi academy, and even though Adolf had, like me, immediately dissociated himself from those days and their watchwords, had left home and was leading his own life in a spiritual seminary, yet the whiff of family still clung to him, clung obdurately to his priest's cassock, a stain like sweat on the skin but not to be removed by any bath, and it adhered to me too, that odour of the Judejahns and Pfaffraths and Klingspors. The Klingspor sisters were our mothers, and that meant a century of nationalist maunderings, military drill, German bourgeois constraint, which turned into horrible frenzy and megalomania each time it burst from its narrow bounds. It was weakness that made me turn up for this appointment. I felt sorry for Adolf in his priest's garb. I saw it as a disguise he'd slipped into, out of fear. The kind of thing someone gets into when he's on the run and is afraid of being spotted. But where was he running to? Was he content with running away, as I was, had he resigned himself to a life spent on the run from something, but with no destination? I found incidental pleasures on the way, or I told myself I did, but Adolf didn't really master the new life of freedom from family, freedom from obeisance to a tradition, it seemed to me, and I felt inclined, in spite of the selfishness I preached to myself – and sometimes thinking of myself seemed to be the only way of remaining pure, which begged the question whether purity was the point – against all my own selfish interest I felt inclined to help Adolf, to support him. But could I? Could I even cope with my own life? And then I thought: If Adolf and I can't cope with life, then we should at least unite against those unscrupulous people who want to rule because they are unimaginative, against the real Pfaffraths, the real Judejahns, the real Klingspors, and perhaps we could change Germany. But even as I was thinking that, it already seemed to me that Germany was past changing, that one could only change oneself, and everyone had to do that for him or herself, all alone, and I wished I was shot of Adolf.

I crossed the Angels' Bridge to the Angels' Castle, and the angels up on their pedestals, the angels with their marble wings, looked like grounded seagulls with lead in their bellies or leaden thoughts, unable to lift into the empyrean. I couldn't imagine the bridge's angels aloft. Never would they float over Rome, never push open my window, step up to my bed, enchant me with their wing-beat, show me the unearthly light of paradise. The Tiber flowed between the old stone arches, muddy, blackish, turbid, it flowed under me towards Ostia and the sea, it had carried a lot of dead bodies, it was an old and experienced river, and I wasn't tempted to bathe in its waters, which were like the washing-water of an old nympho-maniac crone – no, I was tempted after all because maybe I too would be murdered one day!

Adolf wasn't waiting at the gate of the Angels' Castle. I was glad. That meant I was early. Now I knew I was an hour early, and I was pleased to be there an hour early, I was standing in front of the gate of the Angels' Castle, I was at a loose end, with time on my hands, freedom!

A tour guide sat on a stool in the sun. He was reading *Avanti*. Maybe he was dreaming of a just society. He had pushed his peaked cap back from his face. His face was plump; he looked earnest and dim. His shoes were old, but highly polished. From time to time he would spit between his highly polished shoes.

A horse-drawn cab was waiting. It was unclear whether it was hired or not, or was just waiting for the sake of waiting. The coachman was asleep on the dusty cushions in the back. His open mouth gaped towards heaven. An insect buzzed around him. To the insect, the coachman's mouth must be like the entrance to hell. The coachman's mouth was both alluring and threatening. The horse had a fly-net over its head and ears. It looked down on the paving-stones with the empty disappointed expression of an old moral theologian. Whenever the guide spat between his shoes, the horse shook his head in disapproval.

There was also a large black automobile in front of the Angels' Castle. A thoroughly infernal conveyance. Maybe the Devil had some outstanding business in this former popes' residence. The car seemed familiar to me. I must have seen it before somewhere. But who hadn't seen the Devil's cab at some time in his life? The chauffeur stood beside the car, stiff as a ramrod, in military livery. He had creaking leather gaiters on, well-cut breeches and a short jacket. His face was sharply etched and sunburned. His eyes were cold and suspicious. They were the eyes of a soldier and a sentry. The chauffeur scared me. I didn't like him.

I went to the Tiber embankment. I leaned over the railing, and saw the bathing-ship looking deceptively picturesque on the river. The ship floated on the sluggish water, and it looked like a Noah's ark, a beautiful, dirty Noah's ark. Various animals, young squawking ducks and geese, young cats, young dogs of all breeds and none, lounged peaceably on its decks. On the riverbank, covered with long grass, excreta and shimmering twists of metal, accessible from the bridge by a steep staircase, a boy was chased by two youths and roughly thrown to the ground. The boy and the two youths were wearing skimpy triangular bathing-trunks in an eye-catching, screaming red. The boy was beautiful. The two fellows had poor blotchy complexions; their faces were vulgar and nasty. I knew their sort. They were disgusting to me. They were prostitutes and blackmailers, they were base, murderous and cruel. But I was alone. I wanted to be alone. Only sometimes I yearned for contact, for warmth, for the smell of the herd and the stall, for a world of shared physicality, which I had lost, from which I had cut myself off, a compulsion I thought I was clear of, the boys' world of the Teutonic castle, the smell of the dormitories, the naked bodies of boys in that spartan regime, cross-country running in the early-morning mist in the woods; and then later the world of men – the forts, camps and establishments of the nationalist movements, and the comradeship of soldiers were all comprised in this world. I had said goodbye to all that, I was alone, I wanted to be alone, and Kürenberg had commended the solitude of the creative person to me, but I was criminally drawn to these fellows by my background and upbringing, and they were manifestations of a guilt from which I still had to free myself. So when one of the fellows looked up and saw me up on the embankment, he grabbed the point of his triangular trunks and obscenely beckoned me down the stairs to the bank and the bathing-ship. The fellow had apelike paws and swelling muscles, a sign of degeneration and enervation rather than strength. He was repulsive to me. The other fellow was repulsive to me, too. But the beautiful boy was lying between them, pinioned not by eagles, but by these foul vultures. Zeus-Jupiter was dead, and Ganymede probably was too, I cursed myself, and I climbed down to the Underworld

he had climbed down to the dungeon, down a long passage, the gloomy, sparsely lit track wound its way down into the heart of the papal burg. And then came low arched ceilings, clammy fug, one had to walk with a stoop. Blocked-off doors indicated even worse oubliettes, bottomless pits, terrifying murderpits, deathwells. The walls erupted in chains, rings for the feet, manacles for the arms, iron maidens to embrace one all over, torture instruments dangled from the ceiling, racks, bonebreakers, instruments to rip and flay, next to stone beds on which prisoners had rotted away, and the mouldering flesh and bones had etched the outline of the condemned or forgotten man even into the hard unfeeling granite. And upstairs, there were gala rooms, cushy apartments, ornamented chapels, there dwelt a keen appreciation of the arts, beautiful and holy pictures, carved prayer-stools, the silver candelabra of Cellini, in the library people pored over books, absorbed wisdom, were edified, listened to music perhaps, breathed in the evening air, and right at the top the angel hovered over the castle, the archangel Michael saw the sun, watched the glittering splendour of the stars, and looked out on the celebrated panorama of the Eternal City, and sheathed his flaming sword

Adolf had reached the lowest dungeon. A kind of amphora had been set into the bedrock where a prisoner might stand upright, his head above the floor, but his waste would have gradually climbed up his body, walled up the sinful house of the spirit; climbed up to his neck, and whoever by flickering torchlight had seen the man's head, no more than a head separated from the body by a sewer, a cry would have broken from him, 'Ecce homo. Behold, a man,' and the gaoler knelt down and comprehended the miracle of conversion that had befallen him by grace of the prisoner in the nethermost dungeon. Adolf knelt down by the hollow and prayed. He prayed with more fervour than he had in St Peter's; he prayed for the souls of the unknown prisoners. His cassock lay in the dirt, stones crushed his knees. He believed. The world needed to be saved. He believed. Man needed to be saved. He rose and felt strangely replenished. He was on his way back upstairs, to see the full brightness of light coming out of the darkness, when he heard steps, the confident, fearless steps of someone striding purposefully through his own house, though his house is a dungeon, and Adolf, embarrassed, as though ashamed of being found in this place, tried to leave down a passage, but the passage was blocked off, and so Adolf stood concealed but able to peer through a slit in the wall, to see who it was who so confidently went to visit the nethermost dungeon

the bathing-master was like a faun, fat-bellied, wrinkle-skinned, cunning, I took Ganymede into the cell with me, I loosened the red triangle from his sex, I looked at the boy and he was beautiful, and at the sight of his beauty I was filled with happiness and sorrow

they had reached the cloister at Monte Cassino and were having a merry picnic on the battlefield. Wine was being handed round, the ladies were afraid of getting tipsy, but the gentlemen bragged how much more they had had to drink back then, the best barrels out of the cellars, and one of them remembered it all very clearly, he had been a regimental adjutant, and had overlooked the whole scene, he overlooked it now: there was the monastery, here were their positions, the enemy was over there. All in all it had been a fair fight. The war had destroyed the old monastery, but it had been destroyed in a fair fight. Everyone had fought fairly, even the enemy, and the dead had died a fair death. Dietrich Pfaffrath followed every word avidly. The new cloister with its white walls gleamed against the hillside. Where were the traces of battle? Scaffolding indicated reconstruction, and it was good and elevating to be in this idyllic landscape and to hear of a fair war, after having repudiated Mars. Stimulated by the conversation, Friedrich Wilhelm Pfaffrath spoke of Verdun. He told of the trench-fighting. Trench-fighting had been less fair, perhaps because one hadn't gone into it so sportingly, but the conduct of the war had still been decent, decent and just. The enemy had been decently and justly hated, decently and justly shot at, and if one thought back and remembered – there had been more to it than death, there were comic episodes to narrate, jolly japes from the great slaughter. They fetched more food and more bottles from the car. They ate off a white tablecloth that Frau Anna, ever the thoughtful hostess, had taken along. They drank toasts to one another, the old warriors and the young, and the women drank too. The sun shone, and off to one side stood a donkey, swished its tail against the flies and brayed, 'Ee-aw, victory was yours!' and Dietrich sat there, proud and erect, shoulders back, and he was resolved to answer the call of his fatherland, should it come to that, as no honourable man could refuse; only perhaps by then he might be indispensable to his profession, he was no coward, but he was ambitious and he thought of his career

I looked at the boy, in happiness and sorrow. I didn't dare speak to him. I didn't dare touch him. I didn't dare stroke his hair. I was filled with melancholy, bitter-sweet melancholy and bitter-sweet loneliness. But then the worst of the louts stepped into the cell, water was dripping off him, he stank of the stinking water of the Tiber, as the whole bathing-ship did, rotting and gurgling away at the planks like a thousand greedy mouths. Blotches covered the skin of the degenerate youth, pustules flowered red and poisonous on the slack bed of his vicious face, his eyes were dim, their look was cunning and hard, and the stinking water matted his hair. I loathed him. He was naked, and I abominated him. I hated myself. My boy slipped out of the door. I hated myself. The monster was alone in the cell with me. I hated myself and pressed my body against his corrupt body, put my arm round his damp neck, pressed my mouth against his mean venal mouth. I felt lust and past time, remembrance and pain, and I hated myself

through the slit in the wall, Adolf saw Judejahn step into the lowest dungeon. He saw who it was. He recognized his father. He started, and wanted to rush up to him, and then he was paralysed, frozen, able to watch but no more

Judejahn had wandered through the Angels' Castle, he had seen weapons and armour and military equipment, and little Gottlieb had felt a quiver at so much history, but Judejahn had actually been bored as he went through the rooms, nothing new from the olden days there, he'd seen it all before, no surprises there. He felt confirmed in his calling, and he strolled casually, like someone returning to his house after a long absence, down into the dungeons. In the lowest cellar he placidly went up to the shaft in the rock, the grave for the living dead. There had always been wars and prisons, captivity and death, Peter had died on the cross, and his successors had done their enemies to death in the torture chamber, and so it would continue, and lo, it was good. It was human. Who said it was inhuman? Judejahn listened for a while, and hearing no noise, no footfall, he answered the call and relieved himself into the hole for the poorest prisoner

Adolf saw his father's nakedness, as Ham had seen Noah's, but, like Shem and Japhet, he covered his face with his hands

Eva his mother covered her face with her hands, she didn't want to see the sparkling blue sky nor the shining Roman sun. She stood in black, the ghost from the foggy northland fetched up in Rome, the vengeful Fury, her thoughts on dreadful retribution, the true preserver of the myth of the twentieth century, the Führer's mourner, the true believer in the Third Reich and in its resurrection, she stood by the window, and before her was the yard of the hotel frequented by Germans, and in the yard was a pile of empty bottles. In their hurry to reach Monte Cassino in good time for their picnic, the Pfaffraths hadn't troubled to tell Eva how their meeting with Judejahn had passed off. She had had no message from him. She was alone. In the yard, the kitchen boys and kitchen maids were singing nigger songs whose meaning she didn't understand and whose rhythm troubled her. In the corridor outside Eva's door, a chambermaid said to the room-service waiter, 'That old witch never goes out, why did she come to Rome?' The waiter didn't know why the old witch had come to Rome, either. He shouted some obscenity to the girl. The girl screeched and looked in rapture at the white back of the departing white-clad waiter. Then the girl knocked on Eva's door, went in, and grumpily started sweeping the floor. Eva got in the way of the broom, she stood in the sweepings; she didn't know where to put herself. The girl opened the window, and the nigger songs were louder; the nigger songs were wilder, the nigger songs got into the room, they advanced into the corner which Eva occupied

Adolf wept

I climbed up from the river, up the worn flight of steps, I felt happy to be coming from the water, to be coming from the old and friendly sluggish and sluggardly Tiber; up on the embankment time had stood still. The coachman was asleep, his mouth gaped open, the insect buzzed around the gates of hell, the horse was looking bitterly and thoughtfully at the ground, the guide was reading *Avanti* and still spitting between his highly polished shoes. Only the large black automobile with the Arabic plates had driven away. I was pleased it had driven away; I didn't have to see the martial chauffeur any more, not stand in range of his cold, watchful eye. The Devil must have done his business in the papal fortress; the angels on the angels' bridge still couldn't fly, but they seemed less heavy to me now, less downhearted, they seemed light and floating. The brown water of the ancient god-beholden river which I had now after all bathed in, the clammy embrace of the mythical element, had refreshed me and made me euphoric.

He stepped out of the castle gates, and the sun seemed to dazzle him, because he didn't see me. He was pale, and for a moment I thought it was my own pallor I could identify in his face. Adolf wasn't my mirror-image, or maybe he was, a blind mirror in which one sees oneself darkly. When he saw me, he walked sharply up to me. His angry stride seemed to want to tear his priest's robes. Clouds of dust and material billowed up behind him, and his shoes, clod-hopping country shoes, looked rough and out of place on the Roman pavement. He called out, 'I've seen him,' as though the Devil incarnate had appeared to the priest. He pointed to the gate. 'He was here,' he cried. I understood: he had seen Judejahn, his terrible father. Had he spoken to him? I asked. His face burned. He was embarrassed. So he hadn't spoken to him, he had hidden, and I thought: He's afraid of his father, an analyst would say he hid from the face of God the Father, the Old Testament god of vengeance, he isn't free. I didn't care about Adolf, he was a drag on me, he was a link in the family chain I had slipped off, but his agitation moved me, his effort, his search for a way; only his way didn't lead to freedom. I would have liked to help Adolf, I would have liked to lead him to freedom. But did he want to be free? I made us go on to the bridge. He was dejected, and I pressed against his dejection, crying out, 'Isn't Rome beautiful!' I pointed down to the river and its banks, as though they were mine. I cried, 'Look at the Tiber, isn't it beautiful, beautiful and ancient and beneficial? I've just bathed in the Tiber, touch my hair, it's wet with the good Tiber water!' My hair hung down in strands. He only just remarked it. 'See the angels here,' I cried, 'and imagine them take to the air, flap their black marble wings, fly up to the Capitol and dance with the old gods. Can you hear Pan playing the saxophone, Orpheus strumming the banjo and singing little jungle songs?' Truly, I suddenly found the heavy angels beautiful; truly I could imagine them flying, I could see them dancing a boogie-woogie; I hailed them, even the angels were my friends, I rejoiced, I was free. The sky was bright, a lofty blue dome. It was I who was populating the sky with angels and gods; the heavens were graciously inhabited by angels and gods on my say-so, because it amused me, because I imagined it to myself; I had the celestial jazz band playing on the Capitoline Hill, I dreamed the music, I dreamed the dancing; maybe the sky was black, as pilots say it is, a thin veil, no more, in front of an icy void surrounding our foolish planet – I rejoiced in my dreams because I was free, free to dream, I had permission from myself. I would have liked to throw Adolf into the Tiber, I wanted to baptize him in joy, but as he didn't say anything, but walked silently beside me, buffeting the bridge stones with his tough deacon's shoes, and only looked at me now and then with a strange fixity, inquiringly, searchingly, demandingly, and as I wanted to do something for him, I offered to buy him an ice-cream.

He drank only milk, milk like a child, pasteurized milk, carefully heated to precisely udder temperature. A nurse-maid looked after him, plumped the cushions in his indoor wheelchair, tested the flavour of the milk with a doubtful expression, herself smelling of milk in her blue-and-white-striped nurse's dress, of suckling, of sterilized nappies and baby powder, while he carefully brought the glass to his parchment-coloured face with his parchment-coloured hands, carefully moistened his razor-slash lips with the bland liquid. The sun was shining, but the room was in shadow, and powerful electric heaters produced an insufferable heat which, together with the dull blanketing milk-odour, deadened every visitor's senses. He called himself Austerlitz, and perhaps his name really was Austerlitz, but one hardly thought of him as having a real name at all; no one knew which metal works he owned, or which majority shareholdings, or which manufacturer he represented, perhaps he owned every weapons factory there was, every majority shareholding, or at least he represented them; it remained his closely guarded secret where his stores were, how he delivered was his affair, but the guns got there, and the shells arrived punctually in port. Austerlitz was dependable and businesslike, and his contacts with governments and rebel groups all over the world were as proverbial as his credit. Like Judejahn, Austerlitz was wearing dark glasses, so that the two of them glinted at one another like a pair of silly secretive spectres. They looked like sinister homunculi. The nursemaid had parked a trolley in front of Judejahn freighted with strong alcoholic drinks, ice and mixing-beakers, and he listened happily, his pleasure diminished only by the heat and the milk-fumes, to the list of toys the big boys were making over to the little boys. Quite an array of death-bringing gear, in good nick, was to be had for astonishingly reasonable prices, and it looked as though there were some anonymous donors, shy benefactors of humanity or discreet friends of Death, who were prepared to dip into their pockets so that plucky little tribes, less well-off nations, might be supplied with weapons to keep the threat of war alive in these out-of-the-way places. The embers of war kept glowing. Maybe one day a spark would fly and reignite the world. It was a good investment, Death paid his debts. Judejahn made a careful and informed selection of equipment that would be useful in the desert. His fiduciary standing was acknowledged. But fuelled by the whisky he was drinking against the heat and the gaggy milk-fumes, he grew angry that he was only able to buy for his bunch of Arabs and Yids, for the men he was drilling in the desert fort, and he longed for his homeland, for German forests, for wider responsibilities and a change of scene, which would permit him to go to Austerlitz with far bigger orders. Austerlitz, with a little moustache of milk on the parchment skin over the slash of his upper lip, was of course fully apprised of developments on the important German market. Should he tell Judejahn about the current market sentiment? Judejahn was an old customer. But Austerlitz could wait. Possibilities matured, and since he thought of Judejahn as a man of the second rank, whose time had not yet come, and of whom one didn't know when and where he would make his decisive move, he didn't tell him everything he knew. But he did mention one General von Teufelshammer as belonging to the faithful few, busying himself once more, and he mentioned the little doctor who had formerly reported to the Great Doctor, and now, with idealistic eyes wanted to play the part of the Doctor in the nationalist politics. Judejahn was familiar with both of them, he could imagine them in front of him, the general with his studious expression, pebble glasses, bat ears and little yapping mouth, he could see him as he danced round the Führer, completely straight back, excellent pupil, and prepared to hold the front till the death of the last Volkssturm reservist, and he knew the other fellow too, the little doctor, who was prepared to hold the front till the death of the youngest Hitler Jugend boy. The doctor had visited him in his office with messages from the Great Doctor, a smart alec with a ratty mouth, the mouth of a beaming rat, Judejahn hadn't liked him, not because he looked like a rat but because he'd been to university and was supposed to be a pushy intellectual – well, well, so those two had got together, or they were doing a number, and it was unlikely that they were doing it for his benefit, to prepare the Reich for him. Maybe he'd been dead for too long, he would have to go there himself, put in an appearance in Germany in order to remain a player in the German game, he would have to keep an eye on those prize pupils, which meant that he would have to let Pfaffrath fix it for him, the quashing of the verdict, a formal or tacit pardon. Judejahn no longer needed to be afraid of any jury, they would sympathize with him and be mindful of their own future, but it irked Judejahn that he would have to stick by Pfaffrath and snuggle up to Pfaffrath. He smashed his fist between the glasses. It sounded as though the phials for homunculus production were being smashed. The nursemaid came running up, but Austerlitz waved her away again. He showed Judejahn one last exhibit, which he produced from a little suede pouch, a new pistol with silencer, just on the market. Judejahn fell in love with it – little Gottlieb used to stand and gaze longingly at the window displays of gunshops – he fell in love with the deft little death-bringer, and was loath to part with it. Austerlitz, well versed in the law, duly informed Judejahn that it was against Italian law to sell, buy or carry weapons, but he left Judejahn the pistol as a sample, perhaps in advance of some larger order from the desert. 'And where,' asked Austerlitz with his quiet voice, his infantile grin, drooling at the milky mouth, 'where is there no desert, no jungle?' He didn't ask where there was no death.

The *gelateria* had set tables and chairs in the courtyard; it was pleasant there in the shade, away from the noise of the traffic, and Siegfried and Adolf sat together as though for a Socratic dialogue, in a loggia decorated in the old Roman fashion; around them were broken pillars, ramping ivy, the bruised masks of domestic lares, a little fountain tinkled away, there was the friendly outline of a palm tree, and the plaster busts of gods, poets and philosophers, and the heads of satyrs, statesmen and Caesars, the pretty heads of ephebes and nymphs looked on with battered noses, missing ears and blind eyes, as they chipped away at their granite-hard Sicilian ices. In Adolf, the dejected deacon, who had followed Siegfried with reluctance at first, the ice cooled the burning sensation of shame, he liked it, and with a healthy eagerness he savoured the dissolving of the zestful and aromatic artificial winter fruit on his tongue, and it was Siegfried who was now the pensive one, dipping his spoon and chipping away at the ice, leaving it to melt to a reddish mush on his plate. Feeling refreshed, and finding everything more natural, more innocent, and easier to resolve in the setting of their bower, Adolf turned to Siegfried and asked whether they shouldn't see their parents. Adolf suggested a visit, a personal appearance to say to them, well, this is the way we are now, not perhaps what you had in mind, but quite able to justify the kind of life they were leading. Siegfried exclaimed, 'You must be crazy! I don't want to justify my life! Why should I justify myself to my parents? I wouldn't dream of it!' To which Adolf replied that one always had to justify oneself, whatever the life one was living, to God and to one's fellow-men, and hence why not to one's parents as well. 'Do you think your father's a god, do you think he's even a human being?' asked Siegfried. He was malicious. And Adolf grew excited. 'Those are just words,' he cried, 'you're trapped in clichés just like all the people you think you're superior to because what you say is negative, cynical and hard, but it's empty, and all it tells me is that you're frustrated!' Siegfried: 'Is that what they teach you at your seminary, to diagnose frustration in others as a prelude to their possible conversion?' Adolf: 'I'm not talking about my seminary. I'm talking about you.' Siegfried: 'You can leave me out of it. I live as I please. I don't need anyone.' Adolf: 'Very well, you live for yourself. You think you've found the way. That's all you want. So why are you so prickly? Our parents could just as well say the same thing, that they had lived their lives, gone their own way, and it had all been fun.' Siegfried: 'That's just what they will say.' Adolf: 'But you don't approve of their lives, do you?' Siegfried: 'No, because they inflicted their ideas on others, because they condemned me to a military upbringing, because they started a war, because they brought suffering, and created devastation, because they turned our country into a land of intolerance, stupidity, megalomania, prisons, chopping-blocks and gallows. Because they were murderers, or else they stayed cosily at home knowing full well that people were being murdered.' Adolf: 'And do you think that can't happen again?' Siegfried: 'You bet I do! In my daydreams and nightmares I see the Browns and the nationalist idiocy on the march again. And that's why I want to get on with my own life, while the nationalist god is too weak to stop me. It's my only chance.' Adolf:

134

'And why don't you try to do something to prevent this development that seems so threatening to you?' Siegfried: 'How am I to prevent it?' Adolf: 'By trying to change people!' Siegfried: 'That's impossible.' Adolf: 'You have to try!' Siegfried: 'You try it! Your Church has been trying to do that for two thousand years.' Adolf said nothing. Did he despair? Did he see there was no hope? But then he came back: 'And what about your music? Isn't that your way of trying to change the world?' Siegfried said: 'No. You're mistaken.' But Adolf persisted and asked again: 'Why do you make music, why are you a composer?' Siegfried: 'I don't know'

didn't I know? He was right: it was out of fear, out of desperation, because of the apparitions and terrible dreams, that I wrote music. I guessed, I asked questions, I didn't know the answer, I had no answer, I could give no answer; there was no answer. Music was an enigmatic construction to which there was no longer any access, or just a narrow gate that admits only a few people. Whoever sat inside couldn't communicate to those on the outside, and yet they felt that this enigmatic, invisible construction, built by magic formulae, was important to them. Music didn't exist in order to change people, but it was in touch with the equally mysterious force of time, and thus in time it might perhaps contribute to great changes, but what is a century compared to time, what is a millennium? We measure time from the point of view of our own fleeting lives, so we don't understand what time is. It's possible that it may be friendly, it may be kindlier than we thought, or again it could be a gorgon whose full terrifying visage we still have to see. But aside from time and music, Adolf affected me, because wasn't it my own idea too, that we, the sons, looking for different ways of living, should fight for them too, however hopeless it might appear? I wanted to be reconciled with Adolf.

But

Siegfried said: 'We'll lose to Dietrich. My brother Dietrich will always get the better of us. Even as a priest you'll lose. You'll lose, and then either you'll ally yourself with Dietrich as the representative of law and order, of the state and the strong hand – or you'll just lose. Anyway, I don't believe a single thing you've said! I don't believe in your faith in your dogma, and I don't believe in your faith in mankind. You've turned to God, you turned your coat because you needed a master, and you'll be one of those embittered and disappointed priests who lack faith. You'll seem like a perfect priest. But you'll suffer.' Adolf said: 'I don't know.'

I was ugly, as ugly as Caliban. There was no mirror to hand, no magic mirror; it would have shown me Caliban's face 'wound with adders'. I looked at Adolf's worn, threadbare cassock. I could picture his clod-hopping peasant boots under the table. Why did I torment him? Why did I discourage him? Because I'm discouraged myself, or because my own discouragement makes it easier for me to be an outsider, the Pan pipes for the swamp-dweller? Am I actually looking for a fatherland, or am I just appealing to humanity, like a kind of fog into which I can disappear? I love Rome because I'm a foreigner in Rome and perhaps I always want to remain an outsider, an agitated observer. But other people need to belong, and if you could have a fatherland with none of the yelling, the flags, the processions, the state violence, just minimal rules for all responsible citizens, neighbourliness, wise administration, a land free of duress and free of arrogance toward strangers and its own people, wouldn't that be a home for me? I'll never find such a place. I don't think it exists.

I handed Adolf my ticket for the concert. I told him he could go in his cassock, but I couldn't, I didn't have any tails. I said: 'But I don't suppose you will go.' He said: 'Yes. I will go.'

Laura of the charming smile was on her way to her cash-desk, and, being unable to count, she had miscalculated the time. The bar was still closed; the owner hadn't arrived yet to turn the key in the door, nor were the pretty waiters there in their purple tails, they were all still sitting at home with their families, helping their wives with the house-work, playing with their children, and now, tired and unenthusiastic, they were just beginning to get ready to go to work, to the homosexuals from whom they made a living. Laura stood outside the door, looked around, smiled down the Via Veneto, and smiled at the large black automobile that silently drew up, as though sliding on invisible runners over invisible ice, she smiled to the driver, who leapt out, wasp-waisted, smooth, like clock-work, opened the back, clicked his heels together, and Laura bestowed her smile on Judejahn, whom she recog-nized as the non-homosexual man in dark glasses who had patronized the bar once before, out of ignorance of its clientele, and in a quiet hour. Judejahn had meant to look out for Laura, and, seeing her unexpectedly on the street outside the locked door, he realized what had happened, that she had made a mistake over the time, and he said in English that it was probably still too early, the door was still locked, he behaved as though it were a misfortune, he talked about the whisky that had lured him inside and Laura smiled, sent her beams through the tinted glasses, warmed his heart, thrilled his senses. And the smile embraced the large automobile, like all women she felt the power of the motor, the powerful panther-silent gliding of the conveyance was a sex symbol, gently flattering the owner of the vehicle, to whom one prostrates oneself womanishly, not because the owner is presumably a man of wealth, a good punter, but out of slave-girl instinct, because he is mighty, master of so many horsepower drawing the carriage of his life, and this one also disposed of a driver, who stood at frozen attention before the majesty of his master. What to do? Judejahn was going to suggest a visit to the confectioner's next door, he was hungry and Austerlitz's disgusting cups of milk had given him a craving for cream-puffs, and he imagined Laura's large eyes, her dreamy, lustful smile floating over compotes and tartlets in a spun-sugar atmosphere which he wanted to douse with cognac. But when he asked Laura, he got snarled up in his hesitant, stammering English, little Gottlieb hadn't done his homework, and since he saw her smiling at the car, he asked her to join him for a drive, and she allowed the ramrod-straight chauffeur to hold the door open for her, got in, and, such are women, the smile climbed into a cage.

They glided slowly along, invisible runners on invisible ice. Below them was the sparkling Underworld; raging demons, wicked warlocks, evil sprites, hell's beadles ground their teeth, raked invisible fires, bathed in flames, lustfully rubbed their prongs. And the automobile passed through the Porta Pinciana, they rolled into the grounds of the Villa Borghese, and the captive smile lavished itself on the plush interior, they were transported blissfully through avenues of green, she leaned back, and her companion in his dark glasses might be her King Farouk, her pipeline magnate, he had big hands, he was no homosexual. And he saw her waist, he saw her throat, where he might hold her, he hated this life, he hated this type of woman, they were all right as booty, or in a brothel, you paid your money, you undressed or you didn't bother, you assuaged your hunger, breathed in woman smell over-laid by scent, but you remained aware of the carnality of the procedure, and for afters there was soapy water or a prophylactic injection from the regimental quack just in case, whereas this here was a freelance harlot, her smile suggested women's rights, and equal rights, human rights, faugh, he'd had that. He reached into his pants, this could lead to the enfeeblement of the male, loss of virility, this is the way defence secrets were betrayed, empires ruined, little Gottlieb knew all about that, and Judejahn felt a soft-rough, a rigid-smooth, bump in his pants, it slid into his hand like a mouse, and it was the suede pouch with Auster-litz's silencer pistol. They skated past some water, came to a temple standing by the water's edge. Was this the residence of the goddess of love? Did she live in the park? The day clouded over, the trees took on the blue colour of the Valley of Death, a blue that had frightened Judejahn on the aeroplane flying into Rome, the trusty German forest, silent as this automobile was the tread of jackboots on its mossy and needled floor, and one's comrade walked on ahead in the Black Reichswehr undergrowth, treachery treachery treachery cawed the rooks, one gripped one's pistol in both hands, one's comrade fell to the forest floor, treachery treachery treachery cawed the rooks, up into the tops of the knotty oaks, and on the heath there grows a flower fair, it is my maid with the nut-brown hair, home-sick homesick homesick. The woman sitting beside him wasn't nut-brown, she was ebony-black, a southerner, perhaps a Jewess, most probably a Jewess, a succubus, a polluter of blood, who was laughing, with her mouth now red as blood, white as snow was her face, as white as snow, not quite, not yet, almost as white as the snow at home in the German forest, corpses were white as snow, this park was blue, the blue of the southern park, the agonising melancholy of the Roman trees, with their deathly blue, was insufferable to him. He was riding along the Devil's avenue. Abruptly he ordered the soldierly, erect, almost motionless chauffeur to drive them back to the Via Veneto, back to their starting-point, perhaps back to Eva. By now the bar doors were open, the pretty waiters in their pretty purple tails were flitting round the orphaned till. Judejahn wanted Laura out of the car, the chauffeur opened the door, stood at attention, but Laura was still hesitating. She smiled, slender waist, long neck, she smiled, black as ebony, red as blood, white as snow, smiled her bewitching smile expectantly now, and he arranged a rendezvous with her for the evening. Laura walked smiling to her cash-desk, just her walk appeased the anger of the owner. The poor child couldn't count, and her strange new friend seemed very promising to her.

Black-clad, cut-outs on a shadow stage, the sun fell harshly through the window, they stood and faced each other, two pallid figures, he in his black priest's garb, and she in her black mourning dress, and he was pale because he was fearfully excited to be setting foot in her room, while she was pale because the sight of him startled her. It tormented her to see him, to see him in the hated outfit of a power which, according to her, had shamefully joined forces with the Jewish underworld, overseas plutocrats and Bolshevik animals, to wreck the exalted dream of the Reich, of an Aryan future and German hegemony, perhaps destroying it for good. By now she was used to being confronted by betrayal brazenly not lowering its eyes. German women flaunted themselves shamelessly on the arm of Negroes, and traitors were rewarded with ministries. She was used to it now. She was used to weakness and greed in the words of German-minded people who reached accommodation with everything – spat out in disgust in private, but grew rich from change. But her son? Her son in the camp of the traitors, her son in the womanish robes of the papist enemies of the Reich, her son in cahoots with international conspiracies, fatherlandless as a Jew? It wasn't only a wound that hurt her to the quick, a brand in her heart, it was accusation and self-reproach. Where had the bad seed come from? Her family book had been scrupulously kept, there could be no questioning its Aryan purity. And yet she hadn't managed to prevent Adolf from defecting. She had put him in a Nazi educational establishment, and that hadn't kept him from defecting. The school had been blown apart, and he had defected, in the critical hour of need he had betrayed the work of both his parents. Traitors deserved to die. They were strung up on trees or lamp-posts. Their charge-sheet was hung round their necks. Should she not refuse to see Adolf? There was no bond between them any more, and yet he was her son, flesh of her flesh, now a stranger to her in his hypocrite's black, he had chained himself to the Cross, to the un-German creed from Judaea, there was a cross on his robe hanging from a chain which bound him, he came in enemy uniform, he was the opposite of the son she'd wished for, the continuation of her ancestral inheritance and its avenger, but he was her son, she had let him go out of her house at an early age so that he might mature into a man, and he had become a woman, she felt weak, she didn't show him the door. She asked disdainfully, 'What do you want?' And he, heart beating, his excitement making it difficult to speak, stammered, 'To see you,' as though he might simply pull up a chair and have a chat, each of them simply letting the other be, accepting the other for what he was, but she wasn't of a mind to offer him a chair, to accord him an hour at her mother's knee. She returned to the window, gazed out into the yard at the heap of empty bottles now glinting in the sun, flashing drunken greetings to her, and once more she heard the nigger songs of the kitchen staff, alien and offensive to her. 'Father's in Rome,' said Adolf. 'Then don't let him see you,' she murmured back, 'he never liked papists.' 'I have seen him,' he said. And then, clumsily, 'In prison.' The word tore her from her numbness. It was liberation, ennoblement, acquittal, the word spoke of heroic deeds and an heroic example. Judejahn was in prison, he had been arrested, the old shameful judgement was valid, it would be executed. Judejahn was going to Valhalla, and their marriage was rescued. 'Where is he?' she cried. And when he said he didn't know, she grabbed hold of him, tore at his loathsome robes, 'tell me, tell me', and he told her about the encounter in the dungeon, but left out Judejahn's availing himself of the hole in the rock where the lowest prisoners had been kept, and she, not understanding at first what he was talking about, what prison? what fortress? a papal fortress? the Pope had caught Judejahn? what were these caves Judejahn was descending into, going in and coming out again, at liberty, unmolested, a tourist? And when she did understand, vaguely understand, what had happened in the prison, then she felt deceived, sitting in her room mourning heroes, and she laughed, the Northern Erinys, and called them cissies, the pair of them, father and son, prison visitors, playing hide-and-seek in gaol. Gaols weren't there to be visited, people were condemned to gaol, they killed or were killed in gaol, now wasn't the time to visit the historic prisons of the city, a city Judejahn might have destroyed. 'He could have hanged your Pope too, and he should have blown up that fortress of his,' she screamed at him, as he stood trembling in front of her. 'He could have hanged the Pope, but he was too stupid or too craven, maybe he was already implicated in treason, and the Führer didn't know, the Führer was duped by everyone, he wasn't told that the Pope should have been hanged.' She was a Fury. Should he go down on his knees and pray? Should he pray that she be forgiven for her impious words? He said: 'Calm down, Mother,' and felt the feebleness of the words against her wild ranting. For a time he thought she was possessed by the Devil, but Adolf didn't have sufficient faith to believe in the Devil's actual existence, he doesn't exist, he told himself, and his mother wasn't obsessed by the Devil, but by a fiendish idea. How could he exorcize that idea, how could he free her of her obsession with it? He didn't know. He was helpless. He thought: Siegfried was right, there is no communication. He wanted to leave, he ought to leave, but he felt sorry for her. He felt that she was suffering. He sensed that she was being consumed by her own ideas, that she contained an inferno within her. She didn't need any devil. She was a devil unto herself, tormenting herself body and soul. He would pray for her, although at that moment he lacked faith.

Judejahn arrived. He filled the room. He filled the room with his squat bull-like form. The small room shrank further. It shrivelled up. It was as though the walls were pressing together, and the ceiling dropping towards the floor. Judejahn went up to Eva. He embraced her. He said: 'You're in mourning?' She said: 'I'm in mourning.' And she thought: He's arrived, he's arrived, but not from Valhalla. He said: 'I know.' He led her to the bed. She let herself fall on to the bed, and he sat down beside her. He saw the room, the little room overlooking the yard, he heard the nigger song rising from the kitchen, he saw the vulcanite suitcase, solid and cheap, and he remembered the leather-bound trunks she had once had. He said: 'The Jews are to blame.' And she replied: 'The Jews.' He saw his son in his priest's robes standing in the harsh sunlight, black-ish, dusty, shoddy, he had twisted the rosary round his hands, and was holding the cross up to him, he was pale, and he seemed now to be praying after all. Judejahn said: 'It was betrayal.' And she replied: 'Betrayal.' 'Jews,' he said, 'international Jewry.' And she repeated, 'Jews, international Jewry.' And Adolf saw them sitting, like Laocoön and his sons on the shore in Greece, entwined in the coils of the serpent; the hate-dripping, venom-tongued, giant serpents of their madness had enveloped his parents. He prayed. He said the Lord's Prayer. And she asked Judejahn: 'Will you fight on?' And he said: 'I'll deal with them. I'll deal with every one of them.' She gazed at him, and her swimmy blue eyes saw more than they could see; her eyes came from fog and they penetrated the fog of being. She didn't believe a word. He hadn't come from Valhalla. But Eva saw Death standing behind him. She wasn't afraid of Death. Death would fix everything. It would conduct the hero to Valhalla. Judejahn looked at her befogged face, and he thought: She's aged a lot, as I expected. And then he thought: She's my comrade, the only comrade I ever had. He felt her hand grow warm in his. He said: 'I will go to Germany. I will speak to Pfaffrath. I'll deal with those traitors. I'm the same old Judejahn!' He still was the same old Judejahn, he still was the great Judejahn. He bulked large in the little room. He was the size of little Gottlieb's shadow. Judejahn gave orders. He gave orders to her to leave immediately. She was to go home. He took money from his large wallet, money for the wagon-lit. He gave her the money. He would send her more money later to buy a house. And then he pulled out some more large, dirty Italian banknotes, swollen post-war denominations, and pressed them into Adolf's folded hands. Judejahn enjoyed that. He said: 'Buy yourself something to eat. Or get pissed. Or spend it on a girl, if you're still a man.' The money weighed in Adolf's hands, but he didn't dare refuse it. He clasped the money with his rosary and his crucifix. Judejahn packed his wife's few belongings, and threw them into the cheap, ugly plastic suitcase. She never stirred. She let him get on with it. She was glad he was giving orders, glad to see him take action, but her eyes didn't believe him, they saw Death standing behind him, they saw that he'd been on the way to the heroes' banqueting hall of Valhalla for a long time. Whatever he did and decreed here didn't matter; she obeyed him apathetically, and left the room on his arm, left the nigger song in the courtyard, left her son, that strange being that could only be her enemy. Jews. Betrayal. Priests. Judejahn had paid his son off with money, with dirty notes and inflated denominations; he didn't look at Adolf as he led his mother out of the room. And in the lobby of the hotel frequented by Germans, they ran into the Pfaffraths, the tanned day-trippers, coming home from the battlefield in a state of high excitement, invigorated, inspired and noisy. Friedrich Wilhelm Pfaffrath was surprised and disturbed to see Judejahn in the hotel, and Eva on his arm. 'I'm taking my wife to the station,' said Judejahn, 'I wasn't happy with her room. We'll talk later.' And then Judejahn was glad to stare at his brother-in-law's astounded and bewildered face. This face spurred Judejahn to poke fun, and he called out: 'Going to the concert tonight? Your Siegfried will be fiddling!'

But as though to repay him for his joke, there was

Adolf, a black shadow, who dogged him through the lobby. He was a lanky embodiment of seriousness and sorrow. What could they possibly say to him? They looked away, discomfited. He spoiled the day. His black form was the writing on the wall at Belshazzar's feast. Then Dietrich, after a moment's thought, hurried after his cousin, caught up with him and said: 'Hi, Adolf, you might be a cardinal one day. Best be on good terms with you.'

I didn't have a white tie, but I could have bought myself a white tie, or I should have hired a white tie, there must be people in Rome who make a living by hiring out white ties, but I didn't want to buy a white tie nor did I want to hire one; I didn't see why one had to have a white tie in order to be able to listen to music.

I put on a white shirt. The Trevi Fountain was murmuring. I didn't wash myself; I wanted to keep a little of the Tiber smell under the white shirt. The Trevi Fountain was murmuring. I put on a dark suit. It wasn't a Roman suit. It didn't have the soft cut of Italian tailoring. The Trevi Fountain was murmuring. My suit was a German suit. I was a German composer. I was a German composer in Rome. The opera fountain was murmuring. Water fell into the basin. Money poured into the basin. The gods and mythological beings didn't say thank you. Visitors crossed off the fountain from their list of attractions; they had inspected the fountain, taken pictures of the water and the gods, the fountain had been harvested, it had been committed to memory, it was a holiday snap. To me it was a dream. Little boys fished for the coins the foreigners had thrown into the water. The boys were beautiful; they had rolled up their shorts over their slender legs. I would have liked to sit down on the edge of the fountain in my white shirt and my black suit and my faint Tiber smell. I would have liked to watch the boys; I would have liked to observe how beautiful and how greedy for money the boys were.

There was a great commotion on the approach to the concert hall. I heard the policeman's piccolo trilling. His gloves were like elegant white birds. Lace princesses arrived, veiled dowagers, diamonded coiffures, advertising barons and foreign-ministry barons, notorious conmen, ambassadors grown grey in the transmitting of bad news, Snow White's mother and Cinderella's sisters drove up, they were beauty queens, and photographers blitzed them in flashlight, mincing fashion designers mounted their new business dreams on ambitious mannequins and pushed them forth into the light, famous celluloid features yawned at little rich girls, and all of them were honouring music, they were society, they were indistinguishable one from another, they all had one face. The critics hid behind character masks, and publishers beamed benevolently like full moons. Managers put their sick and sensitive hearts on show. A lorry full of red flags clattered past. Leaflets fluttered over the policeman's white gloves like a swarm of envious grey sparrows. The jungle bastion had fallen. Who cared? The stock market took it well. The Aga Khan didn't put in an appearance. He was waiting for Hokusai's wave in his villa by the sea. But a dozen company directors had come, they knew and greeted one another, their spouses were minor divinities. I had no hat, otherwise I should have taken it off; the people assembling here were my supporters and my patrons. Even industry was represented here; advised by a celebrated pessimistic philosopher, it had endowed a music prize, and after the industry prize there would be a trade-union prize, on the heels of the Ford Foundation there would be the Marx

Foundation, and patronage was becoming increasingly anonymous. Mozart had been in service to some distinguished noblemen, whose servant was I, who wanted to be free, and where were Augustine's great men, who, having done their day's work, gave themselves to music to restore their souls? I saw no souls here. Perhaps their clothes had cost too much.

Maybe I was embittered because I hadn't bought myself a white tie. Who would be delighted by my music? Was it meant to delight anyone? It was meant to disquiet. It would disquiet no one here.

Outside the upper circle there were no photographers. There were young men, young women, and interestingly also a few old people. An artist likes to think he has a following among youth, and he thinks the future's on his side when the upper circle applauds. Would they applaud? Did I appeal to them, those proud poor girls? They didn't give me a look. And the poor young men? They were probably students, future atomic wizards, in constant danger of being kidnapped and worn and torn between East and West, but maybe they were only future dentists and accountants – I probably was longing for Augustine's significant audience. A few priests were there, a few young workers. Would I disquiet them? I would have liked to feel comradeship with the young people, the young scientists, students, workers, priests, girls; but the word comrade had been forced down my throat in my early youth, and made repellent to me. I also thought, seeing the students and workers, 'Proletarians and intelligentsia unite,' but I didn't believe in that, I didn't believe a new world would be created from such a union, Hitler, Judejahn, my family and military service had robbed me of belief in all unions. So I welcomed the few old people who clambered up to Olympus along with the youngsters; they were lonely, and maybe my concert was meant for lonely people.

Kürenberg was waiting for me in the conductor's room. He really was moulded by antiquity. His tailcoat fitted as on a marble statue, and, over the white of the collar, shirt-front and tie, his head looked Augustan. He was sage. He didn't stand around foolishly front of house and study his public. He was above that. What did he care about vanity and craziness? Society had one function for him, which was to support the fairy-tale palace of music, it had to prop up the magic temple of notes like caryatids, and it didn't matter at all out of what misapprehension it did so. Ilse Kürenberg was wearing a simple black dress. It too looked as though it had been pinned on marble. It was like a tight, black skin on a well-preserved marble bust. Kürenberg wanted to dispatch me into the box. He saw that I had turned up without a white tie, and that must have annoyed him. He stood above convention, and he told me that, by scorning the white tie and not subjecting myself to custom, I had given dress and convention a significance they didn't deserve. He was right. I was furious with myself. One should play by the rules and avoid making trouble and giving offence. The bells were ringing in the cloakroom, the orchestra was filing on stage, the one hundred famous musicians were tuning their instruments, and now and then I heard a few notes from my symphony; they sounded like the cries of a lost bird in a strange wood. I was to escort Ilse Kürenberg up to the box, and I said I had given my seat to a priest. I didn't say the priest was my cousin, and only now did it occur to me that Adolf Judejahn would share a box in Rome with Ilse Aufhäuser from our town. Her father had been murdered after his department store had been burned. Adolf's father bore much of the responsibility; he had contributed to the burning of the department store, and he had contributed

149

to old Aufhäuser's death. My father could tell himself that he was innocent of murder and arson. All he'd done was watch. It was my father who'd been sitting in the box seat then. He had cheered on the actors from his box. But it didn't appal me that Adolf Judejahn and Ilse Kürenberg were sitting next to each other now. Why shouldn't they? The tragedy had happened, next up was the satyr play.

Judejahn had sent Eva back to Germany, he had put her in a bed first-class. The hotel room had been a cage, the compartment was a smaller, moving cage, in which she was caught, the Northern Erinys, black-clad, light-haired, full of lofty sorrow and now certain of her husband's going to Valhalla. But on the platform at Termini, the great Roman station named after the hot baths of Diocletian near by, the Termi, the fog cleared for a while under the neon lights of the great structure, the befogged face cleared – the second sight, the ghost-seeing sight, the werewolf eye which already saw Judejahn as a dead man – and she beheld him from the compartment of the train that was to carry her across the Alps, northwards and home, she beheld him and recognized him as he really was in the gleaming neon, a stout, grizzled man in dark glasses, and she cried: 'Take off those dreadful glasses and climb aboard, climb aboard the train and come away with me!' And he whiningly objected that his passport was not valid for Germany, and his false name would be exposed, and she said crossly: 'You don't need any false name, you don't need any dark glasses, you don't even need a passport. The border guards will say: "The General's coming home. We're proud to welcome you home, sir," and they'll stand at attention to you, and let you go wherever you want, and they'll be proud of having spoken to you, and at home they'll welcome you with a 21-gun salute, and no one will be able to

lay a finger on you.' Eva saw his return home. She saw
this was his only chance of returning home, and he understood her, he knew she was right, there was his return,
there was Germany. 'The General's home, we're proud to
have you back among us, sir.' That was how it was, those
were the words the border guards would call out. But
Judejahn hesitated, something was keeping him in Rome,
in the city of impotent priests. Was it Laura, was it fear?
No, it wasn't fear, Judejahn was without fear, and of
course it wasn't Laura who was keeping him either, it was
something else, maybe it was the desert, the barracks at
the edge of the desert where he was in command, and if
they received him with 21-gun salutes in Germany, the
echo of guns faded and died, and so too did the crack of
live ammunition, and then it would be Monday morning,
and what would he be then, a Judejahn without power, an
old Gottlieb sitting among malcontents and yesterday's
men. Judejahn was afraid of time, he was afraid of his age,
he could no longer imagine victory – and so he said to Eva
that he would let Pfaffrath fix it, Pfaffrath would prepare
for his home-coming, and the fortune-teller's gaze closed
in on Eva once more, and the fog and the befogged face
both descended, she knew now that Judejahn no longer
believed, he no longer believed in the border guards, he
no longer believed in the twenty-one guns, no longer in
Germany, and the second sight overcame Eva, the ghost-
vision, and a dingy Death on a lean nag drove the hero
towards Valhalla, while her train carried her north to the
Alps.

After an awkward and fraught farewell, Judejahn left for
the hotel favoured by Germans to ask his brother-in-law
Pfaffrath to arrange his return home for him, but at the
hotel he was told that the party had gone to the concert;
and indeed, spurred on by Dietrich, who, nettled by the

photograph in the newspaper, wanted to check on his brother's situation, also prey to their own curiosity, and motivated by a mixture of unease, doubt and pride, they had got the porter to make reservations for them right at the back, and had got there without incident. Judejahn with his mission unaccomplished asked to be driven back to his palatial hotel, and on the way there it occurred to him that his appointment with Laura was not for several hours and that it might be amusing to watch brother-in-law Pfaffrath's boy playing the fiddle. That laughably disreputable event might help him through the boring time before his rendezvous, and it would furthermore strengthen his position *vis-à-vis* his brother-in-law if he had witnessed it and seen for himself the family's degeneration. So Judejahn ordered a ticket for the concert through the hall porter, and, as the call came from an expensive hotel, the booking was for a seat in the front row. However, as he had no white tie, people tried to prevent him from taking up his seat. Judejahn, not understanding the usher's Italian, only feeling the man was being obstructive, and feeling himself in the right after shelling out for a surprisingly expensive ticket, barged the featherweight usher out of the way. What did the miserable lackey want? Judejahn tossed him a banknote, strode into the hall and sat down demonstratively in his seat. Once there, he noticed that he was surrounded by people in evening dress and he thought for a moment he was sitting among the musicians, in the ranks of the very clowns who were to amuse him and who did their work in tails and white tie. However, as the orchestra was tuning up on stage in front of him, that hypothesis could not be sustained, and Judejahn was left to wonder at the formality of the proceedings. Little Gottlieb was impressed; he felt intimidated. But Judejahn wasn't having any intimidation, he sat back even more expansively in his seat, and looked aggressively round the hall. As once before, in the corso hour on the Via Veneto, he had the feeling he was sitting amongst crafty Jews and rootless spivs. Foppish bunch, he thought. He recognized the new society, the new society of traitorous Italians, the scum that had floated to the top after the disgraceful betrayal of Mussolini. So it was in front of these people, who belonged in prison, in a concentration camp, in a gas chamber, that Siegfried Pfaffrath would be fiddling away! Judejahn tried to spot his nephew on the stage, but he couldn't find him. Perhaps Siegfried wouldn't appear till later, the lead fiddlers always arrived late, they were a stuck-up and pampered bunch; they could do with a little discipline. Judejahn saw that right away. The only music he had any use for was martial music. Why didn't they play a jolly march, instead of boring the audience with their endless tuning? He went on looking round the hall, and in the only box he discovered his son, Adolf, and sitting next to him a woman who took Judejahn's fancy. Had Adolf given her the money Judejahn had pressed into his praying hands? Was she his lover? Or was he her fancy man? He hadn't thought of the priest as anyone's possible lover. It confused him.

It confused Dietrich as well, seeing Adolf up in the box. How did he come to be up there? Had the Church given him a seat? Did they want to make an exhibition of Adolf on account of his name? As a significant turncoat, a major convert? Did they have plans for him? Maybe Adolf was a sharp cookie, and he would become a bishop – a powerful fellow in the making. How should he play it? And what about the woman sitting next to him in the box? Dietrich couldn't quite make her out from where he was sitting. And his parents couldn't quite, either. Was she with Adolf? And where was Siegfried? Would he have had any information for them? Questions. So many questions.

On sitting down, Ilse Kürenberg had given a friendly nod to the priest sitting up in her box, but subsequently his face disturbed her, it was a nightmarish face, she couldn't say why, but it was a face from terrible dreams. She thought: He looks like a flagellant, a flogger. She pictured him whipping himself. She wondered: Does he whip others too, does he whip heretics? But surely he wouldn't do that, nor would a priest whip Jews. And then she thought: Perhaps he's a mystic. And then: He may be a Catholic clergyman, but he looks like the rebellious Luther.

But when the music started she was sure he really was a mystic, a German priest and a German mystic, because Siegfried's symphony, for all its modernity, contained a mystical urge, a mystic's sense of the world, though tamed by the classicizing Kürenberg. But Ilse Kürenberg now found why the original composition remained disagreeable to her, in spite of the clarity of the interpretation. There was too much death in those sounds, and a death without the merry dance of death present on antique sarcophagi. At times the music attempted a joy and sweetness like those of the old tombs, but then it seemed that Siegfried had blundered, written down wrong notes, chosen the wrong tone; in spite of Kürenberg's cool conducting, it became harsh and excessive, the music was cramped for space, it screamed, it was fear of death, a Northern dance of death, a plague procession, and finally the passages dissolved into one wall of fog. Compositionally it wasn't botched, in its way it showed talent, Ilse Kürenberg had a fine ear, the music excited her, but there was at its heart a foggy mystery, a perverse dedication to death, which was repugnant to her and excited her in spite of herself.

How boring the music was! Was it even music, or were they still tuning up, under the supervision of the band-leader now? And was that the main piece? Siegfried didn't appear. Had he pulled out? Judejahn felt let down. He'd been cheated of his pleasure. Hunger squeezed his stomach, thirst parched his tongue, but little Gottlieb didn't have the nerve to get up and leave. He felt paralysed. The sound of the orchestra paralysed him. The noise made it impossible for Judejahn to think, he couldn't decide who the woman was next to Adolf, he couldn't make up his mind whether he would sooner sleep with Laura or with this woman in the box.

They were shocked. They were shocked and disappointed. The music was not like any other music they had ever heard. It didn't resemble any notion of music that the Pfaffraths had. It didn't even resemble the notion the Pfaffraths had of the kind of music their son might make. But what notions did they have? And if they had any, then what were they expecting now? Beethoven's too fre-quently dusted-off death-mask over the twelve-valve radiogram in the music corner of their living-room, or Wagner's portentous beret-wearer, manifestly kissed by genius? The two older Pfaffraths missed the sound of elev-ation, the high, exalted tone and the clear harmonies, they looked for the warm flow of melody, they listened in vain for the music of the spheres, music from some higher region, accessible as they thought to their hearing, a region they didn't inhabit, nor did they ever want to, but which they pictured to themselves as an optimistic sky, a rosy dome over the grey globe. Here on earth you had to live soberly and sensibly, and, if need be, resolutely taking responsibility for all man's inhuman cruelty, and so, correspondingly, the more loftily the pink superstructure had to float over the all too human. The Pfaffraths believed in the confectioner's temple of art, a sweet substance formed into ideal allegory; it was, so they said, deceiving even themselves, a necessity, which they liked to call 'love of beauty', and music was productive of a cultural feeling of pleasure and a contented drowsiness. But Siegfried's tones made them shudder, they felt thoroughly ill at ease, it was as though an icy wind were blowing over them, and occasionally it sounded like persiflage of German-bourgeois values; they thought they detected jazz rhythms, an imaginary jungle, a nigger kraal full of lust stripped bare, and this jungle of degenerate noise alternated with other bits that were plain boring, truly monotonous sections of disharmony. Did this discord bring pleasure? Did they accept it? Timorous as mice they looked round and were afraid of scandal and outcry, discredit to their family name that, as they knew, was held in such regard at home. But everyone around them still seemed to be sitting there politely, people's faces bore the usual concert expression of reflective appreciation, and a few of them even had absorption written on them. Dietrich thought he could detect some calculation in his brother's music, a conjuror's trick or a mathematical equation he couldn't quite solve; this music hadn't come to the composer in the way the great and beautiful sounds of Beethoven and Wagner must have come to them, this music was manufactured, it was a sophisticated swindle, there was careful thought in these dissonances, and that bothered Dietrich – maybe Siegfried was no fool, maybe he was dangerous and at the beginning of a great career. Dietrich whispered to his parents: 'He's avant-garde!' That was meant slightingly, but it could also be construed as proof of Dietrich's objectivity, his dispassionate and well-informed judgement, even in this department. But the remark caused some twisted foreigner in a curiously tight-fitting smoking-jacket and with a provocative goatee to utter a censorious 'Shh!'

Adolf didn't care for his cousin's music. It made him sad, yes, it tormented him; but he tried to understand it. He tried to understand Siegfried. What was Siegfried trying to get across with his symphony? What was he expressing? All kinds of contradictory things, Adolf thought, beneficent pains, comic despair, courageous fear, sweet bitterness, sick love and a desert furbished with potted plants, the decorated sandbox of irony. Was this music inimical to God? It probably wasn't. There was also the memory of a time before guilt in these sounds, of a paradisal peace and beauty, of sadness at the entry of death into the world, there was much clamour for amity in the notes, no hymn to joy, no panegyric, but still a longing for joy and praise of creation. At times, Adolf felt he could recognize himself in the sounds. It was like a reflection of his childhood in a broken mirror. The Teutonic fort was in the music, the exercise grounds, the woods, sunrise and sunsets and dormitory dreams. But the cynicism and unbelief, the narcissistic flirtation with despair, and the drift into anarchy drove Adolf away from the music. The Church would not approve these sounds; no Council of Trent would have found them exemplary. Did the deacon Adolf approve his cousin's music? He did not approve it. Did he then condemn it? He did not condemn it. It was not God who spoke in those sounds, it was some struggling soul, and so perhaps it was God after all, in one of his incomprehensible monologues that were so confounding to Christ's church.

★

They were whistling, I could hear them whistling, I had crept away to the door of the upper circle, I was waiting right at the back, a beggar by the church door, a beggar at my own music. They were whistling, I wasn't surprised, they were whistling in all manner of keys and like street-urchins with their fingers stuck in their mouths, they were whistling, my students, my young, imperilled nuclear physicists, my poor proud young girls, I had expected nothing else, the young priests were not whistling, but I think they should have whistled too. I had dreamed of a pure creation, but I had been tempted to meddle in the struggles of this world. I don't know whether a pure creation is possible, an immaculate conception from absolutely nothing, it's what I dream of, and maybe it's pride and delusion and the hubris of Icarus, and my wings broke before they could fly. Icarus must needs be arrogant. It is the arrogance of physicists in their labs, their unimaginative cleverness breaks up the natural world, and Kürenberg wants to encourage me to that destruction because his brain is delighted by beautiful formulae, because he can grasp the lofty laws by which destruction takes place. I don't grasp the rules, and I can't understand the formulae. Probably I'm stupid. How could I work something out, and to whom should I show my results? I still hope to get the right answer without doing the sums, by some inscrutable method which probably would not impress Kürenberg, which would seem dubious and dishonest to him. They were whistling, but downstairs in the stalls they were clapping now, they were shouting out my name, and the shrill whistling in the circle only seemed to encourage those in the stalls to more rapturous applause. Now would be the moment for me to show myself in my white tie. I should have shown myself. Kürenberg kept shaking hands with the first violinist, gesturing to the orchestra, pointing to the wings, from which I was failing to appear, doing everything possible to divert the applause from himself and to calm it down without bringing it to a stop, and with lavish gestures he lamented the inexplicable absence of the composer. One of the poor proud girls near me said: 'I could spit in his face.' She meant she wanted to spit in my face, the composer's. I understood her; she said it in English. And what did the people downstairs want with me, the gentlemen in evening dress, the ladies in expensive dresses, the critics, the publishers, the managers, what did they have in store for me, did they want to garland me, or did they want to spit at me, too?

Clapping loudest of all, from within a bizarre predicament, was Judejahn. His heavy hands were working like steam-hammers. He would far rather have roared, sworn, and had everyone in the hall and on stage stand at attention or clapped them in irons. He would have stood Siegfried against the base of the Palestrina statue; he would have loved to make Siegfried and the bandleader do thirty press-ups. But little Gottlieb didn't have the self-confidence to yell in the white-tie crowd, to swear, to call for attention and thirty press-ups, and when the upper circle began to whistle, he felt that was insubordination against those in the stalls, against the wealthy, those sitting in the light, whom he had long despised and envied, and whose mad-dening views of art and life he now found himself support-ing with the steam-hammer clap of his palms.

That was how Adolf saw him; from up in his box, he saw his father, he saw his excited clapping, whereas he himself did not know whether to express approval which he did not quite feel, and whether he was even allowed to express approval of such extreme and dubious music while in his clerical robes. The lady sitting next to Adolf kept her hands folded in her lap; perhaps she would find it a provocation on his part if he joined the ranks of the applauders. But Adolf would have joined the ranks of those noisily giving thanks if Siegfried had presented himself on stage, because Siegfried deserved thanks, because he had made evident God's disquiet, and it was greatly to Siegfried's credit that he did not stand in the limelight and milk the applause. How was it though that Judejahn had gone to the concert, how was it that he approved of the music? Had Judejahn understood the language of these sounds? Had the notes moved and delighted him? Did Siegfried and Judejahn suddenly understand one another in the world of music? Adolf knew nothing of the existence of little Gottlieb in his father, and so Judejahn's behaviour remained a riddle to him.

They were unable to account for the applause, they could hear the upper circle whistling, which only exacerbated the clapping in the stalls, they heard foreign-sounding accents calling out the name of Pfaffrath heavily and gutturally, this surely was a degenerate, alarmingly corrupt society, blindly tumbling to its own destruction, that was now celebrating their son's music, but the imminent decline of the Roman upper crust did not disturb the Pfaffraths, on the contrary it strengthened their arrogance, for in their certainty of being good Germans, genetically healthy and not susceptible to adulterated nigger-sounds, they thought the fall of what was rotten in Europe was to the advantage of their own nation, which would soon become hegemonous once more, and thus, blinkered by national folly and with the torture of having to listen to the music and the fear of witnessing a scandal to the revered family name for now both behind them, the Pfaffraths too put their hands together in honour of their son and brother. Dietrich could not understand why Siegfried, being summoned, did not appear. And, like everything he didn't understand, it disquieted him. What meaning was there behind his elusiveness? Was it cowardice, or could it be arrogance? Dietrich wanted to know, and he suggested seeking Siegfried out backstage.

I had slowly gone down the stairs from the upper circle. I knew Kürenberg would be angry with me now. He would be angry because I had once again disregarded one of the conventions that kept the art business going, and had failed to bow to the audience. Even without a white tie, I should have gone up on stage. But I did not want to show myself. The applause appalled me. I didn't give a damn about the accolades from the stalls. I felt kinship with the whistles on Olympus; but even those seated there were no gods.

Kürenberg was slumped exhausted in a red velvet armchair. The flashes of the photographers were going off all around him. He did not upbraid me. He congratulated me. And I thanked him and congratulated him, and said it was his triumph, as indeed it was his triumph, and he deflected my thanks, and something wasn't quite right about the way we each in turn resisted the other's flattery, and yet it was his victory, he had dazzled with my score, but for him it was enough to know that he had experimented with a new permutation of a limited number of notes, he had presented one possibility among billions, and demonstrated that music was a living and evolving force among us, and now it was time to try new experiments, and thrust on to new sequences of notes. He was right. Why did I not think of further composition? Was I burned out? I don't know. I was sad. I would have liked to go to my fountain, my Trevi Fountain; I would have liked to sit down on the edge of the fountain, and watch the hectic foolish tourists and the greedy beautiful boys.

Ilse Kürenberg came, and she too congratulated me. But the hand she gave me was cold. Once again I saw in Ilse Kürenberg the sober, sceptical muse of modern music, and I had failed to win the vote of the muse. I wanted to thank her for not giving me her vote, but I wasn't sure how to say it so that she would understand it the way I meant it. But while I was looking for words to express my feelings, I saw such dismay on her face that I was frightened. But then I realized that her shock wasn't directed at me, but that she was looking over my shoulder, and when I turned round to understand her terror, I saw my parents coming up to me, I saw my brother Dietrich coming up to me, and standing behind them was the image that had terrorized my youth, Uncle Judejahn back from the dead, grinning at me as though to say he had been resurrected, and I would have to get along with him now, the old power was back, and waiting at the door was a scared-looking Adolf. There was a Pfaffrath–Judejahn family reunion here, and I felt I was seeing gorgons. I was ashamed. I was ashamed of my family, and I was ashamed of feeling ashamed of my family, and I felt like a dog when the dog-catchers have got him cornered with their nets. My liberty was threatened. My father and mother congratulated me, and they threatened my liberty. They spoke to me, but I couldn't understand what they were saying. My brother Dietrich said, well, I had probably made it now, and his face was twisted as he spoke. He too threatened my freedom. And then I saw my father speaking to Kürenberg, greeting him like an old friend. He reminded Kürenberg of the theatre in our town; he spoke of the town orchestra, the subscription concerts and the good old days of 1933.

Ilse Kürenberg didn't know these people, but in another way she did know them, and it was as though a wall were cracking open behind which ghosts had been walled in. She had never wanted to see them again; she never wanted to be reminded of the ghosts, and now the ghosts were there, they had broken through the wall, demons of a house on fire, revenants of an old murdered father. She guessed that this was Siegfried's family, people from her home town which she had forgotten, local Nazis from a place she didn't want to think about. And she guessed who Judejahn was too, the man in the background, the final-solution man, who was undressing her with his eyes. She thought: Enough of these nightmares. And she thought: There is this symphony which I disliked, there is the priest by the door, a German mystic, maybe a saint, but woe is me if he's no saint, or woe is me if he lapses. And she thought: That one who's talking to Kürenberg is Siegfried's father, the Oberbürgermeister of our town, he was the Oberpresident of our province when we begged him for leniency, and he said he might be the Oberpresident but it was none of his business. She thought: Maybe he bought his shirts in my father's department store, he bought his child's first toys from my father, and when my father's shop burned down, and the shirts and the toys were plundered, then he was satisfied, and when my father was murdered, he made a note of it in the files, and he approved. And Friedrich Wilhelm Pfaffrath, whom Ilse Kürenberg thought of as an accessory to murder and arson, was glad to be in conversation with Kürenberg, who gave polite, non-committal replies, he was glad to be speaking about his community, and he offered the conductor a prestigious engagement in the old still-ruined, but soon-to-be-restored theatre, and he felt offended and thought: That's the way they are, whinging or snooty, when Ilse née Aufhäuser butted in and asked Kürenberg to take her away. The conductor looked round for Siegfried, wanting to invite him for supper later, but Siegfried had vanished from the room.

They waded through paper; there was paper on the Piazza del Popolo, lying in front of the churches of Santa Maria dei Miracoli, Santa Maria del Popolo, Santa Maria di Montesanto, the three Marias that guarded the square, paper lying round the Egyptian obelisk which Augustus had dedicated to the sun, and Sixtus V to the heavenly hosts, the heavenly hosts that guarded the square, paper lying in front of the gate through which Goethe had entered Rome, Goethe was another patron saint of this square, paper lay in the light of the arc lamps making a moonlit night in winter. There had been a demonstration in the Piazza del Popolo, and the leaflets promising people a new spring followed by an unprecedented summer, the oft-evoked Golden Age, the leaflets had fallen to the ground like autumn leaves, and the bold slogans of future happiness had turned to dirt, a filmy crust like dirty snow, a dirty-white winter.

The paper rustled under his swishing priest's robes, and I told him we were crossing a field of promises. I told him the eschatologies seemed to me like a bunch of hay dangled in front of a donkey to induce him to go on pulling a cart. 'But mankind needs to set its sights on something lofty and distant,' said Adolf. 'Think of the strength that the attraction of heaven gave to people in the Middle Ages.' 'Yes,' I said. 'The donkey pulled the cart. It thought it was pulling the cart heavenwards, and soon it would reach paradise, where there were no loads to carry, evergreen pastures, and the beasts of prey were friendly companions. But gradually the donkey realized that heaven was drawing no nearer, it grew tired, and the hay of religion no longer induced it to step out bravely. So lest the cart come to a halt, the donkey's hunger was switched to an earthly paradise, a socialist park where all donkeys will be equal, the whip will be abolished, where there will be lighter loads and improved fodder, but then the road to this Eden turns out to be just as long, the end is just as far off, and the donkey becomes stubborn again. But in fact, he was wearing blinkers the whole time, so that he never realized that he was just going round and round, and that he wasn't pulling a cart but a carousel, and perhaps all we are is a sideshow on a fairground of the gods, and at the end of their day out, the gods have forgotten to tidy the carousel away, and the donkey is still pulling it, only the gods have forgotten all about us.' He said: 'Then you live in a world without meaning.' I said: 'Yes. But does everything have to have meaning?' He said: 'If I thought as you do, I would kill myself.' I cried: 'What for? I'll be dead soon enough anyway, and believe me, while I'm not greatly impressed by life, I dread the idea of being dead. So why should I kill myself? Now, if I was like you, and thought of suicide as a sin, that would mean there was a hereafter! The real inducement to leave this world is a belief in the beyond. If I don't believe in heaven or hell, then I must try to find a little happiness here, a little joy here, beauty and pleasure all here. For me there is no other place, no other time. Here and now are the only possibility for me. And the temptation to kill myself is just a trap someone's set for me. Now who set it? If the trap is there, the trapper won't be far off. Then doubt sets in. The unbeliever's doubt in his unbelief is at least as terrible as the doubt of the believer.

We all of us doubt. Don't tell me you don't doubt. You'd be lying. In the three-dimensional cage we perceive with our senses, there is room for only doubt. Surely everyone feels the presence of a wall, I mean some kind of barrier that separates us from an inaccessible region that may be very close, just next to us, maybe inside us, and if we could find a door to this other domain, a crack in the wall, then we would have a completely different view of ourselves and our lives. Perhaps it would be awful. Perhaps it would be unbearable. The legend says that when we behold the truth, we turn to stone. I'd like to see the unveiled picture, even if I turn into a pillar. But perhaps even that wouldn't be the truth, and behind the picture that petrifies me there would be other pictures, other veils, still more baffling, still more inaccessible, perhaps even still more terrible, and I would have turned to stone, and still not really seen anything. There is something that is invisible to us, alongside the world and our lives. But what?' 'You are looking for God not in His house, you are looking for Him in dead ends,' said Adolf. 'If God exists, He will also live in dead ends,' I said.

We were walking beside the old city wall, down the Viale del Muro Torto. It was windy on the Monte Pincio, and sweet scents blew over from the Villa Medici. Power had established these gardens, power had built the villas, the palaces and the city, power had erected the walls, power had procured the treasures, power had stimulated the arts, the city was beautiful, I was happy to walk along beside the old walls, but power was a terrible thing for those who lived under it, it was an abuse, it was violence, oppression, war, arson and killing, Rome was built on the bodies of its victims, even churches are set on blood-stained soil, no temple, no basilica, no cathedral is conceivable without spilt blood. But Rome is splendid, the temples are magnificent, we marvel at the evidence of power, we adore it once they are dead who wielded it.

It was a poor show. He had disappeared. Without saying goodbye to them. He had gone without saying a word, after they had come backstage to congratulate him, even though his music expressed incorrect attitudes, and had disturbed them; in spite of that they had congratulated him, congratulated him for finding an audience in Rome, admittedly not a serious one, just chaff in the world's wind, rootless followers of fashion, anchored in no culture, but still they had congratulated him and they had wanted to forgive him, forgive him for deserting them at the end of his time as a prisoner of war in England, for breaking with the family and living openly among the enemy. It had been wrong of him to leave, and Adolf had left with him, the defecting sons had run off once more, and they had had a cursory greeting from Kürenberg, who had thereupon left with his Jewess, Aufhäuser's daughter, and then the journalists had pushed off, the photographers with their flashlights, the horde of bizarrely clad and strangely behaved people, the whole gesocks, as Friedrich Wilhelm Pfaffrath yiddishly/antisemitically referred to them. And all at once they were alone in the artistes' room backstage in the Roman concert hall, Pfaffrath with his wife and his assiduous son Dietrich and his brother-in-law Judejahn, they were standing by themselves among the red velvet armchairs, facing walls hung with golden garlands, faded ribbons of erstwhile Italian fame, and paintings of dead composers with coquettishly curled beards, and on one wall was a fresco of a woman, a voluptuous form in chalky colours, Harmony taming the blowing of the winds. They felt oddly irrelevant as they stood in this

167

room, which now seemed ghostly, or rather to turn them into ghosts. Had life given them up, because youth had taken itself off and only Dietrich stayed with them with his twisted mouth, a student and member of a fraternity, but already in his thoughts a civil servant, though less a servant of the state than one who meant to rule it?

Judejahn had given Ilse Kürenberg, the woman in the box, the woman who had sat next to Adolf and had excited his curiosity, an obscene stare. He had pictured to himself the sexual union in which she lived with his son, unchaste under his priest's robe. Now, when she had gone, he asked Pfaffrath whether he knew who she was, and when he heard that she was the daughter of old Aufhäuser, the department-store Jew who had been liquidated, then he regretted that she had escaped; escaped his hands, his boots, his pistol, the borders had been sealed too late, they had always been too generous, the bacilli had been allowed to spread throughout Europe, and they had been the death of a German Europe, a Jewess had sat next to Adolf, a German Jewess was sleeping with his son, who was a Roman priest, it excited Judejahn the way the reader of a legal journal is shocked and excited by the report of a case of racial defilement; Judejahn had no regrets about having killed, he hadn't killed enough, that was his fault, but the fuss that had been made afterwards about his bit of killing, that did preoccupy him, flattered and bothered him, as a scandalous reputation is flattering and bothersome, and it connected Judejahn to his victims to such a degree that the thought of a botched final solution to the Jewish problem, the thought of the mass executions he had ordered, the recollection of the photographs of naked women in front of the mass graves now roused perverted imaginings in him, it was a sin to consort with Jewesses, it was Arthur

Dinter's book *The Sin Against the Blood*, which little
Gottlieb had gobbled up, but the thought of sin tickled the
testicles, stimulated sperm-production, but the association
remained prohibited, unless it be in a dream, in a red mist
that dropped before his eyes, he wasn't thinking clearly,
it was a waking dream, after the completed sperm-
sacrifice, after the lustful hateful liberating thrusts, one
smashed the vessel born of circumcized union, the unclean
container of inexplicable seduction and cabbalistic magic,
which had subtly lured to itself the precious Aryan genes.

Judejahn thought of Laura. She too might be Jewish, he
wasn't sure, he was seeing her that night, but he would
sooner have been seeing Ilse Kürenberg-Aufhäuser instead.
He pictured to himself an encounter in an empty street,
on a bomb-site in front of a dark ditch, full moon, and
sweat beaded on his brow. The Pfaffraths had sat down in
the red velvet armchairs. The drive out to the battlefield
of Monte Cassino, an elevating experience, and Siegfried's
concert, a depressing and confusing one, had exhausted
them. The old-fashioned armchairs were comfortable.
Judejahn too now sprawled on the cushions, and before
Harmony and her winds, in front of the dead Italian
musicians, the faded ribbons and golden wreaths, they sat
as in their parents' drawing-room, as in the Christmas
room of the rectory, as in the best room, which they had
left in order to strive for power, to exercise power and
represent power in trenches, in camps in woods and fields,
in command posts and foxholes, at enormous desks and
imposing tables. Now Judejahn began to speak about how
he saw his homeland, his return to Germany, and they
listened to him attentively, but also with strain and struggling to stay awake. Judejahn intended to set foot in Germany once it had its sovereignty back, and Pfaffrath
nodded, then there would be no danger, no German auth-

ority would execute a Nuremberg sentence, and no German court would condemn Judejahn, and Judejahn spoke of a time to fight and a new movement and assembling the tribes of the faithful, and the finical Pfaffrath called to mind that Judejahn would also be in a position to demand a pension for services rendered to the state up to the rank of general, which was his of right, and if necessary the case should go before a court of law, he had an unanswerable claim on the Fatherland, and the state as presently constituted must not be allowed off the hook.

Thus stimulated by glorious prospects, Judejahn invited them all to have a drink on him. The Pfaffraths were tired. They would have preferred simply to nod off in the old-fashioned armchairs, in the chairs in the best room, and Friedrich Wilhelm Pfaffrath felt as though his father, the Reverend, were sitting there, telling him, as he often had, of Gravelotte and Bismarck and old Kaiser Bill, and the creation of the Reich at Versailles, that historic and treacherous site. But how could they refuse Judejahn, now playing the great man again? They obeyed him, and he stood feet apart outside the concert hall and whistled. It was a signal he trilled into the night, a bar of the desert anthem, and already his black mobile slid up, and the chauffeur, steadfast tan soldier, made tireless by some fiendish drug, leaped out and held the doors open. But the Pfaffraths of course had their own car, the Oberbürgermeisterly official vehicle, and they decided they would follow Judejahn. So Judejahn drove through nocturnal Rome as in days of old, admittedly there were no sirens going, no police protection in the van, no outriders, but once more he had followers. He had brought a phantom to life, the phantom of national greatness, the phantom of racial unshackling, the phantom of dishonour avenged, and once more he bewitched them. Where was he leading them? Into the night. Into temptation, and, like every drive, towards some final destination. He decided to make for the Via Veneto. Why shouldn't he regale his in-laws in the bar with the purple-tailed waiters? The bright lights and the many glittering mirrors would impress them, little Gottlieb knew, and Judejahn could in the meantime, without them needing to notice anything, look forward to Laura's slender waist so easily held in his hands, and the delicate throat of the smiling cash-desk beauty.

After hours of walking, town-walking, night-, garden- and wall-walking, after blind alleys of conversation in blind alleys, melancholic and futile attempts to close in on the invisible, Siegfried had taken Adolf to the bar. He didn't care for these places, he was amused by the queens, their womanish pother, their fake bird-squawking perched on the high barstools, their peacock vanity, their lies, their little jealousies, their endless involved affairs, Siegfried was a pederast, he was no queen, the affections of grown men were disagreeable to him, he loved the bitter, acrid beauty of boys, and his eye liked to dwell on street urchins, dirty and bearing the scratches of their rough games. They were out of reach and invulnerable, and therefore they couldn't disappoint him; they were a visual predilection and an imaginary love, a spiritual and aesthetic devotion to beauty, an exciting feeling of lust and sorrow; embraces like those on the bathing-ship were acts of blind folly, were joyless descents into hell, a crazed attempt to touch the untouchable, the hubris of grabbing the young god in the dirt, for which Siegfried was rewarded by a brief, fleeting euphoria. Occasionally Siegfried had relationships with girls who resembled boys, the fashion of the time favoured that, there were many lovely girls stalking the world in silk or linen trousers, flat-chested and with tousled, boyish haircuts, but in their long, tight trousers they carried the organs of motherhood, biological alchemy was at work, and Siegfried did not want to reproduce. The thought of being responsible for a life, which might be exposed to unforeseeable encounters, chance actions and reactions, and through its own thoughts, actions or further reproduction could go on affecting the future, the notion of fathering a child, this challenge of the world, truly appalled him, and spoiled his contact with girls, even when they used contraceptives, which were themselves disgusting and embarrassing and reminded him of the disgustingness and embarrassment of what was to be avoided. Physical procreation seemed positively criminal to Siegfried, other people might plead irresponsibility and unthinkingness, but for him it would have been a crime. Beauty was stained by seed, and birth was too much like death; perhaps it was a kind of death, the way orgasm dissolving in the rank and organic, amid sweat and groans, was near to death, and one exhaustion was much like another, in the end they were even one and the same, the warm primeval slime of the beginning. Adolf was a little alarmed by the stylishness of the bar, whose character eluded him, he shied away from the candelabra, the glittering mirrors, the purple tailcoats of the pretty waiters; of course he couldn't sit up on a barstool in his clerical robes, and he thought it wasn't fitting for him to sit out on the pavement, on one of the gaudy terrace chairs outside, and so they sat at a table near the cash-desk, and Adolf Judejahn saw Laura smiling.

I don't care for them, but I thought it was funny to see them again, parrots on their perches, my half-brothers, I saw their hysterical merriment, their inborn cattiness, their deep sadness, I saw their crisped hair, their tarty suits, their jangling bracelets, and the American poet who's on a scholarship to Rome, and has spent all year honing a single sonnet, which will eventually be printed in a small university quarterly, he arrived in his pointed shoes, drainpipes and a Directoire haircut with a curly fringe, and he spoke to me about the concert which he had been to, his opinions were clever and inappropriate, but he had been genuinely moved by my music, and I noticed the way he was looking at Adolf, he was curious to see me here in the company of a priest, but I didn't ask the poet to join us, I stood up to speak to him, and finally we agreed to have a drink together at the bar, and I noticed how the very beautiful cashier was smiling at Adolf, till he stared back at her and her smile, as though at a vision. I liked her too, her smile seemed somehow disembodied, a beam from a mysterious source, she was charming, she was called Laura, I knew her vaguely, I had spoken to her, but I wasn't the right man for her, Laura included me among the queers, and because she spent every evening among them, they had become as familiar to her as brothers, and didn't interest her. I hadn't meant to lead Adolf into temptation, I had taken him to a male bar, and I hadn't thought of Laura, but now I wondered whether I shouldn't introduce him to the cashier, he was young, I hadn't thought about his celibacy vow, I didn't even think he suffered on account of it, and if he kept his vow and lived chastely, then that was fine by me, and I preferred to think of him keeping his vow rather than breaking it, but it really didn't matter to me if he broke his vow and got involved with a girl, and Laura was extremely beautiful, it must be lovely to sleep with Laura, I didn't begrudge him that, and God wouldn't mind, there was no need for the Church to hear about it, and if it did, then it would forgive him, but maybe Adolf had scruples, and so it was probably best that he should leave it, especially as it was doubtful whether Laura would consent, and whether she had time for him, but he looked at her so spellbound that I wondered if I shouldn't help him out, my own first night hadn't been celebrated in any way, and I wanted to do something kind.

She watched the priest enter the bar, and as she was a devout Catholic, it upset her that even priests were queer nowadays, Laura assumed there must be some homosexual clerics, but it annoyed her that this one was coming into the bar now, it was indiscreet and surely wrong, even though nothing scandalous took place in the bar. But then she saw Adolf sitting down, she saw him staring at her, and, she could tell by now, she saw that he wasn't queer, and she saw also that he was innocent, that he had come into this bar innocently and non-homosexually, and was now sitting innocently and non-homosexually, staring at her, and there was something about his face that reminded her of another face, the face of another non-homosexual man, but she wasn't sure which man, and the other face wasn't innocent, she smiled, she smiled her loveliest smile, and she thought: Yes, yes, I would do it, it is a sin, but not a grave sin, I could do it and confess my sin. And Laura saw herself as a gift, and she was glad she had something to give, it was possible to give even a priest something, a beautiful present, and Laura knew that the present would bring happiness.

Adolf had told me about the money his father had given him. He had told me about it in the park, and he had wanted to drop the money on the path so that a poor man might find it, and I had stopped him from throwing the money away, and told him that whoever found it would be bound to be a rich man, a miser or a usurer. And then

174

Adolf had told me that Judejahn had given him the money so that he could get himself a girl. And I now said to him: 'You won't be able to afford the girl at the cash-desk for that money. That'll only buy you a cheap girl, not one here on the Via Veneto.' He said I was beastly, and I said I wasn't being beastly, and he blushed, and then he asked me if I only knew love as lewdness, and I said no. I said: 'I know no lewdness.' And he didn't understand me, and he went on and told me the Greek words for the various types of love, which they had taught him at the seminary school. I was familiar with his Greek terms, and I said I was looking for Phaedrus myself. Anyway, let him try it, let him taste the bitter-sweet drink, I went to Laura, and I bought a coupon for the bar, and I asked her whether we might walk her home later, and she smiled as though she'd seen an angel.

She really couldn't count. All her numbers, times and obligations she got wrong, all the hard, sometimes harsh calculations of life. Judejahn had led the Pfaffraths out to the chairs on the pavement; that way he could check up on his date in the bar, unobserved. Laura saw him, the man with dark glasses, and he seemed to her a promising stranger, a highly auspicious acquaintance, but today she wanted to give herself to the young priest, tonight she wanted to do a good deed, she wanted to offer herself to the young priest, who was so sad and so innocent, and in the morning she would go to her confessor and tell him she had given herself to a young priest, and when Judejahn looked at her questioningly, she shook her head. He went up to the cash-desk and glowered at her. What was going on? What was that whore up to, making a fool of Judejahn? Unfortunately, he didn't have the words, he didn't have the words in any language, and Laura smiled, she found it flattering that the dark-glasses man was furious, and besides she liked sleeping with men in the daytime more than at night, when she was tired out by figures and wanted to sleep, and so she told him to meet her in the morning if he liked, and she wrote the appointment on a piece of paper, ten o'clock in front of the CIT office at the station, she would meet him there, and he didn't understand what this whimsy was about, maybe one of those dirty rich Jews had outbid him, he felt like bawling her out, but little Gottlieb was afraid to raise his voice in the bar, and Judejahn put the piece of paper away in his pocket, and then he asked for a coupon for the bar, a coupon for a Napoléon cognac, they were drinking wine outside, but he planned to get a large Napoléon down him at the bar.

He squeezed between the stools, he barged against me, I was sitting at the bar, talking to the American poet, we were discussing the concert again, which had affected him deeply, and he was telling me about Homer and Virgil, and how he was weaving references to Homer and Virgil into the sonnet he was working on, and that now, having listened to my symphony, Homer and Virgil seemed to him an embodiment of a solitude he kept wanting to run away from, which was what led him to barstools and chitchat, and I turned round and saw Judejahn forcing his way between the barstools. I was surprised, and he seemed to be surprised too, we stared at each other, and then I should have dropped my gaze, but I thought it was funny, seeing Judejahn in the homosexual bar, in the circle of my damnation, and I felt like taunting him, and I said: 'Are you queer then, Uncle Judejahn?' His face contorted itself and he looked around, and only then did it dawn on him

that this was a homosexual hang-out, and he hissed at me:
'I always guessed you were one of those perverts!' Had he
always guessed it? And could he guess why? Did he think
of the Teutonic castle, the boys in their soldiers' uniforms,
how beautiful they were when they took off their battle
jackets, how they stopped being little ranks and became
boys again once they were naked, lads yearning for love
and tenderness, and their young bodies full of longing?
Judejahn didn't offend me. Why did I do it? Why did I do
it? Did I hate him? I didn't even hate him. It was over. I
didn't want to be reminded of it. The Judejahn of my
boyhood had been a terror. The Party man had inspired
fear. The General had been fearsome. Now I thought he
was just an old scarecrow. Why didn't I let him be? I was
free, after all! But he had made me a Junker type, and I
knew some Junker expressions, and I was very tempted to
tell him he was a prize shit, but now I was being intemperate, the family made me intemperate, I was intemperate in
the Pfaffrath manner, I hated myself, and I was intemperate in an inverted way, I hated myself, and I told him:
'Adolf is here, too!' And he followed my glance, and we
saw Adolf sitting alone at his table, conspicuous in his
priestly robes, all on his own among the cooing and bicker-
ing queens, and he saw him gazing at Laura, and I said to
Judejahn: 'He's going to spend that money you gave him
on a girl.' And then I saw that Judejahn's face was apoplectic, it was puffed up and purple, and I thought: Are you
having a stroke? And I thought: Don't have it here. And
I thought: It would be funny if Judejahn had a stroke at
the violet bar. Was it a triumph? It was no triumph. I felt
flat. I didn't care whether Judejahn suffered a stroke or
not. His hand trembled as he gave the barman a coupon.
I thought: He's an old fool. And I sensed: He's a ghost. I

felt something almost like pity for Judejahn. It was strange. Maybe I was getting sentimental.

He knocked back his cognac, a river of fire flooded his guts, little tributaries spread into his belly, rage rage rage and pain were in him, all that stood in the way of an explosion of rage was little Gottlieb with his respect for swanky surroundings, even if it was just a squalid palace of venal lust. It was bad enough, Siegfried's impertinence. Judejahn still felt capable of smacking the cissy in his unpatriotic intellectual face. But a new foe had risen up against him, crept into position, a foe of whose approach he had not managed to hear in the time of his power and who could not be discerned from the barracks in the desert either, because even there he had had power, though it was power of smaller dimensions, he had given orders, issued commands, he hadn't faced rivalry, but now the enemy was at hand, he showed his face, he launched himself to strike – it was age! Judejahn was not enraged to find his son among homosexuals. Nor did it occur to him to be amused to find his son, the deacon, seated among queers. He only saw that his son, the hypocrite, had snatched the whore from him, and Judejahn wasn't so much embittered about being cheated of his fornication, as surprised, surprised and incredulous to find himself losing out to this weakling in the womanish dress of a priest, whom he had so despised that he didn't even properly hate him, he felt ashamed of him as of some disfigurement, a funny hunchback making him ridiculous, and the boy was preferred to him. Judejahn kept looking across at the strangely empty table at which Adolf was sitting alone in Laura's lovely smile. Judejahn felt as though he were seeing an evil and dangerous fata morgana, a sand phantom, untouchable, impregnable, cruel, grotesque and deadly.

But in fact it was his arch-enemy, it was no ghost, and yet it was a ghost, the arch-deceiver, who had disguised himself as a priest to deceive the foolish father. It was youth rising up against Judejahn, green youth had betrayed him. One lot of youth had died, Judejahn had gobbled them up in the war, they were all right, they hadn't deceived him, they were in no position to deceive and betray him, they were safely in the grave. But a new generation had betrayed him, and went on betraying him, and now it was robbing him, took away his chance of victory, stole his woman, the woman who at all times was the property of the victor, the overpowerer, and whose possession was a sexual emblem of victory, a warming sense of power and subjugation. Was Judejahn now the old stag who had lost his doe to the young buck, left to crawl into the undergrowth to die? Not yet he wasn't. That was priests' ruses. He'd been duped. Judejahn wasn't the old stag losing his horns and crawling off, not by a long chalk he wasn't. He was the better man. His deeds spoke for him; but how could he tell Laura of his deeds, his victories, his campaigns of devastation? The whole world had witnessed Judejahn's doings, no one seemed to want to remember them. Was it just a matter of eloquence now, the tongues of venal cowards, while the deeds of the brave had already been forgotten, were already a zero in the hole of the past, where even rivers of blood dried up, and atrocity mildewed and crumbled away? What could Judejahn do? He could have the bar cleared. Nonsense, he could not have the bar cleared. He couldn't even go to the cashier to get a token for another cognac. He felt giddy, and he feared ridicule, he feared the ridiculous scene of a meeting with his priest son. Judejahn gripped the brass rail of the bar as though he had to hold it in order not to collapse, not to drop dead or blindly lash out from

179

a position of utter hopelessness. Ah, delivered unto the enemy's hands.

I saw his hand clutching the brass rail, I saw him longing for another drink and not daring to let go of the rail, and I told the barman to give Judejahn a cognac, and the barman poured the cognac because he had me down for a queer and so he trusted me to pay for the cognac later. Judejahn took the glass. Did he know it came from me? He knocked it back with an upward thrust of his buttocks as though he were doing a knee-lift. For a moment his eyes were glassy. But then his eyelids narrowed again to sly pig's slits. The sly pig's eyes were looking at me. They looked round the bar. They looked at Adolf, they rested on Laura, and I was amazed to see him so agitated. Why was it such a terrible blow for him to see Adolf here? Was he such an over-protective father? I hardly thought so. Judejahn didn't want to protect anyone. And since he hated his son's priest's robes, it should have amused him to find the hated cassock in such unsavoury company. Now he left the counter and walked through the bar. He squeezed past Adolf and the cash-desk, and I kept an eye on him so that I could intervene if he started yelling at Adolf. But Judejahn walked right past him without appearing to notice him, and Adolf appeared not to see him either, he had forgotten about me too, he was sitting in Laura's smile as under a giant sun, the wonderful sun of an innocent paradise.

They sat on the pavement in front of the bar, the night streamed past them, rich Rome, elegant Rome, the Rome of the magnates and ostentatious foreigners, the Via Veneto paraded past the rows of chairs belonging to cafés, bars, hotels and pricey clubs, and lights glittered everywhere, the chestnuts flowered and rustled, and stars shone over the great city. To begin with, they had been impressed by everything, even the waiters in violet tails, but then an aura of disrepute spread over the chairs, the twittery voices, the jangling bracelets, the scent of curled hair and womanishly manicured hands that rested on the acquiescent hips of others. Friedrich Wilhelm Pfaffrath was aghast. He dared not give a name to what he suspected, and he thought under no circumstances should Judejahn have brought Anna his wife to such a place. Dietrich also was indignant, but outrage and indignation about morals and seediness had a positive effect too, they stiffened the spine, they made a man hold his head high, decency was sitting among Mediterranean licentiousness, and the Goths would prevail. Dietrich was tormented by curiosity and desire. Curiosity asked him what might have caused Judejahn to seek out this establishment. He wasn't a queer. But maybe he had some secret contacts here, underworld informers, since spies and informers often came from corrupt backgrounds; one exploited them and, having gained power, eliminated one's despicable if useful helpers. Lust cried out for the passing girls. On high heels they teetered past, in tight skirts that exposed their thighs, they were as bred and spirited as circus horses, expensive mounts, talented tricks. Dietrich imagined it for himself, but he knew how to count, and he reckoned that it would come expensive, at any rate it would cost more than he was willing to shell out, and so he hated the girls instead, he found them shamelessly provocative and their walking the public street at night was a scandal, and he thought greedily and bitterly of the publication in his suitcase, the illustrated magazine with the disclosures that brought about relief and slumber. Finally Judejahn emerged from the strange aviary. Something must have angered him, because his breathing was laboured, the veins on his brow stood out, and his hand trembled as he reached for the wine bottle. And then he insulted them, he called them names, because Germany had not yet awoken, because young people were not yet marching, because young people were insolent to their superiors and were going to the dogs. How could they defend themselves? They had never been able to defend themselves against Judejahn. Friedrich Wilhelm Pfaffrath was pathetically vulnerable to any loud-mouth who banged on about the nation, because the nation was an idol, a Moloch to whom one sacrificed reason and life and even property. The Roman chestnuts rustled in the balmy spring night. When would flags start to rustle again? Fervently Friedrich Wilhelm Pfaffrath wished for it, flags were lofty symbols, they were the nation surging ahead, but now perhaps he was growing old. When he heard Judejahn's tirade against himself and the nation, he was seized by a peculiar mild disgust for Judejahn's flags that were soon to rustle again, and he felt as though the mild Roman chestnuts were tittering like old ladies. He thought of his mother, the vicar's wife, who had been left cold by National Socialism. Perhaps she was now watching him from the starry firmament. She had been a firm believer in the hereafter. Rationally, Pfaffrath rejected such a possibility. Even so – if his mother was looking down on him, if she had found him and was watching him, would she feel sorry for him? Judejahn was accusing Pfaffrath of cowardice and disloyalty. At this transfigured moment of the night, tired, exhausted, full of elevating and strange impressions, Pfaffrath accepted his reproaches. He had been cowardly and disloyal, but not in the way his raging brother-in-law had in mind. It now seemed to Pfaffrath as though he had lost his way in his early years, as though there had been another road for Germany and for himself than the military road that Pfaffrath had gone down; another German possibility, which he had disregarded for years, now lay before him in the landscape of youth clarified by a trick of memory, and it was this other possibility that he had betrayed, and the other Germany had been lost for ever. The chestnuts were whispering to one another of his cowardice, his treachery, his failure, as the lindens were at home. But for men the reproachful voice of the night passes with the nocturnal trembling of trees, and after a refreshing night's sleep Pfaffrath will once more feel without stain, an upright German man and an Oberbürgermeister, free from guilt, guiltless towards his ancestors, guiltless towards his children, guiltless towards his own soul. But now, in this transfiguring hour of the night, he asked himself whether Siegfried and his symphony hadn't sought the better home, and whether the notes jarring in Pfaffrath's ear hadn't held a dialogue with his own youthful soul.

I disturbed him in his reverie, I disturbed him in his devotion to Laura's smile. Once more I was moved by Adolf. I put my hand on his arm, my hand on the sleeve of his black cassock, but he pulled back his arm and said: 'You don't understand.' I said: 'Yes I do, you've discovered a new pain in yourself.' He asked: 'Do you really know?' I said: 'Yes.' I had ordered him a glass of vermouth, and he had his vermouth and he asked: 'Do we have to go now?' I said: 'Her name's Laura. We'll leave with her.' He looked at me, and his mouth quivered, and he said: 'You don't understand me.' I said: 'I do understand you.' And I thought: He thinks it will be enough to look, and he's right, looking is bliss, and if he remains resolute, and doesn't go to bed with her, then he'll have gained something. I thought: He will have gained something, but he will think he's lost everything. I thought: What would have happened to him if the Teutonic castle hadn't collapsed along with the Nazis? I thought: Would he even have seen Laura then? I thought: He is on a difficult path. I didn't know whether he would carry on on that path. Carry on to where? There are many *viae dolorosae*, a whole bewildering street map of them.

He observed them secretly from his car. They left the bar. They walked down the Via Veneto, below its gradually extinguishing lights, under the rustling trees, the girl in the middle. Judejahn's car followed them, a black shadow that slowly crept up, came level with them, and then slipped back again. They passed Judejahn's great hotel, and behind the American embassy they turned left, down the Via Venti Settembre. Judejahn gave up the pursuit. He had wanted to be sure. He had certainty – his son had ousted him with that whore. His son was sleeping with a Judaeo-Roman whore. It was ridiculous to be indignant about it. He was aware of that. He thought: Well, what if he is. It would suit him fine if Adolf slept with a girl, might make a man of him. But he had been defeated, he, the great Judejahn had been beaten, had been repulsed, his writ did not run, the world was in rebellion! That was what stirred up a flood of pointless oaths in him. His son sleeping with a girl didn't bother him. He didn't see why it should. He thought all priests were hypocrites and randy goats. He would avenge himself. He would avenge himself on all priests and all whores. He had himself driven up to his hotel. He went up to his luxurious room. Little Gottlieb was very pleased with the room. Benito the cat yowled a greeting to Judejahn. He was hungry. Judejahn was furious that the beast had been given nothing to eat. He stroked the cat, ran his fingers through its mangy fur, and said: 'Poor Benito!' He rang for room service, swore

at the waiter, he ordered raw mincemeat for the cat, and
champagne for himself. It had to be champagne. Little
Gottlieb had always drunk champagne in the officers'
mess. Little Gottlieb had toasted his victories with champagne. He had drunk champagne in Paris, in Rome, in
Warsaw. In Moscow he had drunk no champagne.

They walked silently through the night. They didn't
touch. The tall buildings were silent. They were friendly.
The paving stones lay benevolently at their feet. They
heard the bells of San Bernardo striking; then Santa Maria
della Vittoria and Santa Susanna sounded the hour. But
they weren't thinking about time. On the Piazza della
Esedra they passed through the semicircular arcades. The
shop-windows were behind grilles. The shop-keepers
were worried, they feared the night and robbers. The displays were lit up. Treasures lay spread out. Laura did not
desire them, she desired none of those treasures, marked
with high price tags behind the locked grilles. Her smile
was a beacon in the night, it filled the night and it filled
Rome. Laura smiled for the city and the world, *urbi et orbi*,
and Rome and the night and the world were transfigured.
They crossed the square, and Laura dipped her fingers
into the water of the fountain, dipped them into the little
Fountain of the Naiads, and as though with holy water,
she, a devout Catholic, anointed the brow of her silent
deacon with the water of the naiads. Then they stepped
into the shadow of an ancient wall where night birds might
nest. They stood in front of Santa Maria degli Angeli close
by Diocletian's baths. Siegfried listened for screech-owls.
He thought, compositionally, that the too-wit-too-woo of
the death bird belonged here, but all he heard was the cry
of the locomotives from the station near by, full of sorrow
and full of fear of so much distance. How distant they were

one from another, the three who were gathered together to face the night. Siegfried looked at Adolf and Laura. But did he see them? Was he not projecting himself on the shapes of his companions? They were thoughts of his brain, and he rejoiced that he had thought them. They were kind thoughts. As for them, did they see each other? It was dark in the shade of the ancient bath-house masonry, but in front of Santa Maria degli Angeli there was the gleam of a light everlasting, and by that light they tried to see one another's souls.

I left them alone together, what business did I have with them? I had brought them together, what further business did I have with them? I strolled over to the station. I stepped into its neon glare. Let Adolf pray in front of Santa Maria degli Angeli. '*Ut mentes nostras ad coelestia desideria erigas.* Mayest thou lift up our hearts to heavenly desires.' Had I led Adolf into temptation? I had not led Adolf into temptation. There was no temptation. In the baths, in the National Museum, there were pictures of the old gods, now securely locked away. They were well-guarded. Had I given pleasure? I could not give pleasure. There was only illusion, momentary tricks of the light. I went to the platform. A train stood ready. The third-class carriages were overcrowded. In first class there was a single thin man. Would I be the man in first class? Perhaps he was a bad man. Would it be me? I didn't want to travel in the overcrowded third-class carriages. Florence–Brenner–Munich. Did the journey tempt me? It didn't tempt me. I went into the *albergo di giorno*, situated like a neon grotto beneath the station. The nymphs of the grotto manicured the hands of gentlemen. I love the Roman barber shops. I love the Romans. At all hours they think of their beauty. Men came here to have their hair cut, to have themselves shaved, permed, manicured, massaged, covered with unguents, sprinkled with scents; they sat with sober expressions under barbers' hoods and glittering hair-dryers, as hot sirocco winds blew over their hair. I had nothing to do. I asked for a compress. I asked for a compress because I was bored. My face was wrapped up in a steaming hot towel, and I had hot dreams. I was Petronius the novelist, and I spoke in the public baths with wise men and with boys, we loafed on the marble steps of the steam room, and talked about the immortality of the soul, there was a mosaic on the floor, a bright and skilful piece of work. Zeus the eagle, Zeus the swan, Zeus the golden shower – but the mosaic had been laid by a slave. My face was wrapped in a towel dipped in ice water, I was Petronius the novelist, I enjoyed the conversation of wise men and the beauty of boys, and I knew there was no immortality, and that beauty decays and I knew Nero was mulling things over, and I knew how to place the blade against a vein – the last marble step was cold. I left the grotto, I wasn't beautiful, I went into a waiting-room somewhere, and I drank a grappa, because Hemingway recommended grappa, and again it tasted to me like German rotgut from the time before the currency stabilization. I bought a newspaper at the big station news-stand. The jungle fastness had fallen. The delegates were leaving Geneva. My little Communist with her red kerchief was striding proudly through Rome. She wasn't leaving. Why should she leave? This was her home. The headline said: What now?

Kürenberg had made a lot of telephone calls, he had spoken to critics and arts administrators, he had spoken to agents, and to the organizers of the congress, and to the prize committee and the prize-givers, it was all very political and very diplomatic, and all the officials were secretive and self-important, but Kürenberg had had his way, Siegfried was to receive the music prize, not the whole prize, but he was to get half of it; for diplomatic reasons, the prize was to be shared. Kürenberg told Ilse that Siegfried was getting the prize, and Ilse Kürenberg, who was running a bath, didn't care whether Siegfried got the prize or not; it didn't upset her, but neither did it give her any pleasure. She thought: Have I been infected, have I been contaminated by this meanness, by the simple-mindedness of thinking in groups, infected by the mutual enmity of groups, by the vicious idea of collective guilt, am I against Siegfried and his music, just because he belongs to that family? He isn't happy with them. I know he's left them behind. But why do I see the others when I see him? She thought: I don't want revenge, I never did, revenge is sordid, but I don't want to be reminded, I can't stand to be reminded, and Siegfried can't but remind me; he reminds me, and I see the killers. The bath was full, but the water was too hot. Ilse Kürenberg turned off the light in the bathroom. She opened the window. She was naked. She liked walking through the room naked. She liked standing naked by the open window. The wind moulded itself round her firm, well-kept body. Her firm body stood firmly on the floor. She had withstood the storm. The wind would not carry her away. There was something in her, though, that longed to be carried away.

The champagne was finished, he felt no intoxication, the victories had gone flat. Judejahn felt a dull roaring, like buzzing in his ears, but affecting his whole body; his blood pressure must be dangerously high, he walked over to the window, and he looked across at Rome. Once he had almost ruled Rome. Certainly he had ruled the man who had ruled Rome. Mussolini had been afraid of Judejahn. Now Rome had given Judejahn a mangy tomcat. A whore had run away from Judejahn. He was unable to have her shot. A whore had run off with his son, who was a Roman priest. Judejahn could not have any priests shot, either. He was powerless. Would he fight to regain his power? It was a long road. The road was too long to be travelled twice. He admitted it to himself now. The road was too long. Judejahn could no longer see the objective. The objective grew blurred. A red mist drifted round the objective. A whore had slipped away from Judejahn, and now a naked Jewess was displaying herself to him; the Jewess should be stood in front of a mass grave, but there she was triumphantly, mocking Judejahn; she loomed nakedly over Rome. He saw her in the clouds.

After standing together for a long time in the lee of the ancient masonry – many times the clock of Santa Maria degli Angeli had struck, the locomotives had screamed, perhaps an owl had hooted too, but they had heard nothing – Siegfried's music suddenly resounded again in Adolf's ears, and he touched Laura's face, he tried to hold her smile, a high note, humanity, sweet rapture, and then he was frightened, and he ran off into the night, which was to be long and without smiles.

The angels had not come. The angels from the Angels' Bridge did not take up the invitation of the old gods. They did not dance with the old gods on the Capitoline Hill. I should have liked to see Stravinsky sitting at a black grand among the broken pillars. At the black concert grand, the Maestro would have played his *Passacaglia*, surrounded by the rather off-white marble wings of the angels, and under the great pure wing-beat of the gods, all light and air; but the angels had stayed away, the gods hid themselves, clouds loomed in the sky, and Stravinsky merely said: '*Je salue le monde confraternel.*' The music congress was received on the Capitoline Hill. I thought we must have looked funny in our suits, and the gods hidden behind the ruins, the fauns in the shrubbery and the nymphs among the rank weeds probably laughed a great deal. It wasn't they who were old-fashioned, it was us. We were old and foolish, and even the younger ones among us were old and foolish. Kürenberg winked at me. It was as if to say: 'Take it seriously, but not too seriously.' He was in favour of letting the agents get on with it, so that one might occasionally take the muse of music out to dinner in an expensive restaurant. The prizes were presented by the mayor of Rome, a mayor like my father, and he gave me my half-prize. He gave me a half-prize for my symphony, and I was surprised that he gave me the half-prize, and I thought, Kürenberg arranged that, and I was grateful to Kürenberg, and I thought my father would be proud of me for a whole day, because the mayor had given me the half-prize, but my father would never understand why the mayor had honoured me. I was glad of the prize-money. I would use it to go to Africa. In Africa, I would write my new symphony. Maybe I would play it to the angels in Rome next year: the black symphony of the Dark Continent. I would play to the white angels of Rome on the old hill of the gods. I know Europe is blacker really. But I want to go to Africa, I want to see the desert. My father won't understand the idea of travelling to Africa to see the desert, and to hear music from the desert. My father has no idea that I'm the devout composer of the Roman angels. The Council approved Palestrina's music, the congress honoured my music.

No reveille woke him, it was the yowling tomcat that startled him awake, Judejahn's head was growling, the desert fort was a long way off, Africa was a long way off, Germany was still further away, he awoke in Rome with a throbbing skull, with feeble limbs, with rage at waking at all, with a taste of perfume in his mouth that came from the champagne and the flat victories, mixed with sourness, with something acrid, with cellular decay, and behind his brow the image of the room shook, his feet and thighs trembled, but the virile member was erect, charged, stuffed with blood, it burned in unappeased irritation. He showered, scrubbed himself down, he thought in officers' slang, a yomp now, field exercises, but he was sweating in the shower, he couldn't get his skin dry, the sweat kept pouring off him, shimmering in little beads, Judejahn gasped for air, and the air of Rome was too soft. Hair of the dog was the old drinker's adage. Judejahn ordered a half-bottle of champagne, the champagne of victories. He asked for a lot of ice to go with it. He threw bits of ice into the glass. Judejahn's hand shook. He drained the bumper in a single draught. Now he saw clearly. Fogs vanished. He had a rendezvous with Laura. That was important. What if she'd slept with Adolf. He needed her, Jewess or no, he needed her to free himself from his distressing visions. He rang for the black ambassadorial car, but a while later a call came from the soldierly chauffeur, in clipped tones, without a trace of feeling, reporting a mechanical fault that would take all day to repair. Judejahn had heard the voice of Death. He failed to recognize it. He swore.

One of the churches where one might confess in many tongues was the old church of Santa Maria degli Angeli, the house of worship by the walls of the baths, and Adolf

Judejahn knelt in the confessional of the German-speaking priest, and he told the German-speaking priest what had passed the previous night outside the church doors between himself and Laura, and, as nothing had happened that might cause the Church to be seriously angry with a deacon, Adolf was admonished to avoid temptation in future, and he was given absolution. He looked through the grille of the confessional at the face of his confessor. The face of his confessor looked tired. Adolf would have liked to say: 'Father, I am unhappy.' But the priest looked tired and dismissive. He had heard so many confessions. So many travellers came to Rome and confessed things they wouldn't entrust to their confessors at home. They were ashamed before the confessors they knew. In Rome they were strangers and felt no shame, and that was what had made the priest's face so tired. And Adolf thought: Will I one day be as tired as that as I sit in my confessional, and will my face look so dismissive? He thought: Where will I have my confessional? In a village? In an old village church among shady trees? Or is it not my vocation, am I spurned, spurned from the start? Adolf had wanted to push Judejahn's money into an offertory box, but, just as he was about to do so, he changed his mind. His action was not spiritually motivated. He did not trust the Church's care for the poor. The Church's ministry to the poor was vinegary, vinegary as all poor relief, and it smelled of soup-kitchens; the money went into watery soup for the poor. Adolf wanted someone to have joy of the money. He pressed his father's dirty notes into the wrinkled hands of an old woman who was begging for alms at the church door.

Judejahn was waiting. He was waiting on the station concourse, outside the CIT office, but Laura didn't show. Did she mean to jilt him in the morning as well? Was she lying in a seamy embrace with Adolf? Rage was bad for his health. Judejahn still had trouble breathing. From time to time the mist returned, a poisonous mist of red gas. Maybe mist like that would blow round the world in the next great war. Judejahn went to a refreshment wagon and asked for a cognac. He stood in front of the refreshment wagon for travellers as before the supply wagon on the battlefield. He knocked back the cognac. The red mist lifted. Judejahn looked across to the CIT, but Laura still wasn't there. Judejahn passed the news-stand. He saw the magazine *Oggi* hanging up, and there on the cover of *Oggi* was a picture of Mussolini. His old friend looked battered, and Judejahn thought: I look battered today as well. Behind Mussolini stood a man in an SS cap. He stood behind Mussolini like a minder. He stood behind him like an executioner. You could clearly see the death's head on the cap. Who was the fellow? Judejahn thought: He must be one of my officers. In the picture, the SS man had lowered his gaze, and Judejahn couldn't identify him. The man was probably dead. Most of his men were dead. Mussolini was dead. He had died a grisly death. A grisly death had been planned for Judejahn too. But Judejahn was alive, he had given them the slip. He was alive, and time was on his side, and just then Laura appeared. There was her smile, and for an instant Judejahn thought, Let her go, but then he thought again, She's a Jewess, and the thought excited him.

And Laura saw the highly promising stranger, and she thought: What present will he give me? Now she was looking at the displays in the shop windows. A girl needed jewellery, a girl needed clothes, even a girl who can't do sums needs sheer stockings, and she was used to being given things every so often. Every so often she went on little fishing expeditions, in all innocence and usually in the mornings, she didn't have a steady boyfriend, and after the queers in the evenings, it was nice to spend the morning in bed with a real man, you needed that for your health, and later she would confess it in all innocence, and old men weren't bad, true, they weren't beautiful, but they weren't bad, their old men's love filled the morning, and besides they were more generous than the younger men, who wanted something for themselves, and Adolf had disappointed her, the young foreign priest had been a disappointment, they had been so happy in the night, but then the priest had run off, he had been afraid of sin, and Laura had cried and from now on she was sticking to old men; old men weren't afraid of sin and they didn't run off. It was hard to communicate with Judejahn, but she managed to make him understand that they were going to a hotel near the station.

Kürenberg had invited me to the fine restaurant on the Piazza Navona. He wanted to celebrate my prize with me. He apologized for the fact that his wife wouldn't be breakfasting with us, and I understood that Ilse Kürenberg did not want to celebrate with me, and I understood why. The restaurant was still empty at this hour, and Kürenberg ordered a selection of sea-creatures that lay on our plates like little monsters, and we washed down the monsters with a dry Chablis. It was our farewell. Kürenberg was off to Australia. He was conducting the *Ring* cycle during the Australian season. He sat opposite me cracking the shells of the monstrous sea-creatures, sucking out their savoury juices. Tomorrow he would be up in the air with his wife, eating an airline dinner, and the day after he would be eating in Australia, sampling the curious sea-creatures of the Pacific Ocean. It's a small world. Kürenberg was my friend, he was my only true friend, but I had too much respect for him to treat him like a friend, I was quiet in his company, and he perhaps thought me ungrateful. I told him I wanted to go to Africa with my prize money, and I told him about my black symphony. Kürenberg approved of the idea. He recommended a place called Mogador. The name Mogador sounded good. It sounded black. Mogador was an old Moorish fortress. But as the Moors are no longer powerful, there was no reason why I shouldn't go and live in their old fortress.

She had wondered whether he would take off his dark glasses in bed, and when he did take them off, she giggled, but then his eyes frightened her, they were bloodshot, and she shrank from his treacherous greedy expression, from his lowered bull's brow approaching her, and he asked her, 'Are you afraid?' and she didn't understand him, and she smiled, but it wasn't her wholehearted smile, and he threw her on to the bed. She hadn't thought him capable of such passion, usually the men she slept with for the presents that a girl so badly needs didn't get so excited, their bed scenes were pretty placid, but this man threw himself at her like an animal, he opened her up, he tugged at her skin, and then he took her brutally, he was brutal with her, even though she was slender and delicate. He was heavy, he lay heavy on top of her body, which was so light and so good to hold, and she thought of the queers, thought of the queers in the bar, their soft movements, their fragrant curls, their colourful shirts and jangling bracelets, and she thought, Maybe it's good to be queer, maybe I should be queer too, this is horrible, he stinks of sweat, he stinks like a ram, stinks like the dirty old billy-goat in the stall. When she was little she'd gone to the country once, she'd gone to Calabria, she had been scared and she had missed Rome, her wonderful city, and the house in Calabria had stunk, and she'd had to watch the she-goats being taken to the billy-goat, and on the wooden staircase a boy had exposed himself to her, and she'd had to touch the boy, she hated the country, and sometimes she would dream of the billy-goat, and then she wanted to touch the boy, but the boy had horns that butted her, and the horns broke off, in her dream the horns had broken off like rotten teeth. And she cried out, 'You're hurting me,' but Judejahn didn't understand as she cried out in Italian, and it didn't matter that he didn't understand because it hurt, but it hurt pleasantly, yes, now she wanted this sacrifice, the old man was satisfying her, the promising stranger was delivering in a quite unexpected way, now she pressed herself against him, heightening his excitement, streams of sweat ran down from the ram, they ran on to her body, they flowed down her breasts, and collected in the little dip of her belly, they burned a little, but it didn't hurt, and the man was angry, he whispered, 'You're a Jewess, you're a Jewess,' and she didn't understand him, but in her subconscious she understood him, when there were German soldiers in Rome the word had meant something, and she asked '*Ebreo*?' and he whispered, 'Hebrew,' and laid his hands round her neck, and she cried, '*No e poi no, cattólico*,' and the word *cattólico* seemed further to inflame his rage and his lust, and in the end it didn't matter, rage or lust, she floated off, and he drove himself into exhaustion, gurgled and threw himself aside, drained, knocked out, half dead. She thought: It's his own fault, why did he have to show off like that, old men don't usually try so hard? But soon she was smiling again, and she stroked the sweaty hair on his chest because he had tried so hard; she was grateful to him for having tried so hard; she was grateful to him because he had given her pleasure and because he had satisfied her. She went on stroking him for a while. She felt his heart beating; it was a valiant heart, exhausting itself for her woman's pleasure. She got up and went over to the basin to wash.

Judejahn heard the water splash, and he sat up in bed. The red mists were around him again. He saw Laura standing naked in the red mist, and the black basin of the wash-stand was the black ditch into which the executed victims fell. The Jewess had to be liquidated. The Führer had been betrayed. Not enough people had been liquidated. He staggered into his clothes. She asked: 'Don't you want to wash?' But he didn't hear her. He wouldn't have understood her, anyway. In his trouser pocket was Austerlitz's pistol and silencer.

Now the pistol would decide everything. He would clean up. The pistol would restore order. He just needed some air first, he was panting and trembling too much. He staggered over to the window, pulled it open, and leaned down over the street, which was full of thick red mist. The street was a canyon, and at the bottom of it were automobiles squealing and clattering, making a fiendish racket and looking like creeping monsters under the red mist. But a clearing appeared in the mist directly before him, a tunnel through the fog, and there at the open French window in the large hotel opposite stood Ilse Kürenberg, the Aufhäuser girl, the Jew girl, the escapee, the woman in the theatre box, the woman he had seen naked at night in the clouds above Rome, there stood Ilse Kürenberg in a white dressing gown, a little back from the window, but he saw her naked, naked as she'd been in the night, naked as the women in front of the ditch, and Judejahn emptied the magazine of Austerlitz's pistol, he was the firing squad, he fired all the shots himself, he didn't just give the orders, orders were disregarded, he had to do his own shooting, and at the last shot, Ilse Kürenberg fell, and the Führer's command had been executed. Laura screamed, a single scream, and then a flood of Italian burst from her lips, and splashed away with the washing water in the red mist. Judejahn found his way to the door, and Laura wept into the bedding, she wept into the sweaty warm pillows, something terrible had happened, but she didn't know what, the man had fired a gun, he had fired out of the window – and he had given her no present. She was still naked, and she now held the pillow over her head, because her face was no longer smiling, and she wanted to choke her crying. On the rumpled bed she looked like the headless, beautiful body of the headless Aphrodite Anadyomene.

He had not seen her naked, and so the naked body did not remind Adolf of Laura, nor did he even think of Laura's body, he thought of her smile as he stood in front of the headless Aphrodite Anadyomene in the museum of Diocletian's baths, the headless Aphrodite was still holding the ends of her two plaits in her raised hands, as though trying to secure her head by her plaits, and Adolf wondered what her face had been like, and whether she might have smiled like Laura. They bewildered him. The cold marble bodies all around bewildered him. This was Siegfried's world here. A world of beautiful bodies. There was the Venus of Cirene. She was flawless. Anyone could see she was flawless. A firm, well-made body, but cold cold cold. And then the fauns and the hermaphrodites in all their physicality. They didn't rot away. They didn't turn to earth. They weren't threatened by hell. Even the head of the Sleeping Eumenide didn't speak of terrors. It told of sleep. Its story was of beauty and sleep; even the Underworld had been friendly, only Hell was something else. They had no knowledge of Hell. Was it right to threaten, to terrorize, in order to rescue the soul, and was the soul lost if one responded to beauty? Adolf sat down in the garden among the stone witnesses of antiquity. He was excluded from their society, his vows excluded him, his faith excluded him, for ever. He wept. The old statues looked on, dry-eyed.

He staggered across the square. With every step, he felt he was sinking into a bottomless pit, sliding down, for ever, he had to clutch the air in order to stay up. He knew what had happened, and he didn't know what had happened. He had fired shots. He had contributed to the final solution. He had fulfilled the Führer's orders. That was good. And now he had to hide. Final victory hadn't been secured yet. He had to go into hiding again, he had to go back to the desert, only the red mist was in the way. It was hard to find a hiding-place in all this red mist. There were some ruins. In Berlin he had hidden in the ruins. In Rome, you had to pay an entrance fee to be admitted to the ruins. Judejahn paid the entrance fee to the museum in the baths. He went though some passages, climbed a flight of stairs. There were naked figures standing in the red mist. It must be a whore-house. Or a gas chamber. That would explain the red mist. He was in a large gas chamber full of naked people who were being liquidated, in which case he had to get out of here. He wasn't supposed to be liquidated. He wasn't naked. He was the commandant. The hell hounds had turned the gas on early. What a pig's breakfast. He had to take action. Discipline must be maintained. Gallows must be erected. Judejahn reached a room that was the command post. The mist lifted. There were old mirrors here. The mirrors were blind. He stared into the blind mirrors. Was that him? He couldn't recognize himself. There was a purple face. A swollen face. It looked like the face of a boxer who had taken a lot of punishment. He had lost his dark glasses somewhere. He didn't need them any more. But then he saw a better mirror, and he recognized himself in it, he stood in front of the mosaic of an athlete, there was his face, his neck, his shoulders, it was his reflection from his prime looking back at him, he had stood in the arena, he had fought with a short sword, he had finished off a lot of adversaries. And there was Benito too. He saw the mosaic of the cat with the bird. Benito had had a lot to eat. The world wasn't such a bad place. They had done a lot of killing and eating together. They could be satisfied with themselves. Judejahn staggered into the garden. Naked women, naked Jew women were hiding behind the hedges. It wouldn't do them any good. Hedges didn't protect you against liquidation by Judejahn. He had to make his way through – and then he collapsed.

Adolf had seen him coming, with fear and trembling he had watched his approach, and then he saw him collapse, he fell down as though poleaxed, and Adolf ran to him, and the heavy body of his father lay there lifelessly. Was he dead? His face was purple. A museum attendant arrived, and he called to another attendant, and together the three of them carried Judejahn into a shed where plasterers restored the ancient plastics, and they laid him on the ground in front of a relief on a sarcophagus. The relief depicted a triumphal procession, arrogant Romans with humiliated German warriors tethered to their horses. The Roman plasterers stood around Judejahn in their white coats. One plasterer said: 'He's dead.' And another plasterer said: 'He's not dead. My father-in-law took a while to die, too.' The attendant went to telephone the first-aid post at the station. His father was not yet dead, and then the most important thing occurred to Adolf: there was Hell there was Hell there was Hell. And now there wasn't a moment to lose, he ran through the garden, he ran through the gates, he ran into the church of Santa Maria degli Angeli. The German-speaking priest was still there. He was reading in his breviary. There was no one kneeling at the confessional. Stammering, Adolf asked him to give the Last Sacrament to his father who was dying, and the priest understood and made haste; he fetched the holy oil, and went with Adolf to the server, and they hurried as quickly as they decently could, and the ticket inspectors let them pass, and the attendants took off their caps, and the plasterers respectfully stepped aside. Judejahn lay there lifelessly, but he wasn't dead. Sweat and secretions dribbled out of him, preceding his dissolution. He was purging himself, cleansing himself. Purgatory is the winnowing fire. Had he reached it yet? Judejahn lay in a deep coma. No one knew what was happening to him. Was he riding to Valhalla, were devils coming for him, or was his soul jubilant because deliverance was at hand? The priest knelt down. He went on to perform the extreme unction, and grant conditional absolution as was right for one who had lost consciousness. With the oil that a bishop had blessed, the priest anointed Judejahn's eyes, his ears, his mouth and the palms of his hands. The priest prayed. He prayed: 'Through this Holy anointing and its most tender mercy, may the Lord forgive you whatever sins you have committed through your sense of sight, through your sense of hearing, of smell, of taste and touch.' Judejahn did not move. Was he not moved by the words of the priest? Judejahn never moved again. He lay there motionless, and the Roman priest commended him to God's mercy, and his son in the cassock of a Roman priest prayed for his father – two envoys from the enemy.

The ambulancemen came, and a doctor closed his eyes. The ambulancemen were dressed in field-grey, and they carried Judejahn off as though from a battlefield.

That same evening, Judejahn's death was reported in the press; its circumstances had made it world news, though the fact of it can have shocked no one.